SHE CAME FROM WEST VIRGINIA

A Historical Novel
of the
Civil War

Paul Dodd

FIRESIDE FICTION
2007

FIRESIDE FICTION
AN IMPRINT OF HERITAGE BOOKS, INC.

Books, CDs, and more—Worldwide

For our listing of thousands of titles see our website
at
www.HeritageBooks.com

Published 2007 by
HERITAGE BOOKS, INC.
Publishing Division
65 East Main Street
Westminster, Maryland 21157-5026

International Standard Book Number: 978-0-7884-4051-9

CONTENTS

FOREWORD

When I was a graduate student, in the 1970's, I did an extensive research paper on the separation of the Virginias during the Civil War. As I delved deeper and deeper into the subject, I became increasingly fascinated by the drama and intrigue involved in the formation of the state of West Virginia.

I discovered that, initially, there was a two-thirds majority among the leaders in Virginia's state government that favored staying loyal to the United States. I found that the eventual decision to secede was not as much the result of a change of mind, but rather, was more the result of a careful plot and political strategy carried out by the determined minority of secessionists. Not only did they eventually get a convention vote to secede; an action that could be taken only after ratification by a vote of the people of the state; they were able to get state officials to act immediately, ignoring the rules set by the convention.

This book chronicles the actions of some of the leaders of loyal Virginians who, considering secession from the Union to be unconstitutional and an act of treason, took matters into their own hands by establishing a Reconstituted Government of Virginia in Wheeling and eventually acting to carve the new state of West Virginia out of the Old Dominion.

I have taken the findings from my research effort of long ago and woven them into a historical novel featuring a fictional family, the Blakes, and a fictional community, Melford Creek. I have attempted to reflect the living conditions and life situations of that time and location. I hope that the book faithfully reflects the viewpoints of the people who were, firstly, Virginians loyal to the United States and only secondly, advocates of the creation of a new state.

i

The following historic characters are mentioned in the book:

Laura Ann Jackson Arnold
Jonathan Arnold
Edward Bates
Henry Ward Beecher
John Bell
Jefferson Bennett
Robert Bennett
Montgomery Blair
John Breckinridge
Arthur Boreman
James Buchanan
Simon Cameron
Alexander Campbell
Archibald Campbell
John Carlile
Salmon Chase
Jefferson Davis
John Davis
Dennis Dorsey
Robert Garnett
Horace Greeley
Joseph Hooker
R. M. T. Hunter
Andrew Jackson
Mary Anna Jackson
Thomas J. Jackson

John Janney
Thomas Jefferson
Andrew Johnson
Joseph Johnson,
Adoniram Judson
Robert E. Lee
John Letcher
Abraham Lincoln
George Lisle
J. M. Mason
George McClellan
Irvin McDowell
George Meade
Francis Pierpont
Roger Pryor
Samuel Richmond
Tuck Richmond
William Rosencrans
Dred Scott
William Seward
William Sherman
Harriet Beecher Stowe
John Tyler
Gideon Welles
Waitman Willey

SHE CAME FROM *WEST* VIRGINIA

1 *THE OMINOUS CLOUDS OF WAR*

"I'm afraid that we face dark days ahead, gentlemen. This election could well start a firestorm that consumes our entire country."

The date was August, 16, 1860, and the speaker was Waitman Willey, a staunch Unionist lawyer from Morgantown who was in Richmond seeking to solidify Virginias position of support for keeping the country together. He was staying at Mrs. Etta Hatcher's boarding house, the boarding house where twelve year-old Andy Blake was living with his father, Jeremiah, while they were in Richmond with Jeremiah's boss, former Virginia State Senator and United States Congressman John Carlile.

Waitman Willey was a prominent Virginian, one with whom Andy had been impressed when he had accompanied his father to a Union rally in Morgantown and he was excited to get to see him again. He was a compelling man with a wide handsome face well weathered by the wind and sun. He had thick, dark brown hair that began graying at his temples and gradually lightened down to his almost white beard. As Andy studied him he thought him to be the most determined person that he had ever observed.

Although dressed in the proper attire for a lawyer of his status, Willey did not look nearly as dapper today as he had looked on that day in Morgantown when Andy had first seen him. His black suit was in need of pressing, his white collar which should have been stiff with starch was limp, and his high top shoes were scuffed and the heels were worn, all of which told Andy that Mr. Willey had been on the road for quite a while and that he was more concerned with the issue of the day than he was with his appearance; much more!

Willey spoke with the strong, authoritative voice of someone who had spent many hours in court presenting legal arguments and who had made numerous impassioned speeches throughout the state of Virginia defending the Constitution of the United States. His major contribution to state government, thus far, had been the sharing of his expert knowledge of constitutional law, having served twice as a delegate to Virginia state constitutional conventions.

Andy was impressed, but puzzled, by the small distinguished audience that Willey had handpicked and was addressing as they sat in the ornately furnished private back parlor of the boarding house.

Mrs. Hatcher was wise in the ways of politics, having lived for thirty-five years with her politically astute husband, Albert. Albert Hatcher, by being a friend and advisor to numerous members of state government, had been able to benefit from knowing about many things before they occurred and this, combined with his natural business acumen, had enabled him to amass a sizable bank account and purchase a number of desirable properties in Richmond.

Etta had been a very aware silent partner in Albert's profitable politically connected career until his death in 1849. She was left with a sizable inheritance and could have lived the rest of her years in quiet comfort but found that she missed the excitement of the political whirl.

She decided that the thing she should do was to sell most of the properties and most of her slaves that she had inherited from Albert and renovate the largest of her properties into a grand boarding house that would cater to the needs of the politically powerful of Richmond.

She soon acquired an elite clientele and she was able to manage the boarding house quite nicely with the help of, as she expressed it, "six of the best slaves God ever granted to anybody."

Her most trusted slaves were Sadie, who was in charge of the kitchen and known throughout Richmond as a cook without equal, and Jubal, who Andy assumed to be Sadie's husband. Jubal, the proper and polite butler, served the distinguished guests who were coming and going at the boarding house. In addition, she owned Jesse who managed the livery, and three teenage girls, Mandy, Flora, and Hilda, who took care of the housekeeping and serving.

This meeting was only one of many discreet gatherings which Mrs. Hatcher had hosted, especially now with the air full of tension over the upcoming presidential election and the anticipation of the uncertain days which lay ahead.

As he surveyed the group, in addition to his father and Waitman Willey, Andy knew his father's boss, John Carlile, and he recognized Governor John Letcher, and Assemblymen John Davis and Arthur Boreman, but the other ten or twelve men were not the usual political allies that he was used to seeing. He knew some of them were, like Waitman Willey and Arthur Boreman, from other parties and, thus, traditional political opponents of John Carlile, the Governor, and Assemblyman Davis.

"The country is being torn apart by the abolitionists on one hand and the rebellious elements on the other and it will take nothing less than a miracle to save the Union," Willey continued. "If that fellow Lincoln gets elected, and it looks more and more like he might, I think that you can count on at least half a dozen states trying to secede."

"Well," enjoined Governor Letcher, a thin, balding, scholarly looking man, "thank God, Virginia won't be one of them." The Governor's strong statement was greeted by murmurs of agreement and a hearty "amen" or two from the group.

Andy was having considerable trouble figuring out just exactly what was going on. He was proud that his father was associated with such a powerful person as John Carlile and he understood that his father and the former Congressman were spending most of their time in Richmond these days doing everything in their power to strengthen the Unionist support in Virginia. But he just could not comprehend why this particular group had gathered.

Andy knew that his father and Carlile were a part of the Jackson wing of the Democratic Party and they were always mapping out strategies of how to gain advantage over the other parties and even the Calhoun wing of their own Democratic Party. But here they were, meeting secretly with a leading member of the Unionist Party and some of his key allies. It struck Andy as curious, indeed.

"John," Willey asked of the Governor, "how do you see the election coming out here in Virginia?"

The governor paused for a moment, pursing his lips and adjusting his glasses on his thin nose and then answered, "Waitman, the Union support is so splintered here it's hard to predict the outcome. In sharp contrast to that, the Calhoun bunch is well organized and they will undoubtedly get out a strong vote for Vice President Breckinridge. Even though Senator Douglas will get a lot of votes, we Jacksonians simply cannot carry the state with him at the top of the ticket. It looks to me that, although Senator Douglas will get a good vote and, much as I hate to admit it, Lincoln will get a few votes, the best hope for the Union to prevail in this election rests with the Constitution Party and John Bell, even if he is an old Whig."

"Oh, forgive me Arthur, that was a slip of the tongue. I suppose I just described you, didn't I?" the Governor joked, smiling at Boreman as everyone laughed, and then added seriously, "The worst thing that could happen would be if John Breckenridge carries the state. Every young hot-head in Virginia who's looking for a fight is supporting him and if he wins they will surely make things difficult for those of us who are trying to keep the country in one piece."

"Arthur," the Governor continued as he turned to Assemblyman Boreman, "why don't you bring Waitman up to date on the situation in the state legislature?"

"We've got better than a two to one majority in favor of staying with the Union," Boreman answered, "but we'll lose half of them the minute the federal government tries to use force on any state. Those are the ones who are with us in wanting to keep the country together, but they don't believe that the Constitution gives the federal government the right to use coercive force against a state, even to keep it in the Union."

"That's precisely why I believe that we are in the best position of anyone to save the country," the Governor said. "We have to make sure that force is not used and I'm confident that we can do it."

As the evening wore on toward midnight and the discussions became more complex and the air in the parlor became thicker and thicker with the aroma and smoke of the men's pipes and cigars, Andy began to nod as he sat quietly at the back of the room.

Suddenly he was jolted awake as John Carlile pounded his fist on a table. Carlile was usually calm and calculating, which seemed to be appropriate for his almost boyish appearance. His young looking face was clean-shaven and he kept his black hair neatly trimmed which made him stand out prominently amidst the long hair and elaborate beards and mustaches that most men sported.

Andy awoke to hear him say in an uncharacteristically loud, emotional voice, "Gentlemen, no matter what we say; this thing is not going to be settled peacefully. It will be miraculous if blood is not spilled before it's all said and done. Virginia is the key to this whole affair and I believe that we hold the balance as to whether this country will survive or not. Our resolve must be unwavering and we must preserve the Union, no matter what it costs."

"John," the Governor said reassuringly in a calm voice, "I believe that Divine Providence has placed us in just the precise location where we can do the very thing you are asking for. We can prevent the bloodshed you fear and, in the long run, preserve the Union. What we have to do is increase the size of our state militia and guard our borders, both north and south, to prevent any hostile force from crossing over to the other side. Neither side will dare challenge Virginia and after there's some time for both sides to cool off, things can be settled without war."

"I think that you have expressed our hopes well, Governor," Willey said, "and I think that your statement is an appropriate benediction to our get-together tonight. I want to thank each of you for being here and for your commitment to preserving the Union." He then added, "As you go from here tonight, it might be better not to leave as a group. It would be a good idea for you to stagger your departures, so no suspicion is raised about our meeting."

The next few minutes were spent in the exchange of small talk and private conversations as the members of the group gradually departed quietly into the dark Richmond night. John Carlile then commented, "Jeremiah, it looks like you have a boy that needs to be put to bed so why don't we meet for breakfast around seven so we can discuss the events of the evening."

Jeremiah looked at his tired son and thought for at least the thousandth time how much his light haired, blue eyed son favored his beautiful late mother and how very proud of him she would be.

Jeremiah had let Andy stay up hours past his normal bedtime because he wanted his son to have a measure of understanding of the momentous events that were occurring. He recognized that Andy was very bright but as is common with young people, sometimes too quick to form an opinion.

Tonight was an exceptional opportunity for Andy to hear opinions other than just from his father and to be better prepared for what now appeared to be rough days ahead. This was a lot for a boy of twelve to digest, Jeremiah thought, but there is no way to shield him. Before this thing is all over, he will need a strong foundation and tonight's meeting should be helpful.

After everyone had left, and before going to their room, Jeremiah and Andy went out into the dark to the privy behind the boarding house so they would not overtax the capacity of the chamber pot in their room. Before coming back inside, Andy paused for a long moment, looking up at the stars while deep in thought, and then commented, "This has been quite a night, hasn't it, Papa?"

"It surely has, Son," came the reply. "It surely has. Now we had better get to bed; we've got a lot to do tomorrow."

2 *LORD, THIS HAS TO BE MY SARAH*

Jeremiah Blake had come into the world in a cold, drafty house in the community of Melford Creek, in Harrison County, Virginia, in the winter of 1825. He was the first child born to the Reverend Abraham Blake and his wife, Sally, and they accepted him as a gift from God. Sally was attended at childbirth by a neighbor, Mrs. Fannie Wilson, who served as the midwife for the neighborhood, and by Abe's mother.

During the four hours of Sally's labor in the front room on a bed located near the fireplace, Abe stayed in the kitchen praying and pacing, entering the front room only when his mother yelled to him to bring more wood for the fire.

"You should have stuffed some rags in the cracks in this room," his mother complained. "I can feel that cold wind coming right through the walls."

As soon as Sally's moans and screams ceased and he heard the first cries of his new child and his mother's, "Thank you, Lord," and then Mrs. Wilson's, "Oh look, it's a little boy," he rushed into the room.

Although Abe had long ago followed the Biblical admonition to pray for wisdom and, thus, considered that he was gifted of God to know everything he needed to know, he suddenly realized that God had left out some crucial bits of knowledge. As a farmer, he had observed innumerable animal births and was skilled in assisting these births, when needed. But this scene was different. First, he looked at his tiny helpless infant with a matted mop of black hair, covered with blood and mucous and attached to the umbilical cord. Then he turned to his Sally lying exhausted in a bloody soiled bed. This was a far cry from seeing a mother cow grooming her newborn calf which then gets up and begins walking around, virtually self-sufficient, within a matter of minutes after birth.

Abe kept his attention on his eighteen-year-old wife because he could not bring himself to watch while his mother and Mrs. Wilson cut and tied the cord and cleaned the baby.

"You look well, Sally," Abe lied for one of the few times in his life as he looked at his beloved wife, pale and lifeless, "how do you feel?"

"I feel wonderful," she replied weakly. "I have never been so happy. I thought for a while that I would surely die but I prayed and God gave me the strength and now, just look at His handiwork."

When the baby was wrapped in a blanket and placed in the awkward arms of his father, Abe's mother asked him what he was going to name the baby.

"His name is Isaac," Abe said emotionally, but without hesitation.

"No, Abe," Sally said in a voice hardly louder than a whisper. "We are not going to name him Isaac; his name is going to be Jeremiah, after my father."

Although Abe did not protest, he was never happy with the decision to name his boy Jeremiah. Through the ensuing years whenever he and his son would find themselves in strong disagreement, Abe figured that things would have turned out different if he had only put his foot down that day and named him Isaac. After all, he was certain that Isaac was the name that God wanted the boy to have.

But on that day, the day the child was born, Abe was so drained by the ordeal and so in awe of the miracle which had just occurred that, for one of the few times in his life, he did not insist on his role as Sally's superior and being the sole decision maker for his family. So this usually unyielding, dominating husband silently, but unhappily, accepted the fact that he had little choice but to acquiesce to his wife's wishes.

Abe Blake was a hard working farmer during the week and a fiery Methodist preacher on Sunday. He was a very stern, extremely pious man who expected others to believe and live as he did. Everything in Abe's life was directed by his interpretation of the Bible and what he knew of the example set by John Wesley.

Since his name was Abraham, early on in his life he most

assuredly assumed that God would provide him with a wife named Sarah and a son named Isaac, like his Biblical namesake. He had never considered marrying anyone with a name other than Sarah until one Sunday morning at the Methodist Church in the community of Nutter Fort where, at the age of twenty-five, he was newly assigned to preach.

Wanting to make a good first impression, Abe selected one of his most successful sermons using the text from Colossians 3:2: "Set your affections on things above, not on things on the earth." As he was delivering his sermon, though, he had some difficulty observing the text himself as he became distracted by a person in the congregation who was simply the most beautiful girl that he had ever seen.

He could not prevent his eyes from turning toward her radiant face encircled by soft brown curls, which fell below her hat made of white crocheted lace. At the end of the service as he was greeting everyone upon their departure at the door of the church, his heart raced as he silently informed the Almighty, "Lord, this has to be my Sarah," as she came closer and closer to him.

"God bless you sister, and what is your name," the young preacher asked in an almost breathless voice as he weakly shook her hand in greeting.

"My name is Sally Stevens, Brother Blake," she replied in a crisp and confident voice, and as soon as he heard the name, Sally, Abe's mind started spinning out of control.

Instantly he was questioning his long held belief that God had a Sarah out there for him and he suddenly realized that if God actually did, he would now be disappointed because there was no way she could measure up to this Sally. At that moment, Abe, for the first time in his life, not only questioned his firm premise, he was on the verge of questioning God when Sally added, "Actually, my name is Sarah, but everybody calls me Sally. My papa started calling me Sally Good'in when I was little and I guess it stuck."

As Abe rode toward home that afternoon, he urged his horse into a trot and improvised as he lustily sang, bouncing along in the saddle, "O happy day, that fixed my choice, on thee my 'Sarah' and my God." He had never been so sure of his calling or so confident that he was the "apple of God's eye" as he was on this glorious day.

He was as giddy as a faithful follower of the teachings of John Wesley would permit himself to be as he went to the second verse of the song and rephrased it to, "Tis done, the great transaction's done; I am the Lord's and 'she' is mine." It was the greatest day that the young preacher had ever experienced. He now knew what older preachers had been talking about when they said they had "undergone a mountain top experience," because now he was "undergoing" one of his own.

Since Abe had no doubt, whatsoever, that God had ordained the events of this day and had revealed to him his Sarah, it never occurred to him that maybe God had not shared this wonderful news with Sally. Nothing could dampen Abe's enthusiasm or his assurance that he was smack-dab in the center of God's wonderful plan.

"Sally," her mother said to her as the Stevens family was walking the two miles to their home after church, "it appeared to me that the young preacher was quite taken by you. What did you think?"

"Why, what makes you say a thing like that, Mama," Sally replied with a tinge of embarrassment in her voice.

"Well," Mrs. Stevens said with a slight smile, "I couldn't help but notice that he was looking in your direction a lot during the sermon and I'm not sure but what his voice was a little bit quivery when he was talking to you at the door after church."

"Oh, Mama, you're just imagining things, that preacher wouldn't be interested in me and I'm sure not interested in him. Besides, I'm way too young for him," Sally protested, while at the same time wondering about the weak hand shake she had received from a man who had been so forceful in the pulpit just minutes earlier. And she had to admit his preaching voice and his greeting voice were quite different.

By this time Sally's younger sister and little brother had gotten into the act and were skipping along, chanting, "Sally's gonna marry the preacher, Sally's gonna marry the preacher."

"I most certainly am not," Sally yelled at them as they ran on ahead toward the house which was now in sight, "and you better stop saying that or I'll smack you good when we get home."

Jeremiah Stevens, Sally's father who was a quiet and thoughtful

10

man, as was typical for him, did not acknowledge that he had even heard any of the conversation or teasing. He just kept his steady pace toward home and Sunday dinner, and if he had any thoughts on the matter he kept them to himself.

Despite Sally's protestations, during the next two weeks she did give a lot of thought to the new preacher. She was forced to admit to herself and to herself alone that he was a right nice looking man, tall and slender and well dressed in his black suit and starched collar. And his preaching was certainly impressive.

After reading his text from the Bible, she had noticed, he never looked down at the pulpit again. He just got into a rhythm and, without as much as a moment's pause, preached nonstop for nearly an hour. She figured that she could not have been distracting him very much for his words and demeanor were so compelling that hardly a person stirred and when he gave the altar call at the end of the sermon, the front of the church was crowded with people praying and repenting.

Yes, she thought, the Reverend Abraham Blake is an interesting man, and if I were a couple of years older I might be interested, but not now when I am only sixteen. I don't care if Mama keeps reminding me that most of the girls my age are getting married, I am not ready yet.

Neither her private thoughts about Brother Abraham Blake, nor her sibling's teasing, nor her mother's frequent references to him prepared Sally for the next preaching Sunday, two weeks later. Although she secretly admitted the possibility that Brother Blake might be somewhat interested in her, she had no idea that he already considered her to be his possession, in accordance with a divine plan.

Maybe it was because she was preoccupied with her thoughts about the young preacher that she did not pay attention to the fact that her mother was unusually busy in the kitchen on Saturday and early Sunday morning. If she had noticed, she might have figured out that her mother was determined to get ahead of all the other women of the church, especially those with eligible daughters, and secure Brother Blake for Sunday dinner at her house.

When Brother Blake greeted Sally on this Sunday, she was puzzled as, instead of receiving a weak handshake like she had experienced two weeks before, she suddenly felt her right hand being clasped tightly in both of his. As he said, "God bless you Sister Sarah," he smiled at her in a knowing way as if they were the only two persons in the world who were aware of some great secret.

Dinner at home was equally uncomfortable for Sally. Yes, her mother had succeeded in getting the family to church early so she could be in the front of the line in inviting Brother Blake to dinner, and once she got him there she was determined to make the most of the opportunity to impress him with the attributes of her near old-maid sixteen year-old daughter.

Sally had little appetite that day. She was feeling more and more anxious and uneasy with the way things were going. She was relieved when her mother asked her to help clear the dishes and put away the food while her father and the preacher went into the parlor and the younger children went outside to play. After the kitchen chores were completed and Sally's mother insisted that they both join the "men-folks" in the parlor, Sally had no choice but to comply.

No sooner had they sat down than the pent-up enthusiasm and joy of Brother Blake just burst forth.

"I am so glad that God led you to invite me here today, Sister Stevens," he said. "There has been something constantly on my mind since I was here two weeks ago and it has been the subject of my unceasing prayer. Ever since I felt God's call into the ministry, I have been asking Him to provide me with the helpmate that He has prepared for me. Now I believe that He has revealed that one to me and I know that I will never be able to fully express my gratitude to Him for what He has done. Brother Stevens, I believe, beyond the shadow of a doubt, that it is God's will for your daughter, Sarah, to become my wife and I would like to ask you for your blessing."

This bolt of lightning set off a series of reactions. As Sally impulsively jumped from her chair and started to run out of the room, her mother grabbed her with a suffocating hug and started crying and murmuring, "Thank you, Jesus," as her father just stared straight ahead.

When her father finally moved, he did not turn toward the preacher, instead he turned to his stunned daughter still in her mother's arms and asked, "Well, Sally Good'in, how does all of this strike you?"

"Papa, I don't know," was her startled reply. "I certainly don't want to marry somebody that I just met."

"He hasn't talked to you about any of this, has he?" her father asked.

"No, Papa, not a single word," Sally said.

"But we can't go against the Lord," her mother said, revealing her sentiments in the form of a warning, "and if the Lord has showed Brother Blake that this is His will, we better pay attention to it."

"Now you just hold on for a minute, Blanche," Mr. Stevens said, "and let me say a thing or two." Then, turning to the preacher, he continued, "Now then, Brother Blake, you strike me as a pretty good feller, but like Sally says, we hardly know you. So for you to come in here and spring a thing like this on us is more than we can deal with here today. It looks to me like the girl ain't near ready to consider marrying you, and until she is ready, you ain't getting my blessing. My advice to you is to back off and come at this thing a little slower. I ain't questioning if it's the Lord's will or not, but if it is the Lord's will, He might not be in as big a hurry as you are. If it is His will, it still will be next month or next year. Now, if you prove to be half the man I think you are, in time the girl might change her mind and want to marry you, but until then, to my way of thinking, you've got some waiting and some wooing to do."

Bitter disappointment and humiliation engulfed Abe as he hastily said his good-byes and angrily dug his heels into the sides of his horse and headed for home. How could he have been so wrong? How could he have been so stupid to think that a person as beautiful and graceful as Sally Stevens would want to marry him? Had he, because of his sudden infatuation, presumed on God? He was sure that Sally would never forgive him for this day and he was almost ashamed to ask God to forgive him for his stupidity, but finally he did.

For the next two weeks, Abe searched the scriptures for an answer or a sign that would give him guidance as he prepared to face the family that he was certain now had total disdain for him. As was his habit, when he found himself in need of solace, he turned to the Psalms and, although he had read them many times, he was surprised to find that so many of them were mirror expressions of

13

his anguish.

He read: "Out of the depths have I cried unto thee, O Lord. Lord, hear my voice." He turned the page and read: "Lord, I cry unto thee: make haste unto me; give ear unto my voice." And on and on as Abe was settling comfortably into a state of holy despair, feeling like the persecuted saints of old until he began reading from the fortieth Psalm: "I waited patiently for the Lord; and he inclined unto me, and heard my cry. He brought me up also out of an horrible pit, out of the miry clay, and set my feet upon a rock, and established my goings. And he put a new song in my mouth."

Abe accepted this passage as his sign. What he needed, he knew, was a new song for neither his mouth nor his heart had been able to sing since that awful Sunday.

Armed with the insights wrought out of two weeks of desperate prayer and study, Abe once again stood before the congregation at Nutter Fort.

Brother Blake preached quite a bit quieter this Sunday that he had two weeks previous. What his sermon lacked in enthusiasm, though, was more than made up for by the substance and self-reflection in this Sunday's message. Using the fortieth Psalm as his text, he exhorted the people to be patient, always waiting on the Lord instead of rushing headlong into decisions which will achieve our wants. Instead, he encouraged them, "be humble and faithful and always appreciate the gifts that we receive in God's perfect time."

Without making any specific reference to the disastrous events of his last Sunday here, he admitted to the congregation that he needed to hear this sermon himself and that God was using events in his own life to show him the truth of the text.

Not knowing what to expect, Sally approached the rear of the church with great apprehension but was surprised and relieved when Abe took her hand firmly and said, "God bless you, Sister Sally, I hope you have a good day."

"Thank you, Brother Blake," Sally responded. "You have a good day, too."

Sally then heard her father, who was just behind her, say, "Brother Blake; I liked your sermon today. Sounds to me like you might be getting on the right road."

Well, Sally thought as she walked home, if he hates me, he

didn't let it show. I wonder what that means?

As the weeks and months passed, Sally slowly began to look at the Reverend Abraham Blake with different eyes. His sermons from his heart began speaking to her, but it was mostly his actions that began to attract her.

Despite his humiliation on that Sunday at her home, he treated her with total respect and showed no signs of resentment toward her. This, coupled with the obvious overt efforts of every other young woman in the congregation to get his attention, caused Sally to slowly begin giving encouraging signs to Abe to see if he was still interested in her.

He was. They were married later that year in April, just before Easter, 1824.

Jeremiah was born the next February on that dark, cold, blustery day.

3 *THE BOY HAS A SPECIAL GIFT*

As Jeremiah grew up hearing his parents talk about the day he was born, he came to believe that the cold, harsh nature of that day was an omen of what his life would be. Throughout his life, despite his brilliance and the successes he achieved, Jeremiah would be plagued time after time by periods of darkness and melancholy.

His mother Sally was, by nature, a warm and loving person but during the early years of Jeremiah's life she seemed to be sad most of the time and as much as Jeremiah tried, he just could not do enough to keep her from her sorrows.

Jeremiah could not have known just how much his mother's life had changed when she married his father when she was barely seventeen. She had exchanged the relative ease of life in a warm and loving family in the community of Nutter Fort for the stark reality of eking out an existence with her preacher-husband on a hilly, rocky farm on Melford Creek. Their only means of support other than what they grew on the farm came from the small "love offerings" that Abe received from the churches where he preached.

At the time of their marriage, Abe was still struggling to build a house on land that he was buying from his father, paying for it by sharing his crops with his parents. Although Abe's father and two brothers were helping him with the house construction, none of them were skilled builders and the introduction of Sally to the rather crude, unfinished house on her wedding day was a shock, to say the least.

Living with her new husband was not easy, either. Although Abe loved Sally deeply and was thankful for her, he believed that God had ordained that, as a man, his role was to be the unchallenged "head of the house" and that his wife was to be his "obedient vessel." Nothing in her childhood growing up under the protective care of her gentle, supportive father had prepared her for a life with this stern, closed-minded husband. If there had been a way, any way at all, she would have left Abe and returned to the comfort of her parent's home.

What Jeremiah did not realize was that, although his mother was often sad, he was her greatest treasure and probably the only reason that she did not take desperate action or lose her mind.

Sally's demeanor changed for the better when Jeremiah was ten years old and her second child, Rebecca was born. Jeremiah recognized the change in his mother's attitude and was glad for it, yet it troubled him. Why did this new child make her happy when he perceived that he had not? Neither Abe nor Sally had ever given Jeremiah a hint of any of his mother's intervening pregnancies and even if he had known, he was too young to connect her sadness with the trauma of experiencing one miscarriage or stillbirth after another. Jeremiah would weep when he was older and he realized what had been happening the times his father had taken him to the Wilson's to stay for a day or two and took Mrs. Fannie Wilson with him back to his house.

It saddened him that he had given very little thought to the fresh mound of dirt on the hill behind the house each of those times when he returned home. This had occurred every couple of years and he could only imagine the deep sorrow and feelings of defeat that his parents, and especially his mother, must have felt and suffered through in virtual silence.

But what he reasoned in his ten year old mind was that maybe only girls can make mothers happy and maybe his mother's sadness was not due to what he had done but just because he was a boy. But then he thought about their neighbor, Mrs. Fannie Wilson, the midwife who had helped deliver him; she had a family of nine boys and no girls, and she was the happiest woman that he knew. Nope, Jeremiah concluded, there has to be something wrong with me and he thought of little else during his dark periods.

This feeling was reinforced two years later when Jeremiah's second sister, Rachel was born. It was not until Jeremiah was fifteen years old and his baby brother, Joshua, was born that he could see that the birth of a son could bring happiness to his mother.

Abe Blake was a remote father. He never seemed to be satisfied with Jeremiah's behavior or work effort. Sinless perfection was the only mode of conduct that Abe would accept, and as hard as Jeremiah would strive to please his father, he was constantly falling short. When it came to carrying out his assigned tasks on the farm, it seemed that he simply could not do them as fast or as well as his father demanded. Abe practiced his firm belief in the Biblical admonition not to "spare the rod and spoil the child," so Jeremiah frequently felt the sting of his father's harsh words or, worse, the sting of his belt, a stick, or his meaty hand.

Jeremiah's happiest days, then, were not at home with his sad mother, or in the fields with his harsh father, or at church on Sundays listening to his father's long sermons, some of which scared Jeremiah nearly to death. His happiest days, instead, were at the small one-room log school house, presided over by a young teacher, George Talley, where he could lose himself in his studies. If it had not been for school and Mr. Talley, Jeremiah would have expected nothing more than to live a sad, laborious life and then, probably, be consigned to the Devil's Hell.

George Talley had seen something special in the small sad boy as soon as he started school. Mr. Talley lived in the community and, like Abe Blake and every other man on Melford Creek, was a farmer so he knew Jeremiah and his parents well. He also knew the reason for Sally's sorrow and he often worried about the severity of discipline that Abe meted out to Jeremiah.

Mr. Talley had realized that this was not an ordinary student, even when Jeremiah was only six years old. He had never had a student who took everything so seriously and gave himself so totally to his studies. By the end of Jeremiah's fifth year in school, he had completed all the work that Mr. Talley expected of his eight-year students.

"Well, Jeremiah," Mr. Talley commented near the end of Jeremiah's fifth year, "you have created a dilemma for me. I don't know what to do with you for I have taught you everything that I have to offer and you are barely twelve years old, much too young to go out into the world. What do you think we should do?"

"I would very much like to continue to come to school," Jeremiah answered, realizing that the alternative would be to spend every day of the year at home until he was old enough to strike out on his own. Although he now had two little sisters, Rebecca and Rachel, and the mood in the home set by his mother was much cheerier, he knew that all of his waking hours would be spent in the fields doing backbreaking labor under the critical eye of his father. "Is there any way that I could still come?" he asked.

"I have been thinking a great deal about that," his teacher said as he considered the slight, dark haired boy who was so eager to learn and so unsuited to face the harsh life on Melford Creek that seemed to be his inevitable fate. "If your parents are agreeable to it, I would like for you to continue to attend school and help me with some of the instruction. You could tutor some of the students who need help. In addition to that, I would like to make available to you all of the books that I have and guide you in your reading to help you prepare for college."

"College?" Jeremiah said, at once excited and frightened at the thought. He knew that he wanted to continue learning but the concept of college had never seemed to be a possibility. "I don't think Papa will think much of that idea."

"Why don't we talk to him and your mother," Mr. Talley said, "and then we'll go from there."

"College?" was Abe's astounded response to the proposal being presented to him by Mr. Talley. "Why on earth should he go to college? How much education does a person need? I believe that a body can pray and the Lord will give him the wisdom he needs. I never went to college, but the Lord still called me to preach and there ain't no higher calling than that. I did get to go to school long enough to learn to read and write, but my papa couldn't write his own name and I just pray that I'm half the preacher that he was. George, you've told me that this boy can read and write and cipher better than anybody you ever taught, and you know that he has learned the Bible here at home and at church and now he's becoming a tolerable hand on the farm, so what's this talk about college? And if he was to go away, who's going to help me here, tell me that?"

"Brother Blake," Mr. Talley answered calmly, carefully choosing his words, "first off, he would not leave for another four or five years, and secondly and most important, the boy has a special gift. God has given Jeremiah the best mind of any student that I have ever taught and I believe that we would be robbing him and robbing God if we did not give him the opportunity to fully develop his abilities."

"Well, I don't see it and I ain't having none of it," was Abe's angry response. "If the farm ain't enough for him, he can preach or teach like me or you, but he'd still be here where he's needed."

"Abe, I have something that I must say," Sally said, in a voice more determined that Jeremiah had ever heard before. "I don't disagree with you very often, but I ask you to listen to me for I think that this is a time when I have to speak up. I have known for a long time that Jeremiah is a special child and, like George says, he has a wonderful gift. Even before he was born I began asking God to show us His will for Jeremiah. I think we should thank George for his generosity because I believe that this is how God has answered my prayer."

"You do, huh?" Abe said angrily, but did not comment further, realizing that Sally, as she did on rare occasions, had made up her mind on the matter and if there was going to be peace at home, he would have to swallow a bitter pill. It was much later that Abe pondered the irony of Sally's successful use of the "it is God's will" argument in contrast to his failed use of the very same argument on that humiliating day when he first proposed marriage.

It was when Jeremiah was twelve that his father figured he was strong enough to be of some help when he took corn, wheat, or buckwheat to the mill down in Lewis County to be ground into flour and meal. The mill, owned by the Jackson family, was the closest place for Abe to get his grain ground and the Jackson's did the grinding for their portion of the resultant flour and meal, which they could then sell.

The sight of the mill was breathtaking to Jeremiah. The most impressive item was the giant wooden wheel being turned by the waterfall created by a dam across the millstream. His curiosity led him to inspect the inner workings of the mill and see how the interlocking cogs from the water wheel connected to the large shaft in the center of the heavy millstone, which slowly turned, grinding the grain. He had never seen anything quite so impressive.

The next thing he noticed was a boy not much bigger than himself covered from head to toe with white dust, who was hard at work bagging flour.

"Who is that boy, Papa?" Jeremiah asked.

"I think he's one of the Jackson's," Abe replied. "He's always here so he must be a relative. Mr. Jackson ain't never been married so he ain't his son."

Abe and Jeremiah had arrived shortly before noon and when Jeremiah saw the lad leave his station and go toward the bank of the mill stream to eat lunch, Jeremiah took his sack of biscuits and meat his mother had fixed and went to join him.

"Howdy," Jeremiah said. "What'cha doing?"

"Looking for a shady place to set while I eat," was the curt reply. "Who are you?"

"I'm Jeremiah Blake from up at Melford Creek," he answered. "I came down here with my papa this morning."

"You papa must be Preacher Blake," the boy observed. "I feel sorry for you having a preacher for a father. He gets after me all the time for some of the words I say."

"It's not too bad, I reckon," Jeremiah lied, "what's your name?"

"Thomas Jonathan Jackson, but I go by T. J." the boy answered.

"Does your papa work here at the mill?" Jeremiah asked.

"My papa is dead," T. J. responded, staring straight ahead across the stream. "He was a lawyer in Clarksburg but he died when I was two. My mama's dead, too, that's why we live here with our uncle."

Jeremiah was momentarily speechless. What had started out as a casual conversation had suddenly become very serious. What should he say next?

"You said, 'we,'" Jeremiah blurted out. "Who else is there?"

"My sister, Laura Ann," T. J. said and Jeremiah noticed a softening in T. J.'s demeanor when he began speaking about his sister. "She's eleven and I'm thirteen. We got an older brother, Warren, and when Mama died he went to live with her people and me and Laura Ann was sent here. I'm glad she came here with me so I can look after her."

"I'm twelve," Jeremiah blurted out, again not sure what to say.

"Huh?" T. J. asked.

"I'm sorry, I didn't know what to say and you told me how old you were so I just said that I'm twelve years old," Jeremiah explained.

"Okay," T. J. said as he jumped up and went to the edge of the stream. "Can you skip rocks?"

21

"I sure can," Jeremiah responded proudly. "Sometimes on the West Fork I can have them skip ten or twelve times."

"Let me see you skip one," T. J. said, challenging him.

"Okay, just as soon as I find the right rock," Jeremiah said as he searched for the perfect flat round stone.

When he found a stone that suited him, Jeremiah threw it with a sidearm motion and it skipped across the water like a dragon fly and landed all the way on the other side of the mill stream. Proud of his accomplishment, Jeremiah knew that T. J. would be hard pressed to top it. However, T. J. did not acknowledge the beauty of Jeremiah's achievement nor did he immediately try to skip a stone. Instead T. J. issued another challenge.

"Let me see you skip one left handed," he demanded.

"I don't know if I can or not," Jeremiah replied, somewhat puzzled. "I reckon I can try."

With that, he selected another stone and awkwardly slung it into the stream where it simply plunked and sank to the bottom.

This obviously pleased T. J. who quickly picked up a stone and threw it with his left hand and it skipped three times before sinking.

"How can you do that," Jeremiah asked.

"I don't think that a person's left side needs to be weaker that his right side," was T. J.'s answer, "so every time I do something with my right hand, then I make myself do the same thing with my left hand. I can eat with my left hand, write with my left hand, and drive nails with my left hand. I figure if I use it as much as my right, I'll be as strong in one as the other."

"I never thought about that," Jeremiah said, "I might try that myself."

"Well," T. J. said abruptly, "I gotta be getting back to work now. I'll see you the next time you come down here."

After they had loaded their bags of flour on the wagon and headed the horses toward home, Abe turned to Jeremiah and asked, "What did you think of the mill?"

"It's really something," Jeremiah replied and then jumped into the subject which most interested him. "Did you know that Jackson boy's papa and mama are both dead and he can skip a rock with his left hand?" He then proceeded to relate, non-stop, to his father all that he had learned about his new friend that he had found to be so fascinating.

The next four years, from age twelve to age sixteen, were great years for Jeremiah. He was a natural teacher and enjoyed tutoring some of George Talley's students, but his greatest pleasure came from his reading.

Under Mr. Talley's watchful eye, Jeremiah studied the history of the great civilizations of the world and Greece and Rome captivated him. He studied the military exploits of Alexander the Great, Julius Caesar, Hannibal, Charlemagne, Napoleon, and, his favorite, George Washington. He read the writings of leading American authors and writers from old England.

He developed a special fascination with government and politics. He pored over every text he could find which told about the founding fathers of the United States and laid in bed at night entertaining himself with "what if" scenarios.

What if the Trojans had not let in the horse and had defeated the Greeks? What if Hannibal's elephants had not turned and trampled his own army? What if the American Revolution had not been successful? What if the Constitution had not been accepted by all of the states? What if George Washington had wanted to be a king? What if the Church of England or his own Methodist Church or some other denomination had been selected as the national religion? What if President John Adams had not been willing to turn the government over to Thomas Jefferson, a man that he feared would destroy the country? Why had the founding fathers not dealt with slavery? What? Why? When? Jeremiah's thirst for knowledge was insatiable.

During these years Jeremiah looked forward, more and more, to the trips to Jackson's Mill where he had found that he and T. J. thought alike about a lot of things and they had become the best of friends. T. J. was also a student of history, especially military history and the boys never seemed to have enough time to fully share their personal slants on what had, or could have, or should have happened in history.

"What are you going to do for a living," T. J. asked Jeremiah the fall when he was sixteen and Jeremiah was fifteen. "You're so smart, you ought to be a professor, or teacher, or something like that."

"I'm aiming to go to college, maybe next year," Jeremiah responded, "and I suppose I could be one of those things or maybe even a lawyer like your papa. What about you?"

"I've never told anybody this but Laura Ann, but I am gonna be a soldier, and not just any old soldier, I intend to be a general," T. J. said resolutely. "My aim is to go to West Point. I know that ain't gonna be easy. I only went to school for four years and I don't come from a rich family, but that's what I'm shooting for."

"How do you think you can get that to happen?" Jeremiah asked.

"I'm kin to some big politicians in Clarksburg that my papa was working with when he died. I'm hoping that they can help get me appointed," T. J. speculated.

"Boy-oh-boy, that would certainly be something," Jeremiah said and then chuckled, "can you imagine; 'General T. J. Jackson and Jeremiah Blake, Attorney at Law.'"

"Well, I don't know about you, Jeremiah Blake," T. J. said with a steely glint, "but I am determined to be General T. J. Jackson. You be sure and remember that."

"I certainly will, General," Jeremiah said as he stiffly saluted his friend and they both broke into laughter.

It was a few days after his sixteenth birthday, in February, at the supper table when Jeremiah decided that he could not postpone any further the painful task of announcing his plans to his father.

"Papa," he said, "Mr. Talley helped me send off my letter of application to college and if I get accepted, I'm fixing to leave this summer."

"Oh, you are, are you?" was the sharp response. "Well, where are you going and how are you going to get there and how are you going to live after you get there?"

Jeremiah took a deep breath, determined not to be put off by the reaction of his father, which was not unexpected.

"You know about the Buffalo Seminary up in the panhandle," he said. "It is going to be called Bethany College from now on and Mr. Talley says that most of the other colleges in Virginia only accept students from rich families but Bethany is going to be open to everybody. I figure I ought to go on up there this summer so I can look for a place to live and work while I'm there." Then he

24

continued, hesitantly, "I was thinking that maybe you would let me take ol' Molly with me."

By the time Jeremiah had finished talking, his father was livid.

"Boy, don't you know that the Buffalo Seminary is Alexander Campbell's baby," Abe yelled. "No wonder he's changing the name and opening it up to everybody, he wants to make Campbellites out of you and everybody else he can get his hands on. If you go up to that place, you'll come out of there a Campbellite or an abolitionist, or both. Don't you think for one minute that I'm gonna let you take my best riding horse to go off on no fool escapade like that."

Abe was so worked up that even Sally knew that this was not the time to enter the discussion. Her look of sympathy in Jeremiah's direction did give him some hope. When she set her mind to it, Jeremiah knew that she could sway even the immovable, all-knowing Reverend Abraham Blake.

It was early May at the end of a day spent burning brush piles and planting corn on a freshly cleared "new-ground" that Abe commented to his son, "If you're aiming to get to that college by summer, you best be doing something about it. You still got your head set on that?"

"Yes I do, Papa" Jeremiah replied.

"Well, you are going to need a good horse, so I suppose I'll have to manage somehow without ol' Molly," Abe said. "You and her always got along good together, anyhow."

Hot tears welled up in Jeremiah's eyes. Nothing in his father's demeanor over the past two and a half months had given the slightest hint that this day would ever arrive. He had envisioned leaving, on foot, with his mother crying and his father's angry voice echoing in his ears. Now, instead, it looked like he was going to depart with some semblance of his father's blessing and favorite horse. He would have been less surprised if the Second Coming that his father preached about so much had occurred. Jeremiah had a sudden urge to embrace his father, but he refrained because such a show of affection had never taken place between them so he just said gently, "Thank you, Papa; thank you ever so much."

"I think it's your Mama you want to be thanking," was his father's reply as they walked toward the house.

4 *THE SEVENTY MILE ODYSSEY*

Jeremiah left for Bethany in late May, after a lot of hugs and kisses from Rebecca and Rachel and a long, tearful embrace and endless admonitions from his mother. The last thing he did before leaving was to transfer little Joshua from his arms to the arms of their mother and solemnly shake hands with his father. A great sense of adventure swept over him as he began his pilgrimage from the only home that he had ever known to traverse the forbidding seventy or so miles to his new life at Bethany College.

He was acutely aware that he had only barely been out of Harrison County in his entire life. Since he was twelve he had accompanied his father each time he took a wagon load of grain to Jackson's Mill, but that was just across the line into Lewis County. But now he was on his way to the big city of Wheeling, located on the mighty Ohio River and he was going to college! His melancholia was forgotten; he could not contain his excitement.

He spent the first night of his trip with his grandparents, Jeremiah and Blanche Stevens at Nutter Fort. Their home was one of his very favorite places. The house was inviting and young Jeremiah always felt a sense of safety and reassurance when he was there and this night was no exception.

His grandfather listened intently as Jeremiah told him of his dreams and aspirations. He said that he did not know exactly what his future would be but his grandfather was proud to hear of his hopes of studying the law and government and then returning to Harrison County to be of service in some way. As he talked, Jeremiah was struck by the difference in talking to his Grandpa Stevens and trying to talk with his father or his late Grandpa Blake, neither of whom ever seemed to have the patience to listen to the opinions of a young boy.

Grandma Blanche outdid herself for supper, fixing Jeremiah his favorite meal of chicken and dumplings, capped off with fresh strawberry shortcake made from the tiny wild berries that she, herself, had picked that day.

For breakfast the next morning, she made a big pan of biscuits, which she served with fried ham and red-eye gravy. After Jeremiah had eaten all he could hold, she insisted that he have another biscuit or two with honey, or jelly, or molasses, or "something sweet."

Jeremiah's grandfather followed him out to the barn as Jeremiah was getting ready to leave.

"Son, do you have any money?" the grandfather asked.

"None to speak of, Grandpa," Jeremiah replied, to which his grandfather responded, "Well, just how do you expect to pay for your college once you get there?"

"I'll have to work and earn my own way. At least that's what I've been thinking," Jeremiah said. "Mama always told me that I should do my best and trust God to provide the rest, and I guess that's what I'm planning on doing."

"I'm glad your mama told you that because that's what I told her many a time and I guess she didn't forget it," the grandfather said. "But I hope it wouldn't hurt your feelings none if me and your grandma helped you a little bit just to get you started. You take this here envelope and you open it up when you get to the college because I have an idea Mr. Alexander Campbell might want some money right away."

After Jeremiah and his grandfather had saddled Molly, he went to tell his grandmother good-bye and she handed him a small package and said, "Honey, you need to find someplace to put this in your things. I've fixed you a little something to eat while you're traveling."

As he headed Molly north he turned and waved to his grandparents. Filled with their warmth and love, he felt a huge lump form in his throat and tears streamed from his eyes. In all of the excitement of his preparations and leaving, he had not stopped to grasp the totality of what was occurring until this moment. Seeing his gentle, aging grandparents waving to him and realizing how much they loved him and what great expectations they had for him was suddenly overwhelming.

Jeremiah had a good day to travel and his horse was fresh so they made good time. When the sun was about straight overhead he found a shady spot near a small stream and stopped. After he let Molly drink her fill, he removed the saddle and tied her where she could graze. Then he opened the package that Grandma Blanche had given him and, just as he expected, he found a number of large biscuits filled with thick slabs of ham. After he had eaten he laid down and rested for about an hour and then replenished his water jug from the stream and saddled up Molly to continue the trek north.

By nightfall, he arrived in the community of Old Hundred. He surmised that whoever named this town was surely a Methodist because that was what Methodists sang in church every Sunday. He amused himself by singing it under his breath as he looked for a place to spend the night:

"Praise God from whom all blessings flow,
Praise Him all creatures here below;
Praise Him above ye heavenly hosts;
Praise Father, Son, and Holy Ghost."

Jeremiah was pleasantly surprised when he saw a sign on the side of a chestnut clapboard building that said "Hendry's Blacksmith Shop." He was especially glad to see that there was still some smoke coming from the chimney because one of Molly's shoes was coming loose and he was concerned that the smithy might not still be in his shop.

"Hey there, young feller," a booming voice came from inside the darkening shop, "what can I do for ya?"

"One of ol' Molly's shoes is coming loose and I don't have any way to fix it myself. Thought maybe you could help me," Jeremiah answered.

"Let me have a look at 'er, I bet I can take care of it in a jiffy," the smithy replied as he came out into the daylight.

"What brings you to Old Hundred?" the smithy asked as he lifted up Molly's front hoof and examined the situation.

"I've come up from Melford Creek on my way to Wheeling, well, Bethany really. I'm aiming to go to college up there," Jeremiah explained.

The smithy looked up from his work into the boyish face of the skinny lad before him and said, "You look to be a mite young to be going to college. You must be a smart one, huh."

"I don't know about that," Jeremiah replied embarrassedly, "I figure I might have a lot of trouble keeping up once I get there."

"Aw, I'll bet you won't," the smithy said as he used his pincers to wiggle and then pull out a loose, bent nail and then, after shifting the shoe slightly, with a few expert taps with his hammer he replaced it with a new nail and quickly secured the shoe.

"There," he said as he lowered Molly's hoof to the ground and lifted each of the other three hooves to inspect them. "She's as good as new. That should see you to Wheeling with no trouble."

Jeremiah expressed his appreciation with the common, "I'm much obliged to you," and then asked, "how much do I owe you?"

"That would cost an ordinary feller ten cents," the smithy said with a smile, "but for a bright young man starting out on his way to make a mark in the world, there ain't no charge."

"Where you planning on sleeping tonight and what are you gonna eat?" the smithy asked as Jeremiah was getting back in the saddle.

"It's a nice night so all I need is to find a place with some grass for ol' Molly and I've got some biscuits and ham left that my grandma fixed me this morning, so I'm think I'm in pretty good shape," was Jeremiah's reply.

"After traveling hard all day, the horse needs some grain," the smithy said, "and a good meal and a feather tick bed wouldn't hurt you none. Come on, boy, you're coming home with me."

Despite Jeremiah's sincere protests, Amos Hendry would accept no payment for his work nor permit Jeremiah to reject his offer of food and shelter for him and Molly. After putting Molly in the barn and providing her with a generous portion of corn and oats, Amos took Jeremiah to the back door of the house and they went into the kitchen.

"We've got company, Bess," Amos announced as he entered the door. "This here is Jeremiah Blake, on his way to college up on the other side of Wheeling, and he's gonna spend the night with us."

"Well, Mr. Blake," Bessie Hendry said as she wiped her hands on her apron and shook Jeremiah's hand warmly, "we're mighty glad to have you but I hope you won't mind putting up with our usual. Not knowing you was coming, I don't have much fixed for supper."

"I appreciate your gracious hospitality, Mrs. Hendry," Jeremiah told her. "I was planning to sleep on the ground and eat ham and biscuits left over from breakfast, so I am sure your usual will be much better than that."

"Why, listen to that boy talk, Amos," Bessie said. "He sounds like he's already been to college. Where are you from, Mr. Blake?"

"I'm from Melford Creek, down below Clarksburg," he answered.

"His papa is a preacher down there, he tells me," Amos added.

"That is just wonderful," Bessie said. "I'll bet you're gonna be a preacher, too, after you get out of college, just like your papa."

"Well, maybe," was Jeremiah's weak reply.

"You young'uns get in here," Bessie suddenly yelled out. "It's time to eat."

Immediately from the front of the house a young boy and three girls came hurrying into the kitchen.

"Mr. Blake, this here's our son Jonas, and he's twelve," Bessie said, "and this is Lily who's ten and this is Violet who's seven and this is little Rose who's five. Folks around here say I must like flowers by the way I named my girls. Jonas says he's just glad I didn't name him Johnny-jump-up. Ya'll say hello to Mr. Blake now, children."

The children shuffled and looked uneasy as they said hello to the visitor who did not look very much older than Jonas and then quickly took their places at the table.

"Since you are a preacher's son, would it be too much to ask for you to say the blessing, Jeremiah?" Amos asked.

Although this was a task which his father always performed at home and Jeremiah knew his father's evening blessing by heart, instead of using it he offered a simple prayer of thanks for the safety of the day, his good fortune of meeting the Hendry's, and for the food that was before them.

The sincerity of the prayer touched Bessie and she said, "Mr. Blake that was a beautiful prayer. I am so glad that you are able to be with us, even for such a short time. Why, you've been a blessing to us already."

The food, the usual for the Hendrys, was all very familiar to Jeremiah. As a matter of fact, he imagined that Mama and Papa, sisters Rebecca and Rachel, and baby Joshua could be having the very same meal of wild greens fried in bacon fat, a big pot of soup beans, boiled potatoes, fresh green onions from the garden, and corn bread, with buttermilk to drink.

After supper, Jeremiah sat on the front porch talking with Amos and Bessie while the Hendry children played in the yard. As the children became less and less wary of the stranger visiting them, Lily, at the urging of the others, approached him and asked if he would like to be "it" in a game of hide-and-go-seek.

"Lily," Bessie scolded, "you young-uns leave Mr. Blake alone. He's traveled a long ways today and he don't want to play no silly games with you."

But Jeremiah was already on his feet and he jumped from the porch into the yard.

"Yes, I would like to be 'it,'" he responded to Lily. "Just don't hide where nobody can find you. If you do, I might leave you there all night. Now you better hurry and hide, for I'm only going to count to twenty."

As the darkness deepened, Bessie had a hard time calling a halt to the games and getting the children settled down for the night. By this time, Jeremiah was no longer a stranger but their very favorite playmate and they clung to him and begged their mother to let them stay up just a little while longer. After relenting twice, Bessie finally succeeded in getting the girls to go to their bedroom and then, by the light of a candle, she showed Jeremiah to the room where he and Jonas would sleep.

As he sank into the softness of the feather tick, Jeremiah reflected over the events of the day and marveled at his good fortune. He was the one born on a dark, dreary day and his life was not supposed to be this good. He would have to think this out more thoroughly sometime when he was not so sleepy, but he sure felt good now.

Jeremiah left the next morning refreshed and well fed with good-bye hugs from Lily, Violet, and Rose, and a stiff handshake from Jonas as well as the sincere assurance from Amos and Bessie

31

that they had been privileged to have him in their home and that he would be welcome there anytime. It had been such a wonderful night that he was sure that he detected that Molly had more spring in her step.

Even though it might take a day longer to reach his destination, Jeremiah had studied his route and rather than going the most traveled road leading directly to Wheeling, he had determined to go straight north from Old Hundred for a ways so he could cross the Mason-Dixon Line and actually be out of the state of Virginia and into the state of Pennsylvania. This was a big event for a youth that had only been in two counties in his life until yesterday.

He was disappointed that there was no visible manifestation of the famous line separating the two states but by mid-morning, after traveling for three hours or so down the narrow roads and country lanes which this route afforded, Jeremiah stopped and called to a farmer who was cultivating his newly emerged corn crop.

"Pardon me, Sir," he called out to the farmer, "am I in the state of Pennsylvania yet?"

"That you be, Boy," the farmer replied as he wrapped the check lines around the handle of his cultivator plow and walked toward Jeremiah at the edge of the field. "Are you lost or is Pennsylvania where you want to be?"

Jeremiah replied, "I'm from Virginia and I'm on my way to Wheeling but I've never been out of Virginia before and I wanted to be able to say that I had been in Pennsylvania so I came up this way."

"Well," the farmer asked, "now that you got here, does Pennsylvania look any different from Virginia?"

"No," Jeremiah laughed, "it all looks about the same. I guess that was why I had to ask you if I was here yet."

After a few minutes of conversation, Jeremiah said that he had better be on his way and asked the farmer for the best way to proceed toward Wheeling.

"Can't say," the farmer said, "I've never been there but I reckon, if I was you, I'd go on up north a ways further and then find me a way to head over toward the river."

Before the day was over, Jeremiah was not certain that his sojourn into Pennsylvania was a good idea, after all. He was navigating more or less by the position of the sun and was spending more time off of Molly than riding her. He had to open and close gates, which was bad enough, but he also had to lay down and then put back up innumerable draw bars which were so much more trouble. He had to explain to person after person who he was and why he was needing to go through their property and getting mostly useless directions toward his destination.

As the day wore on toward evening, he rode into a community and asked the first person he saw, "What is the name of this town?"

"This is Cameron," was the reply.

"Cameron, Virginia, I hope," Jeremiah asked, just to be sure.

"Sure is. What else could it be?" was the man's surprised response

"Thank you, sir, and thank the Lord," Jeremiah said in a relieved voice. "I've been lost over in Pennsylvania since first thing this morning and now I finally found my way back to the right road."

As Jeremiah was getting settled for the night in a field at the edge of town, he noticed that threatening clouds were coming in from the west and he began to search for some sort of shelter. He led Molly and went back toward the center of Cameron where he spotted what he was looking for. The Cameron school house faced east and, unlike the simpler school at Melford Creek, it had a porch with a roof and there was ample grass for Molly in the school yard, so as the thunder rumbled and the rain splashed down, using the saddle as his pillow, he slept like a baby on the porch of the school.

When Jeremiah awoke the next morning, it was already broad daylight. Whoa, he thought, I must have been more worn out than I realized. I never sleep this late.

His stomach told him that it was way past time for breakfast and he had finished the last of his grandmother's ham last night after throwing away the biscuits, which had started to mold. Even though he had always heard bad things about the quality of store-bought food, he knew that he had no other choice if he was going to satisfy the gnawing in his stomach. Before he started out in search of a store he decided to assess his resources.

He first opened his own purse and counted the coins that he had been able to save and had figured would be sufficient to keep him alive until he found work. He then opened the envelope, which his grandfather had given him two days earlier and was amazed to find what to him was a fortune of fifty dollars. Salty tears immediately filled his eyes as he realized the love that had motivated this sacrifice by his grandparents. He quickly closed the envelope and carefully placed it back in his saddlebag and resolved to only use it to pay for college expenses, and proceeded to the only store in town.

"How can I help you, young man?" the storekeeper asked as soon as Jeremiah entered the store.

"What kind of food do you have?" Jeremiah responded.

"You fixing to cook something or just looking for something you can eat on the go?" the storekeeper asked as he looked at the youth and figured out the answer. "If you're looking for something fast, I got soda crackers, cheese, sardines, and some dried apples. I got some pickled eggs in that jar over there and some cucumbers in that barrel of pickle brine."

Jeremiah carefully selected ten crackers, a small wedge of cheese, a tin of sardines, a large pickled cucumber, and two pickled eggs.

"That'll be twelve cents," the shopkeeper said as he tore a measure of paper off his large roll and started to bundle everything up together.

"Let me keep the eggs and cucumber out," Jeremiah instructed as he opened his purse and counted out the coins. This was more than he had planned to spend on a meal but, he figured, his meals at the Hendry's had not cost him anything and what he was buying now would do him all day so he told himself that he could afford it.

Before leaving, Jeremiah wolfed down the two eggs and took a bite of the cucumber. His whole face puckered as soon as he tasted the pickle. He loved the pickles his mother made but they did not taste like this. He had never tasted a pickle made in a brine with dill weed, and if he had not felt that he was on the verge of starvation he would not have eaten the rest of it. He decided that the warnings he had heard about store-bought food were well founded and now he began to worry about the sardines he had bought, whatever they turn out to be.

5 *THE LORD WILL PROVIDE*

Jeremiah arrived in Wheeling on the first day of June in 1841. It was late in the day and he was amazed at the amount of activity going on around him. Shopkeepers were closing their businesses and going home. Farmers who had been selling their produce on the street were heading their wagons out of town. Women who looked to Jeremiah like they were wearing their Sunday finery were walking toward their homes carrying the food items that they needed to prepare their families' evening meal.

Despite his fascination with all of the urban hubbub, Jonathan soon headed Molly straight to the banks of Virginia's mightiest river, the Ohio. As a Virginian, he took pride in the fact that the state border with Ohio was the western bank of the river and that this great stream was wholly within the state of Virginia. He got off his horse and went to the river's edge and, taking off his hat, dipped his hands in the water and gave his head and face a thorough bath.

After sitting on the bank for a while, watching as the boat traffic moved up and down the river, Jeremiah's active mind began to imagine what it would be like if he were a fish, spawned in Melford Creek, which swam downstream into the West Fork River and then into the combined Monongahela River up to Pittsburgh and there turning south into the Ohio River and was just now swimming past this point.

Jeremiah next imagined himself to be in charge of the first European expedition looking with amazement at the vast expanse of the mighty river when he and his men came to this point.

As he pondered that scene he thought that they must have wondered if the other side would ever be settled. Surely they could not have anticipated the awe-inspiring bridge that he was now viewing, truly a marvel, the longest suspension bridge in the world.

And then going even farther back in his imaginings he visualized Indian villages on the island and dotting the river's edge with him and other native men expertly piloting their canoes through the current of the water.

He was moved by the size of the river, its power, and the realization of its timelessness, flowing there long before there were people and then serving equally and magnanimously every culture or generation that happened upon it. Jeremiah had found the city of Wheeling to be impressive and more than a little intimidating, but the river, the river, it was the river that inspired him.

Jeremiah was full of anticipation on the trip to his final destination of Bethany the next morning. He had good, even holy, thoughts about Bethany. As he rode, he thought about the times that Jesus, on his way to and from Jerusalem, would plan his trips to go through the little town of Bethany so He could visit his friends, Mary, Martha, and Lazarus. He pondered on the fact that it was there that Jesus performed his greatest miracle, raising Lazarus from the dead. Bethany, Jeremiah figured, must have been Jesus' favorite place on earth since He chose that place as His point of departure when He ascended to Heaven.

Even though his trip thus far had been largely improvised Jeremiah had, for months, pictured exactly what this day would be; the day of his arrival at Bethany.

The sun was straight overhead when Jeremiah rode Molly into Bethany. There was no question of where Bethany College was located because the impressive building that housed the college was the most prominent feature of the town. What Jeremiah was looking for first, though, was a church steeple. His well thought out plan was to find the Methodist Church and seek the assistance of the pastor to help him locate employment and lodging. When he spotted the steeple and arrived at the small white church, he was disappointed to find that instead of being a familiar Methodist Church, it was a foreboding Baptist Church.

"Pardon me, Sir," Jeremiah said as he approached a man sitting on the porch of the house nearest the church. "Could you tell me where the Methodist Church is located?"

"There's not one here in Bethany," was the reply. "The nearest one is over on the river at Wellsburg. Is there anything I can do to help you?"

"I've come up here to go to college and I was hoping to see the Methodist pastor about where I could get some work and a place to live," Jeremiah said.

The man responded, "Well, seeing as there's not a Methodist pastor around here, you might want to ask the Baptist pastor."

"I don't think so, he might not want to help," Jeremiah said with an embarrassed chuckle. "My papa's a Methodist preacher and Methodists and Baptists don't see eye to eye on a lot of things."

"I've heard people say that; why do you think that is?" the man asked. "Do you think that it's because Baptists aren't really saved when all they do is shake the preacher's hand instead of repenting and praying at the altar; or do you suppose it's because Baptists think they can live like the devil and never lose their salvation?"

"I reckon it could be either one or both," the startled Jeremiah said. "You sound so much like my papa you ought to be a Methodist preacher, too."

"Well, I'm afraid I'm not," the man replied with a hearty laugh, "I'm the Baptist pastor, but I know what some of you Methodists think of us. Now, if you're not afraid of putting your salvation in jeopardy, I'd be glad to try to help you. If you are planning to go to Alexander Campbell's college, I figure you're going to need all the help you can get. I predict that by the time he's through with you, you'll think that Methodists and Baptists aren't so different, after all."

Jeremiah was stunned, and embarrassed, and confused. This was not how things were supposed to be happening. The trip to Bethany had gone so well that he thought that maybe, just maybe, he was leaving behind his dark cloud of despair that was always lurking, but now he was sure it was still with him.

What should he do? What choices did he have? He either would have to accept the hospitality of this man who seemed kind enough, but who, Jeremiah knew, didn't really understand the Bible and would try to convert him before the night was over, or he would have to strike out further into the unknown.

Because he was weary from his travels and had no enthusiasm

37

for further adventure, he decided that he had little choice but to accept the offer. After all, he thought, if God could use a Samaritan to help that man on the Jericho road, maybe He could use a Baptist preacher to help me.

"I would be much obliged if you could help me," Jeremiah said. "I guess the first thing I need is a place to spend the night and then if you could recommend someone who could use some help on their farm, I would search that out tomorrow."

"Good," the preacher said. "My name is William Sharpe, most people around here call me Brother Sharpe, but I would be pleased if you would just call me Will. Now, what would your name be?"

"My name is Jeremiah Blake," was the response.

"Well, Jeremiah Blake, did your preacher papa name you after the 'weeping prophet' of the Old Testament?" Will asked. "If I'm not mistaken, I believe I can see a bit of sadness in your eyes."

"Actually, my mother named me for my grandfather, Jeremiah Stevens," Jeremiah explained, and then added with a smile, "but you're very perceptive for I do often identify with the Jeremiah in the Bible. George Talley, my teacher back home, once told me that I couldn't enjoy a sunny day in May because I was too busy worrying about the next December storm."

"Well, Jeremiah Blake," Will said as he got up and moved toward Molly, "let's take care of your horse and then you're going to stay with us tonight. Tomorrow we'll go looking for you a place to live."

Will and Rowena Sharpe were in their early thirties and had two small boys, William, Jr. (called Little Will), and Seth. Jeremiah soon overcame most of his misgivings and became comfortable with this new, young family. Once again, as had happened at the Hendry's, Jeremiah was given the opportunity to offer the blessing for the evening meal. He was happy to do so, for he wanted God to hear the blessing and if it came from a Baptist, well, he wasn't all that sure it would even get there.

Early the next morning Will and Jeremiah saddled their horses and set out across the rolling fields outside Bethany. In less than half an hour they came in sight of a prosperous looking farm with a well-kept white house and large red barn. On the way, Will had described the Givens family that lived there.

38

"You might be put off at first by old Ben Givens," Will began. "That man has the wickedest mouth on him of any man in Brooke County. But you'll come to realize that behind all his bluster and profanity he's got some good in him and he does have a good head on his shoulders."

"Now, his wife Jennie is a saint," Will continued. "She and their youngest girl come to church once in awhile and they're good neighbors to the people around them."

"What makes you think that they would hire me?" Jeremiah asked.

"Ben Givens is kinda like the rich farmer in the Bible," Will said. "He's got more than he knows what to do with. He's had a few years of bumper crops and he can't keep up with it all by himself. He's got two grown boys but they left home as soon as they could and got jobs over on the river. There's talk that he might even bring in a slave or two and I don't want to see him do that. Maybe if he hires you that will be all the help he needs for awhile."

"Then, there is one more thing that I have been thinking a lot about," Will added. "Ben and Jennie's youngest boy James, who's about twelve, was born with something wrong with his legs and he can't walk so he's never been to school, never been to church, never been nowhere, really. Jennie's done the best she can to teach him to read and write but she can't take him much further. As soon as you told me what you were looking for I thought of the Givenses. You could be just what James Givens needs."

"What do you mean?" Jeremiah asked.

"I mean he needs someone to give him more of an education than Jennie can do, but more than that he needs a friend who can help prepare him for life," Will answered. "If somebody don't do something soon, I'm afraid he'll get to the place where he'll never come out of the house."

"Well, here we are at the Givens place," Will said as he dismounted his horse and tied him to the hitching rail. "Let's see how it goes."

They were greeted at the door by a most pleasant, rather matronly woman with an ingratiating smile.

"Good morning, Brother Sharpe," she said. "What brings you all the way out here this early in the morning?"

"Ms. Jennie," Will replied, "I've got somebody that I want you to meet. This is Jeremiah Blake and he's looking for a place to live and work while he goes to Alexander Campbell's college."

"How do, Mr. Blake," Jennie said as she extended her hand to him, her smile getting even broader. "I'm glad to meet you. The mister is sure needing some help here on the place but you look a little too skinny to be a farm hand to me. You sure you've worked on a farm before?"

"Just every day of my life, Mrs. Givens," Jeremiah assured her as he returned her smile. "I was born and raised on a farm down in Harrison County."

"Well, ain't that something?" Jennie said apologetically. "You know I didn't mean no harm. It's just that you look so young and you're sorta refined looking so I took it that you might be a city boy. I hope you'll forgive me."

Jeremiah laughed as he told Jennie that he would take her first evaluation of him as a compliment and assured her that he was stronger and tougher than he looked.

Jennie invited them to come and sit on the front porch and wait for Ben to return from his milk run. She explained to Jeremiah that he delivered milk every morning to about twenty-five families in town and was due back shortly.

As he sat down in the porch swing Will asked, "How is James doing these days, Ms. Jennie?"

"Why, he's doing just fine," was the reply. "He reads everything he can get his hands on. He's even memorized the first three chapters of the Gospel of John. Don't you think that's something?"

"It sure is," the preacher responded. "You're doing a fine job of educating that boy." Then he continued, "Where is James and where are your girls? Would they like to come out and visit with us while we wait?"

"I'll bet they would," Jennie said as she got up and went to the door. "James," she yelled, "you and the girls come on out here, we got company."

Jeremiah, not knowing what to expect, was very pleasantly surprised to see two pretty girls emerge as he continued to hear scurrying and thumping sounds that he assumed were being made by

40

James as he came through the house.

Then, as Will was introducing Jeremiah to Lizzie and Lucy, James popped through the door. He was a handsome lad with sandy brown hair and a friendly face and he was perfectly normal above his hips. His body rested on his hips and his legs that were turned outward and nearly parallel to the floor. He moved to the porch by elevating himself in quick hops with his deformed legs and propelling himself forward with his hands and strong arms.

"Well, hello there, James," Will greeted him. "You're sure looking good today."

"Good morning, Brother Sharpe," James said politely. "I'm glad to see you again."

"James," Will continued, "this is Jeremiah Blake. He's a few years older than you and he's about to start college and we've come to see if your papa might want to use him on the farm while he's here."

Jeremiah got up from his seat and reached down to shake James' hand. He had never felt a hand like James' before, heavy and calloused and extremely strong for such a young boy. James responded shyly but with a slight smile that made him look remarkably like his mother.

"I hear that you like to read," Jeremiah said. "What books do you have?"

"I've got a few books left over from when my brothers went to school and now Lucy brings me home books when she goes to school," James replied. "And we've got a Bible and Pilgrim's Progress."

"If I were to live here with you," Jeremiah offered, "after I get into college I could probably see what's in the library there and bring you all kinds of books."

James brightened at that prospect and as he started to respond his father came in sight driving his horse drawn milk wagon.

"Hey, preacher," Ben yelled good naturedly as he got down from his seat on the milk wagon, "did somebody die, or are you out here looking for sinners or money or both?"

"Ben, you shouldn't talk to Brother Sharpe like that," Jennie scolded. "He's brought out a nice young man that's looking for a job and place to live while he goes to college."

"Good morning, Ben," Will said cordially as he shook the farmer's hand. "I agreed to help this young man find some work and a place to stay and I decided to start here with you. I thought you might be able to use him. His name is Jeremiah Blake and he grew up on a farm down in Harrison County."

"Well, Sonny Boy," Ben Givens said, "I won't hold it agin you that you're hanging out with the preacher, here. What I need to know is, can you do the work? Can you milk cows? Can you pull a crosscut saw? Can you use a scythe? Can you stack hay? Can you work horses? Can you split rails and build a fence? These are the things I need done around here."

"You didn't name a thing that I haven't done a hundred times over," Jeremiah answered, "and I'd be much obliged if you'd give me a chance to show you what I can do."

"Now, before you reach any decision, Ben," Will interjected, "Jeremiah will be going to college during the day once the fall term starts, you need to know that."

"Well, I been thinking about going south and getting me a couple of slaves, and I still might, but I need help now so we might as well try this out for a while," Ben said. "Now, Boy, what was your name again?"

"Jeremiah, Sir; Jeremiah Blake," was the answer.

"Well, Jeremiah Blake, you got yourself a job if you don't want too much money," Ben said. "About all I can offer is room and board and, say, thirty cents a day when you work all day. We'd have to adjust that down when you start to college and only help part of the day. How does that sound to you?"

"You are very generous," a grateful Jeremiah answered. "I promise you that I will give you my best effort."

"I'm expecting that and if I don't see it, you won't be around here very long," Ben threatened, and then looking at his wife added, "Now we've got to decide where the boy will sleep. You got any ideas on that."

"Where were you aiming for your slaves to sleep, once you got them?" Jennie asked testily, showing that she was not happy that she had been left completely out of the decision making.

"Why, hellfire Jennie," Ben exploded, "they could have slept anywhere; in the barn with the cows if need be, but you know we can't treat this boy that way."

Jeremiah was startled by Ben's outburst but impressed that, unlike his mother when his father bellowed, Jennie was not in the least intimidated. She turned to Jeremiah and addressed him with a cool, controlled tone.

"Jeremiah," Jennie said, "we have a nice guest bedroom that you can use most of the time. Then, when some of our family folks come to stay for a few days, you would need to stay in James's room with him if that would be okay with you."

"That sounds fine to me," Jeremiah responded, relieved that everything was so easily resolved but apprehensive about what life would be like with this family. He was sure of one thing. It would not be dull.

Before going to bed that night, Jeremiah wrote a long letter to his parents, relating to them all of the wonderful things that had happened to him since he had left home. He was even bold enough to tell his papa about the way he had been helped by a Baptist preacher but he did not think that it was necessary to mention that he was living in the home of the man with "the wickedest mouth in Brooke County."

6 . . . *FIRST LOVE*

Life on the Givens farm took some getting used to.

Although Ben Givens was blustery and demanding, somewhat like Jeremiah's father, Abe Blake had never sworn at him nor called him disparaging names. Jennie was in some ways like Jeremiah's mother but she was tougher and more resilient than Sally Blake and fought with her tyrant of a husband at the drop of a hat. This gave Jeremiah much food for thought. He had always viewed his home as peaceful but he began to consider the possibility that there was peace primarily because his father was seldom challenged.

Getting used to James was a delight. James had a good mind and was well educated in the matters to which he had been exposed and was starved for other matters that Jeremiah could share with him. Nearly every waking moment that he was not working Jeremiah spent with James, discussing the Bible and other books that James had read or exploring the world around them.

Jeremiah soon discovered that it was not James' choice to be housebound, as Will Sharpe had correctly surmised. He was housebound due to a combination of Jennie's over-protective nature and Ben's oblivion to James' potentialities.

But the biggest adjustment Jeremiah faced was living in the same family with the girls, Lizzie and Lucy. Lizzie was seventeen, one year older than Jeremiah, and Lucy was fifteen. Lizzie was striking looking with bright auburn hair and deep blue eyes. She was also brash and outgoing and had become her father's only family help on the farm since her older brothers had left. She was a lot like her father. Her temper could flare up in a second and, if her mother was not in earshot, she would cuss just like him.

Jeremiah had heard people cuss before, but not a lot. Being a preacher's son had given him a wall of protection. Abe Blake did not cuss or use any offensive words; he expressed his anger and frustration in other ways. When they were in the presence of someone whose language became offensive, the Reverend Blake would remark to the person that, "the boy don't need to hear that kind of stuff," and it would usually cease.

So hearing someone cuss was not a new phenomenon to Jeremiah, but hearing a girl cuss certainly was, and a pretty girl, at that.

Lizzie quickly began making Jeremiah the butt of her jokes and constantly badgered him in a way that totally baffled him. She was only one year older than he but she seemed to him to be much wiser in the ways of the world and know things about which he did not have a clue.

She had a beau, Eldon Tompkins, who came calling on Saturday evenings. It was not long until Lucy and James persuaded Jeremiah to join them in trying to spy on Lizzie and Eldon after dark as they sat ever so close together in the swing on the front porch.

Lucy was very different from her older sister. She was more demure and domestic, spending the most of her time in the company of her mother. She was pretty, too, with brown hair and brown eyes and Jeremiah considered her a much more appealing prospect if anyone happened to be looking for a girl friend. He felt that she treated him with the proper respect and he didn't mind at all that she seemed to often be glancing in his direction.

Jeremiah took quickly to the work. He was proud of the fact that he could milk faster than either Ben or Lizzie. He regularly milked five of the twelve cows that Ben had while Ben milked four and Lizzie milked the other three. He and Ben did all of the hay mowing as Lizzie was not very skilled with a scythe but she did her share of the hay raking and putting the hay into the barn or stacking it around a pole in the field.

Ben was pleased at Jeremiah's ability and stamina in the use of the crosscut saw and double-bitted axe. Cutting down the big chestnut trees, sawing them into logs, and then splitting the logs into fence rails was hard work but work that Jeremiah knew well. When they were working together and Ben was swearing as he strained and sweated, Jeremiah remembered how David had calmed King Saul with music and he found that if he whistled softly to himself Ben's swearing became less intense.

By the first of August Ben, Lizzie, and Jeremiah had become an efficient work force. Ben no longer was talking about going south to buy slaves, instead he was making plans to work around Jeremiah's absence while he was in college.

"Since we'll have most of the crops pretty well harvested by then, I think we'll be able to manage," he said at the supper table one evening. Looking at Jeremiah he said, "If you can help with the milking and feeding morning and night, me and Lizzie should be able to keep up the rest."

Then, early in August, tragedy hit. Ben and Jeremiah had felled a big chestnut tree on the hillside, trimmed off the limbs, and sawed it up into logs. While Jeremiah went back up the hill to get their tools and water jug at the stump, Ben started to move one of the logs down the slope and lost control of it and it rolled onto his foot, crushing it horribly.

Jeremiah knew immediately that there was a crisis. He had heard Ben cuss and swear a lot but never like this. He knew from the terror in his voice that this tough man was in terrible pain. He quickly grabbed the cant hook and, with strength that he did not know that he had, actually rolled the log uphill enough for Ben to pull his leg and foot free.

Ben kept on yelling and swearing in both anger and pain. Jeremiah knew that he could not carry this big man back to the house and that Ben could not walk so he tried to calm him and tell him that he was going to get the horses and wagon and would be back as soon as he could.

"Bring some whiskey with you when you come back," Ben yelled as Jeremiah started running toward the house.

Jennie, doing the weekly laundry at her washboard and tub on the back porch, saw Jeremiah running and hurried to meet him.

"What's happened?" she asked excitedly, "Where's Ben? Is he all right?"

"A log rolled on his foot and he's hurt pretty bad," a breathless Jeremiah blurted out. "I'm gonna get the horses and wagon and go back and get him."

"It'd be quicker just to harness ol' Prince and take the milk wagon," Jennie wisely suggested. "Let me get on my bonnet, I'm going with you to get him."

"He said to bring him some whiskey," Jeremiah said, "You got any?"

"Oh, yes, he's always got some somewhere," Jennie said, "if I can only figure out where he's got it hid."

By this time both girls were in the yard and James was on the porch.

"I know where he's got it," Lizzie said as she ran for the barn and then returned with a half full bottle.

In a matter of minutes Jeremiah had the horse harnessed and hitched to the milk wagon and he and Ben's wife and daughters hurried to rescue him.

When they got to him they found that Ben had scooted himself down the hillside for a ways and Jeremiah and Lizzie were able to help him hobble the rest of the way to the wagon and it took all four of them to get him loaded as he cussed every breath.

"Where's that whiskey?" he pleaded. "Did you bring it?"

Jennie handed him the bottle and as he took a long swig she began gingerly removing what was left of his shoe and his sock. The sight of his badly mutilated foot sickened her and she turned her head and began to cry. She quickly composed herself and called to Jeremiah who was driving the wagon.

"Just keep on going past the house and take him into town to Doc Pritchard," she said. "Just stop long enough for the girls to get off."

"I'm going with you, Mama," Lizzie insisted. "Let Lucy stay with James, they'll be okay."

By the time they arrived at Doc Pritchard's office Ben had pretty well anesthetized himself with the whiskey. The doctor came out to the wagon and, after giving the foot a quick examination, helped Jeremiah and Lizzie carry him into the office. As he prodded and manipulated the injured foot there was a fresh outbreak of yelling and swearing from Ben.

"Ben, I know this hurts you," the doctor said, "but I've got to do it to see how much damage there is and what I can do about it."

After a long and thorough examination the doctor shook his

head and said, "It don't look good Ben. You really tore up that foot and ankle. I'm going to try to get your ankle back in place and do the best I can to patch up your foot and then pray that gangrene don't set in so we don't have to take your foot off."

Jennie and Lizzie hugged each other as they cried at hearing the diagnosis. The doctor turned to Jeremiah and said, "Young fellow, I'm going to need you to help me hold Ben while I try to set his ankle. You think you can do that? Jennie, you got any of that whiskey left? If you do, let's give it to him. I figure he's going to need it."

After Lizzie retrieved the bottle from the wagon and Ben was well fortified, the doctor told Jeremiah to hold Ben's leg as still as he could and he began the painful task of trying to put the ankle joint back in place despite the swelling. While Ben swore and Jennie prayed, Lizzie came to help Jeremiah hold the leg still while the doctor pulled and twisted, then probed with his fingers, then pulled and twisted and probed some more, over and over until he finally said, "That's as good as I'm going to be able to get it, I'm afraid. I'm going to wrap the ankle now and then see what I can do for the foot."

After two hours of the doctor's ministrations to Ben's foot and ankle, Jeremiah was totally drained. Despite all the whiskey he had drunk, Ben was remarkably sober and aware of his predicament. Even though he was still in enormous pain as he was loaded into the wagon and took the bumpy ride home, he was considerably quieter. It was sinking into him that his life had been changed by this accident, and not for the better. His active mind was rising above the pain and the remnants of the alcohol and beginning to devise strategies for coping with his new reality.

The three of them got Ben into the house, helping to steady him as he tried to use the wooden crutches that Doc Pritchard had given him. No sooner had he laid down on the living room davenport than he began to bark out instructions.

"Jeremiah, you and Lizzie get right on out to the barn and milk them cows," he said. "I know it's late but it's got to be done. Tomorrow morning you'll have to get up a half-hour earlier since I won't be helping and people will be expecting their milk on time. Jeremiah, you'll have to do the milk deliveries 'til I get able to do it again. Lizzie, you've gone with me enough times to know where all we drop off milk so you go with him the first few times until he knows where to go. Jennie, you and Lucy are gonna have to take a bigger hand in getting the milk loaded and ready to go but I'll be able to set in a chair and help you in a day or two."

Jennie stroked Ben's forehead as she reassured him that everything would get done and Jeremiah and Lizzie headed for the barn.

By six o'clock the next morning the cows had again been milked, the milk put into the cans and loaded and Jeremiah and Lizzie were headed toward town. As Lizzie directed, Jeremiah weaved the wagon along the side streets from house to house. Lizzie jumped from the wagon at each customer's home, got the containers from the porches, expertly filled them from the milk cans on the wagon using a large dipper, and quickly put them back on the porches. The milk was delivered and they were on their way back home in less than an hour.

"I think we handled that pretty well, don't you, Lizzie?" Jeremiah asked.

"I think so," she responded. "I think you handled everything pretty well yesterday, too. I've been thinking that if you hadn't come to stay with us Papa might have been up on that hill alone and if something like that had happened we might not have found him in time."

Now, there's something new, Jeremiah thought. This was probably the first serious observation that Lizzie had made about him and, most certainly, it was the first time she had complimented him.

"Thanks," the suddenly shy Jeremiah replied, "but I think we all did just what we had to do."

"Are you kidding?" she said. "Even if we had found him in time, me and Mama could never have done it alone and by the time we went and got help his leg would have been so swelled up that Doc Pritchard wouldn't have been able to set his ankle. I guess, for a stuck-up old college boy, you did pretty good."

Jeremiah drove on in silence. He was not completely comfortable with the way the conversation was going but he had no idea that it was about to get exponentially more complicated.

49

Lizzie turned toward him and asked, abruptly, "Has anyone ever told you how cute you are? I saw that you were cute the first time I laid eyes on you but I thought you were too young; but now I'm thinking about changing my mind about that. You know, while Papa's not able to be around, me and you could have a lot of fun."

Jeremiah turned and looked quizzically into the face of Lizzie and then quickly returned his gaze to the road ahead.

"What do you mean by that?" he asked, looking straight ahead.

"Oh, you know what I mean," she said teasingly. "I've seen you looking at me. I mean we could do a little hugging and kissing in the barn, maybe. You do like to kiss, don't you?"

That question resulted in dead silence.

"Hey, wait a minute," Lizzie said, "maybe you've never even kissed a girl. Have you? Jeremiah Blake, you tell me the truth now, have you ever kissed a girl?"

"That's none of your business, Lizzie Givens," the red-faced boy answered. "You better stop this teasing."

"Hey! I was right," Lizzie continued, "you've never kissed a girl." Then after a moment's hesitation she said, mischievously, "Well, I think it about time we changed that."

With that, Lizzie grabbed Jeremiah's face in her strong hands turning him toward her and, before he could react, she placed a long, hard kiss squarely on his lips.

"Okay, now when somebody asks you if you've ever kissed a girl, you can tell them, 'I sure have,'" Lizzie said triumphantly, and then asked, "How did you like it?"

"It was pretty good, I reckon," Jeremiah weakly responded as began wondering if this meant he would have to marry her now. "But what about Eldon?" he asked. "Isn't he your beau?"

"Certainly Eldon is my beau," Lizzie said in an exasperated voice. "I'm not talking about you being my beau, you silly thing, I'm just wanting us to have a little fun together."

Jeremiah's frightened thoughts about marriage quickly switched to thoughts of sin and of what the pleasures and consequences might be if he accepted Lizzie's offer.

"I don't know," he said. "It doesn't seem to be the right thing to do, you with a beau and all."

"Okay, bashful boy," as she resumed her usual teasing tone, "I might leave you alone and, then again, I might not. You just better watch out."

The rest of the day went by without any further mention of the morning's conversation, even when they were alone in the barn that evening. Jeremiah was relieved, but also a little disappointed. Lizzie had ignited some fires in him that he had never experienced before and he was having a hard time thinking about anything else.

The next morning was different, though. As soon as they entered the barn, Lizzie set down her milk pails, threw her arms around Jeremiah and held him closely as she kissed him passionately. Jeremiah was overwhelmed by the moment and, instead of just accepting the kiss as he had done yesterday, he surprised himself by dropping his pails and putting his arms around Lizzie, returning her ardor.

Suddenly, the kiss was over and Lizzie very routinely went about her milking duties while Jeremiah needed some time to clear his head. He did not know what to say so, despite the fact that he felt like singing or shouting, or running and jumping, he said nothing and expended his pent-up energy by milking his first cow in record time.

Lizzie did not bring up the subject of the morning embrace during the milk run and Jeremiah was too tongue-tied about the whole situation to begin a discussion. The day of fieldwork went by, concluded by the evening milking and still nothing was said. Did it really happen, Jeremiah thought?

As soon as they entered the barn the next morning, Lizzie again initiated a long embrace and lingering kiss.

"My, my, Mr. Blake," Lizzie said in a teasing, breathless voice, "you sure do kiss good."

Jeremiah knew that he should make some response but he could not get a word out. Instead, he immediately grabbed a bucket, sat down, and began milking vigorously.

By the next morning Jeremiah had enough courage to initiate the embrace and he was walking on air.

Then Saturday came.

"What time is Eldon coming over, Lizzie?" her mother asked as they were finishing supper.

"Sometime around eight, if he gets all of his work caught up,"

Lizzie replied.

A hot stabbing pain shot through Jeremiah's chest. As the week had progressed, he had put Eldon completely out of his mind. Now as he faced the cruel reality that was Eldon, he thought for a moment that he would not be able to draw another breath. He had never before felt such anger and he suddenly hated Eldon so much that he felt that he could kill him on the spot.

He was thankful that James was anxious to use the rest of the day's light to spend time with him and his books and the two of them retired to the back porch.

Sometime after nine o'clock, as it was getting dark, Lucy came to where they had been studying and whispered that it was time for them to slip around the house and spy on Lizzie and Eldon.

"You two go ahead," Jeremiah said. "I don't feel like doing that tonight."

"Aw, come on," Lucy urged, "I'll bet we can catch them kissing."

Rage and jealousy engulfed Jeremiah as he again refused to go with Lucy and James and, instead, took Ben's hound dog and walked up to the top of the hill behind the barn where he sat down and suffered.

The scene at the barn on Sunday morning was not pleasant. When Lizzie reached for Jeremiah, he pushed her away and went to milking without saying a word. The milk route was run without Jeremiah responding to anything Lizzie said to him.

Finally, in desperation as they neared home after the deliveries, Lizzie said, in a voice unusually soft for her, "Jeremiah, if you'll just talk to me, I'll go to church with you and Mama and Lucy today."

This got Jeremiah's attention. Lizzie, like her father, avoided church at almost all cost. Since Jeremiah had come to live with them, Jennie and Lucy went with him to church almost every Sunday. Each Sunday morning, as Jennie was clearing away the breakfast dishes, she would always ask Ben and Lizzie if they wanted to go to church with her and they always declined. Now Lizzie was offering to go without her mother's urging. That must mean something, but Jeremiah was not sure what it meant.

"That would make your mama happy," was his cool response.

"But would it make you happy?" Lizzie asked.

"I reckon so," Jeremiah responded. "It wouldn't hurt you to go to church once in a while."

Jennie was overjoyed that Lizzie accompanied them to church and Pastor Will Sharpe was particularly happy to see her.

"Lizzie," the preacher said to her, "I've been expecting to hear from you that you and Eldon were planning on a wedding sometime soon. You know how I love to hitch up young people."

"Thanks, Brother Sharpe," Lizzie said quietly, obviously embarrassed by Will's boldness. "Nothing's been set yet but when there is, we'll let you know."

That was it for Jeremiah. Heartache or no heartache, he knew that he had to deal with the situation. It is a wonder the cows got milked that evening. As soon as he and Lizzie got to the barn, he let his emotions burst out. For the first time in his life he heard himself sounding like his father, raging and accusing Lizzie as the cause of his anger and hurt.

"How could you treat me like you like me when you are planning to marry Eldon?" he exploded, hardly able to say the name of his enemy.

"Please forgive me," Lizzie pleaded. "I didn't think it would get out of hand. You were so cute I thought it would be fun to tease you and see what it was like to kiss you but I didn't think about this happening."

"What do you mean?" Jeremiah yelled. "What did happen?"

"It looks like you got pretty struck on me," she replied, "and I guess I outsmarted myself because I've become pretty struck on you, too. Now what are we going to do?"

Jeremiah's anger started to cool as he heard that Lizzie did, indeed, like him, too. He was almost surprised to hear himself say, "Well, if you are going to marry Eldon, we've got to behave. We still have to work together but we can't let ourselves get involved with each other. I think I can handle the milk route by myself so we won't be together as much and maybe that'll help some."

"I guess that's the best thing to do," Lizzie said, fighting back the tears. "I just wish you were old enough to get married, I would ten times rather have you than old Eldon Tompkins."

Lizzie's admission moved Jeremiah to tears. Suddenly he

didn't hate Eldon anymore, instead he felt sorry for him. Now they were both crying. His anger was gone as he had now looked into the soul of Lizzie who had been such an enigma to him.

"Could you tell me why you would prefer me over him," Jeremiah asked, hesitantly.

Lizzie recovered quickly. Her answer indicated that she had regained her composure.

"Well, for one thing, college boy," she said as a sly smile replaced her tears, "you are a way better kisser than he is. Now, when you start kissing all those other girls, you promise me one thing. You promise me that you'll remember who it was that taught you how to kiss in the first place. Now I guess we'd better see if you can still milk as good as you can kiss."

7 . . . *THE BAPTISM*

Jeremiah did the milk run by himself for the next few days. Ben and Jennie wondered among themselves why this sudden change had occurred in the way things were being done but, wisely, did not question either of the young people.

The solitude gave Jeremiah time to reflect on his short, but intense, romance with Lizzie. He was sure that he would never love anyone else in his life and that he would never get over the hurt. But he also realized something else, he missed having company while he made the deliveries.

After giving it a lot of thought, he decided to make a bold move; he would try to get James to accompany him. He planned his strategy and approached the subject just as Thursday's supper was ending.

"James," Jeremiah asked, trying to sound casual, "how would you like to go with me tomorrow morning?"

"You mean on the milk wagon?" James responded. "Yeah, I'd like to do that for sure."

Jennie, reacting as the protective mother that she was, immediately voiced her disapproval of such a ridiculous idea.

"Why, James can't go on the milk wagon, Jeremiah," she said in an exasperated voice. "Whatever made you think of such a thing? You don't know what might happen to him; he ain't never done nothing like that and he could get awful bad hurt. Besides that, he couldn't deliver the milk or nothing so what good would he be? People would be looking at him and talking. A lot of people in town ain't never even seen him. No, he can't do that."

"Now you just hold your horses, Jennie," Ben said. "This

might not be too bad of an idea. Since I've been laid up with this foot of mine I've been watching the boy and thinking a lot about him. When I was up on that hillside waiting for y'all to bring the wagon and I started to scoot myself down the hill, I reminded myself of James, pulling myself along with my hands. I realized that a body can do about anything, even if all his parts ain't working like they're supposed to. I been watching him ever since that day and he gets around about as good as any of us; reminds me of a water bug scooting across a pond. Maybe he could do a lot more than we've give him a chance to do. I don't see no harm in him going on the milk run. Jeremiah won't let him get hurt, will you, Jeremiah?"

The next morning Jeremiah reached down and took James' hand and, with a quick lift, helped the strong, agile boy hop up into the wagon. Jeremiah then got him up into the seat beside him and they headed to town with the rest of the Givens family looking on from the front porch.

As soon as they got out of sight of the house Jeremiah asked, "Have you ever driven a horse?"

"No, I never have," James answered.

"There's nothing much to it," Jeremiah said, matter-of-factly, as he handed the check lines to James before the boy had time to become apprehensive about a new adventure.

"What do I do?" James asked. "I don't know how to do this. You better do it."

"Right now you don't have to do anything," Jeremiah said, reassuringly. "Ol' Prince is doing all the work. He even knows where to go since he's been doing this route longer than I have. Just hold the lines and when you want him to slow down, give them a little tug and when you want him to stop, pull back and say 'whoa.' When you want him to go right or left, pull the line on the side you want him to go to. That's about all there is to it."

When Jeremiah did not take the check lines back from James when they were offered, James clung to them nervously as first and, then when nothing disastrous happened, he began to feel the excitement of being in control.

When Jeremiah pointed out the first customer's house, James barely tugged the lines and the experienced horse came to a stop. Jeremiah quickly jumped down, delivered the milk, and then bounded back onto the wagon.

"Click your tongue and tell Old Prince to 'git-up,' James," Jeremiah told the boy. "We've got a ways to go."

Jeremiah considered his experiment a rousing success. He offered to drive the wagon back to the farm once they got in sight of the house but James insisted that he complete the trip. Ben was sitting in the rocking chair on the porch with his bad leg resting on a cushioned stool when he suddenly yelled, "Hey, Jennie, get out here. You ain't gonna believe this."

Jennie rushed through the front door in time to see the milk wagon come into the yard, being driven by James who was wearing the biggest smile she had ever seen on his face.

"Look at me, Mama," James said excitedly as he brought Prince to a halt beside the porch, "I can drive the wagon. Jeremiah showed me how and it's easy. And all the people we saw was real nice to me."

"That's good, Honey," Jennie said emotionally. "I'm glad you're all right. I prayed for you all the time you was gone." Then turning toward her husband she said in an accusing voice, "Ben, did you know that Jeremiah was gonna let him drive the wagon? Do you think that's a good idea?"

"No, Jennie," Ben answered slowly, " I didn't know that he was gonna let the boy drive the wagon, but I've learned to not ever be surprised by things that Jeremiah does. It appears that Jeremiah's been seeing something that we've been overlooking. Instead of keeping him cooped up and babying him all the time, we probably need to find out what all else our boy can do."

From that day on, James was the driver of the milk wagon. Ben put his fertile mind to work and hobbled out to the milk loading area day after day to put together a platform with wide steps that James could use to get up to the level of the wagon. After he had accomplished that, he installed a strong wooden rail across the wagon that James could grasp and then hop from the platform onto the wagon.

The next Sunday, James went to the Bethany Baptist Church for the first time since he was a baby. Jennie was a nervous wreck. She wasn't sure that some of the people there even knew about James' existence, much less if they would accept him. She cringed at the thought that people would be talking about her behind her back and the children would make fun of James. These were the reasons she had never taken James out in public before, she thought, and now because of Jeremiah's influence, this was being done against her better judgment.

Jeremiah helped James as he hopped up the steps into the church and Jenny quickly perched him in the least conspicuous place on the back pew between her and Lucy. To her chagrin, Brother Will Sharpe spotted them immediately and rushed to greet them.

"James, James, James," he exulted, "I am so glad to see you. I have prayed that the day would come when I would see you here in church and today my prayers are answered."

"It was Jeremiah that talked me into it," James answered. "If it hadn't been for him, I'd never have done it."

Much to Jeremiah's satisfaction, Jennie discovered that most of her fears and apprehensions were unfounded. After their first looks of surprise, all members of the congregation were warm in their greeting of James and she went home with a profound feeling that a great weight had been lifted from her. The events of this day, more than anything that had ever occurred before, caused Jennie's eyes to begin to open to see that James was more than a beloved burden; he was a remarkable young boy who did not need protection as much as he needed nurturing, just like her other children.

During their study time that afternoon, James had many questions for Jeremiah. James had read the Bible but had never had any instruction in it. Will Sharpe's sermon and the other events of the service raised many issues in his young, inquiring mind.

"Why did those people go to the front of the church after the sermon?" James asked.

"They were responding to Brother Sharpe's invitation to accept Christ and join the church," Jeremiah said and realized immediately that he needed to reword this "church talk."

"Let me try to explain it in another way," he continued. "God wants us to know that Jesus died to pay for our sins and we need to give ourselves to Him and serve Him instead of just doing things for ourselves. Baptists make you go and shake the preacher's hand and then be baptized to show that you accept what Jesus did for you. Does that make sense to you?"

"I think so," James responded. "I've read all about Jesus dying and coming back from the dead and I've prayed a lot when I've been scared or lonely. What else do I need to do?"

James had led Jeremiah into deeper theological water than he was comfortable with. However, he chose to plow on.

"It doesn't sound to me like you need to do anything, much," Jeremiah ventured. "Now if you wanted to be a Methodist you'd be told to pray and ask God to forgive your sins and wait until you get an answer from him."

"What kind of an answer?" James asked.

"I don't know for sure," Jeremiah said. "I guess it's kind of a good feeling that God gives you if you really mean it when you pray."

James probed further.

"Well, what do I need to do to be a Baptist?" he asked.

"Tomorrow when we deliver milk to Brother Sharpe's house, we'll talk to him about it," Jeremiah said, relieved to have arrived at a reasonable conclusion of the conversation.

The next morning when Jeremiah delivered the usual amount of milk at the Sharpe residence, he knocked on the door and waited until the sleepy-eyed preacher came to the door.

"James wants to know what he needs to do to become a Baptist," Jeremiah blurted out, and then added, "He knows a lot about the Bible and I told him how Methodists repent and pray through but I thought you ought to talk to him."

Will Sharpe, barefoot and half dressed, did not hesitate but immediately climbed up into the wagon with James and gently covered the basic tenets of Baptist theology and asked James if he believed and accepted Christ's sacrifice for him. When James answered in the affirmative, Will put his arm around him and said a brief prayer.

"See you both in church on Sunday," Will said, cheerfully, as he went toward his house.

That was awfully easy, Jeremiah thought. Is God really that accessible? Maybe some people, especially the real bad sinners need to cry and pray for a long time but a relatively innocent young boy like James wouldn't have to, he reasoned.

There was not a dry eye in the church the next Sunday when, at the end of the sermon, James hopped and scooted to the front of the church and reached up for Brother Sharpe's hand.

"James came to the Lord on Monday morning on the milk wagon in front of my house," Will announced to the congregation, "and now he has publicly professed his faith in Christ and wants to follow Him in baptism and become a member of this church. What is your pleasure?"

"I move that he be accepted for baptism and, after baptism, into full fellowship of the church," intoned the head deacon, routinely.

"Do I hear a second?" the pastor asked, and after hearing a number of seconds said, "All those in favor of receiving him, say 'Amen.'"

A loud unison "Amen" was heard and after the benediction everyone crowded to the front of the church to give James the "right hand of fellowship."

On the next Sunday afternoon it seemed like everyone in Bethany and the surrounding countryside had showed up on the banks of the creek for James' baptism. The entire Givens family was there, including the skeptical Ben.

The crowd first sang one verse of "There is a Fountain Filled With Blood," then Will read the brief account of Jesus' baptism by John in the Jordan River, prayed a short prayer, and took James by the hand and helped him into the water.

When they got into where the water was slightly above Will's knees and well up on James' chest, Will lifted his right hand over James' head and said, "Upon your profession of faith, I baptize thee, my brother James, in the name of the Father, Son, and Holy Ghost," and deftly tipped James backward under the water and quickly up again."

After the chorus of "Amen's" died down, Will said, "We read in the book of Acts that the Ethiopian said to Philip, 'Here is water; what doth hinder me to be baptized?' And Philip said, 'If thou believest with all thine heart, thou mayest.' So today, I extend that invitation to everyone here. If you believe; here is water. Is there anyone else here who wants to be baptized?"

Suddenly there was an emotional, high pitched, "I do, Preacher," and the crowd watched in shocked amazement as a tearful Ben Givens hobbled as fast as his bad foot and crutches would carry him down toward the water. Seeing his crippled son surrendering his life, symbolized by his baptism, had melted what everyone had assumed was the heart of stone that resided in mean old Ben Givens.

Will embraced Ben and helped him out into the deeper water and before baptizing him asked, "Ben Givens, have you accepted Jesus Christ as your Lord and Savior?"

"Yes, Preacher, that's what I done just now," Ben replied.

"Then, based upon your profession of faith," Will said, "I baptize thee, my brother Ben, in the name of the Father, Son, and Holy Ghost," and put him under the water.

Jeremiah was used to occasional emotional shouting in his Methodist Church back home but this was his first experience with Baptists shouting. Ben Givens coming to the Lord was an unexpected miracle and the sight of it was too much even for the staid Baptists to contain.

As he was describing this day in his weekly letter home Jeremiah wondered if all this would surprise his papa. At any rate, he thought, this was surely a day to remember.

8 *THE SAGE OF BETHANY*

It was a beautiful fall day in the panhandle of Virginia when Jeremiah Blake entered the hallowed halls of Bethany College. The leaves were turning to rich hues of red, gold, and orange, and provided a backdrop to the college building that seemed to Jeremiah to be the most desirable place on earth.

He had readjusted the milk route slightly, making the last deliveries to homes that were closest to the college so he could make the deliveries each morning and then walk to class while James drove the wagon back to the farm. In the evenings Jeremiah would come to enjoy the three-mile walk as a transition from his academic pursuits to his evening farm chore duties.

The college building contained a library and classrooms. On the first day the entire student body met in the assembly hall and, for the first time, Jeremiah saw the college founder, Alexander Campbell, the renowned "Sage of Bethany."

As President Campbell began to speak, Jeremiah could barely contain his excitement. He was actually in the presence of this famous man who was loved or feared by so many people, a man who had traveled and lectured and debated and published and preached; a theologian, a scientist, a farmer, and an educator. As he watched this fifty-three year old legend and listened to him speak with his distinct Scottish accent, Jeremiah was flooded with feelings of gratitude to everyone who had made this moment possible.

He thought of his parents who had raised him and permitted him to come here, Mr. Talley who had counseled and encouraged him, his grandparents in Nutter Fort who had given him much more money than he needed for tuition, the Hendry's who had befriended him on his trip to college, Will Sharpe who had introduced him to the Givenses, the Givenses, themselves and, lastly, the benevolent God who, Jeremiah now gratefully acknowledged, had been involved with all of the above.

"You are embarking on a momentous journey today," the Sage of Bethany began in a booming voice, "and I cannot tell you what will be your destination, but I am prepared to begin this journey with you and serve as the pilot of your ship while you are here at this institution."

Jeremiah sat mesmerized as President Campbell spoke. He had never been in the presence of such a learned person nor had he ever heard such an eloquent speaker. No wonder, he thought, that my papa was worried about me following this man wherever he wished to lead me.

The Sage spoke of his childhood in Scotland and his Scots-Irish Presbyterian roots. Jeremiah knew that his ancestry was also Scots-Irish but the teachings of John Wesley had supplanted Scottish Presbyterianism in his forebears soon after they had landed in America.

As President Campbell related his impressive odyssey from childhood to the present day, both religious and secular, he explained how each experience had motivated his actions, culminating in the establishment of the college. He discussed how he had become a Baptist and a Baptist publisher but had since, because of his belief that all Christians should be united, had become a Reformer and a participant in what was known as the Restoration Movement.

"You are preparing to journey into a world that has many rifts and warring factions," the Sage stated in his grand oratorical style. "We are living in a world where Christendom is divided by countless denominations and sects. We are living in a country that is divided by the issue of slavery. We are living in a time in which a debate rages as to whether we are first the citizens of the nation or of the state. While you are at this institution you will learn that I will not hesitate to expound on my positions on these and other issues of the day.

"The only religious titles or classifications to which I will ascribe are these: I am a Christian and I am a disciple of Christ. I am a Christian and a disciple of Christ because I have placed my faith in

His death and resurrection and I entered into the Kingdom of God through the waters of baptism. As a result of my convictions, these are the only titles or classifications which I will recommend to others. I consider it a disservice to our Lord and an insult to me when people call those in the Restoration Movement, 'Campbellites.' I have left neither the Presbyterian denomination nor the Baptist denomination to start another in my own name. I believe the true church to be only the church of Christ and it is my desire to further that precept."

Well, there it is, Jeremiah thought, Papa's fear that he would be expected to follow Campbell's religious teachings could be well founded. However, he was relieved that President Campbell did not indicate that he would demand that his students ascribe to his position on the church, denominationalism, and baptism. When I next write to Papa, he thought with a smile, I will be able to tell him that in spite of the eminent Alexander Campbell and the helpful Baptist preacher Will Sharpe, I am still a Methodist.

Next, Jeremiah recognized that what he had been told by his teacher George Talley was accurate as President Campbell expounded on his philosophy of education.

"I believe that education should not be limited to the privileged," he said. "It is not only the black race that needs to be freed from slavery, all men need to be liberated. What are some of the evils that can enslave any man? They are the chains of ignorance, the prisons of superstition, and the walls of prejudice.

"Here at Bethany College you will not be limited to studying only the classics, rather we will endeavor to provide you with instruction in science, in agriculture, in literature, and the languages. My goal for each of you is that you will leave this institution fully equipped to serve your family, your country, and your God."

Then, as Jeremiah was wondering about his papa's other fear that he would become an abolitionist, the Sage launched into the subject of slavery.

"You have, no doubt, heard that I have said that I do not consider slavery to be a sin," he said softly as he began his discourse on the subject. Then, with his voice raising he continued, "I do not consider it to be a sin since it is not so described in Holy Scripture. However, as it is being practiced in our country, I do consider it to be a curse on our society and a Pandora's box which will lead to greater and greater suffering.

"In the New Testament, Almighty God, through the Apostle Paul, gives us instructions, which if followed, would solve the slavery problem. In the Book of Colossians, chapter four, He tells us, 'Masters, give unto your servants that which is just and equal; knowing that ye also have a Master in heaven.' The problem is that this Biblical admonition has not always been followed. Many of the slaves have not been given education or instruction in the gospel and this neglect by their earthly masters is most certainly displeasing to our Heavenly Master. Oft times slave husbands and their wives are torn asunder and sold to different masters, never to be reunited. Small children are taken away and sold, never again to be held in their mother's bosom. The sin is not slavery, the sin is the way in which slavery is practiced."

The Sage continued, "I, myself, once owned three slaves, the result of an inheritance from my wife's father. I taught them to read and after I had led them to a knowledge of the Lord, I baptized them and gave them their freedom. Now, I ask you, does that make me an abolitionist, as many have charged? No, I say, that does not. I hold deep sympathy for the plight of the slave but I am not an abolitionist. Abolitionism is based on the belief that slavery is a sin, and as I previously stated, that is not my position. Yet, slavery should not be, yea cannot be, the perpetual policy of our country."

So far, so good, Jeremiah thought, I don't have to be either a Campbellite or an abolitionist to study here. But, he wondered, if not abolition then how would the Sage propose that slavery should end?

"I am in agreement with much of what Thomas Jefferson had to say on the matter," President Campbell said. "I, like him, find that the black race is both physically and mentally inferior to the white race and, therefore, it would be futile to attempt to make the races social equals. I believe that Mr. Jefferson was wise in advocating that a place be set aside where the freed black man could establish his own society and, had such a place existed, I am confident, Mr. Jefferson would have given all of his slaves their freedom.

"Therefore, my solution to the slavery problem, which I have transmitted to President John Tyler, is that the federal government spend the sum of ten million dollars each year to establish such a site and assist the freed slaves build a separate culture so we can free our country of the hypocritical dilemma in which we find ourselves.

"Lastly, I will address the issue that most divides our country, the issue of first loyalty and primary authority.

"When my father and our family came from Scotland, we came by choice to the nation of the United States of America, not to one of the individual states. We came to America, not for what Pennsylvania or Virginia had to offer but what the nation of the United States had to offer. I am indebted to the state of Pennsylvania for the years that I resided there and I am indebted to the state of Virginia for the opportunity afforded me here, but the opportunities afforded in these states or in any other state are granted first by the Constitution of the United States.

"President Andrew Jackson said it best when he stated that, 'the Constitution of the United States forms a government, not a league. It is a government in which all the people are represented, which operates directly on the people individually, not upon the states. To say that any state may at pleasure secede from the Union is to say that the United States are not a nation.' When state governments say that they can nullify a law enacted by the United States or that they can, at their pleasure, choose to leave the Union, they are in conflict with the greatest document ever written for the governance of a nation, the United States Constitution. Andrew Jackson considered secession to be an illegal act and, therefore, an act of revolution, as do I."

Jeremiah was so inspired by the events of the day and the grand speech by Alexander Campbell that it seemed like his feet barely touched the ground as he walked home to the Givens place. He wished that his friend T. J. Jackson could have been with him today to hear the words of the Sage. He resolved to remember everything he heard and he looked forward to the next summer when he would be going home for a visit and when he could go see his friend and share his newfound knowledge with him.

9

T. J.'s GONE TO WEST POINT

Near the end of the summer of 1842 when the work load on the Givens farm had lessened a bit, Jeremiah saddled up ol' Molly and headed south for a few weeks at home before he again started classes. As he passed the schoolhouse in Cameron he patted his horse on the neck and remarked, "Molly, do you remember the night we spent here? Do you remember that big thunderstorm? A lot of things have happened since then, haven't they?"

He planned his trip so he could surprise the Hendry's on his way home and, as he expected, they insisted that he spend the night with them. As soon as Bessie Hendry came to the door and saw Jeremiah she exclaimed, "Lordy, look who's here," and quickly wiped her hands on her apron before she threw her arms around his neck. Jeremiah noticed that Bessie's girth had greatly increased since he had last seen her. His smile of greeting to Bessie was made broader by the realization that Jonas would soon have a baby brother or the Hendry family would have another "flower" join it.

"Hey, girls," she cried, "come in here and see our company."

Little Rose was the first one to appear and she ran and jumped into Jeremiah's arms. Lily and Violet followed close behind and, perhaps emboldened by seeing Rose's embrace, also greeted Jeremiah with hugs.

"Jonas is down at the blacksmith shop with Amos," Bessie said, "but they should be getting here for supper pretty soon."

When Amos and Jonas arrived, Jeremiah was surprised at how much Jonas had matured in the months since he had seen him. He seemed to be a good three inches taller than before and his work in his father's blacksmith shop had added muscle to his once-thin body. No longer as shy or self-conscious, Jonas gave Jeremiah a warm handshake that was nearly as firm as that of his father's.

"Jeremiah," Amos said, "you look to me to be a whole lot smarter than you were last year. Do you feel any smarter?"

"No, not by a long shot," Jeremiah answered. "About the only thing I learned is just how much I don't know. Spending two semesters around President Campbell was a good way for me to discover just how ignorant I am."

The next morning as he was heading toward Clarksburg, Jeremiah reminisced about the previous evening. He loved the warmth of the Hendry family and he realized that the time he had spent with them at the supper table, on the porch talking with Amos and Bessie, and then playing games in the yard with the children were precious moments, indeed.

Jeremiah and Blanche Stevens were overjoyed to see their grandson when he arrived at their house at Nutter Fort in the late afternoon. They were an avid audience as Jeremiah recounted the highlights of his first year at college.

"Sounds like Alexander Campbell is as smart as folks say he is," Grandpa Stevens asked. "What do you think of his point of view on religion?"

"There are only two things that bother me," Jeremiah responded, "but they're pretty big ones. He believes that a person has to be baptized to be saved and he comes pretty close to saying that people like us who belong to a denominational church aren't going to Heaven."

"Did you go to his services while you were there?" Grandpa Stevens asked.

"No," Jeremiah answered, "I went to the Baptist church. The pastor there was the one who helped me find a job and a place to live with the Givens', so I went to his church. The Givens' go there, too."

"Jeremiah," Grandma Stevens interjected, "you are not going to believe it when you see your sisters and your little brother. Rebecca and Rachel are becoming quite proper little ladies and Joshua is walking everywhere and talking up a storm. Do you reckon he'll remember you?"

"I sure hope so," Jeremiah said as he felt a sharp pang of regret that he had been away from his family for so long and had not fully considered the consequences of his absence until this moment. Suddenly he was very anxious to get home to be with them.

After a good night's sleep and once again enjoying one of his Grandma's bountiful breakfasts, Jeremiah bid his grandparents good-bye and began the last leg of his trip home.

"It's Jeremiah; its Jeremiah; Mama, look who's coming, it's Jeremiah," Rebecca screamed when she saw her brother riding up the road toward their house.

Molly speeded up to a trot as she recognized familiar surroundings and by the time Jeremiah had dismounted in front of the house, he was surrounded by his loved ones.

Jeremiah bent down and hugged his sisters who were now aged seven and five and was then enveloped in a long, tearful embrace by his mother. He was surprised and moved to see tears in his father's eyes as they shook hands and Abe said, "It's good to have you home, Son; you look well."

During this time, little Joshua watched the proceedings and then, when Jeremiah approached him, took off in the opposite direction as fast as his chubby legs would carry him.

"Come here you little skunk," Jeremiah yelled as he ran and scooped up the husky two-year-old in his arms and smothered him with kisses as Joshua squealed with laughter.

"Grandma was afraid you wouldn't remember me," Jeremiah told his little brother, "but it looks like she didn't know what she was talking about. I believe you remember me just fine and you were just playing a trick on me by running away."

Jeremiah was amazed at how different life on the farm seemed now that he was back at home. At first he thought that it was only temporary and that things would revert to "normal" in a few days, but he then began to realize that things were really different.

What was the difference? His sisters were a little older and treated him like he was something special, which was one thing. Joshua quickly became his greatest joy, that was another. His mother seemed happier and more content that he had ever seen her, maybe that was it.

No, he thought, the big difference is in my relationship with Papa. By the end of his three-week stay, after a lot of cogitation on the matter, Jeremiah had it pretty well figured out. There was no question that his father was a bit less critical and demanding of him. He even openly showed some pride in Jeremiah by asking him to recount the conversion and baptism of Ben Givens in the form of a testimony in front of the church.

The conclusion that Jeremiah finally arrived at, though, was that the difference was not due so much to changes in his father as to changes in himself. His time away from home and his experiences with other families and observing other fathers had given him a broader perspective and helped him observe his father less emotionally and more objectively. What he slowly began to realize was that, although his papa had many human flaws, Abe Blake was a man of great faith and faithfulness to his family and to God and the church. Lovable? Maybe not always but always faithful to the things in which he believed.

Now that he was looking more objectively, he could see his father as a person born to illiterate parents with very limited educational opportunities, and a man who had faced a life of hardships. This enabled Jeremiah to peer through the crust of harshness that had been impenetrable to him before. It's not that Papa's bluster has gone away, Jeremiah realized, but, as he was able to understand some of the reasons for the bluster, it no longer intimidated him.

Near the end of his first week at home, Jeremiah headed down to Jackson's Mill to see T. J. He was anxious to share his new found knowledge with his friend and have a long period of discussion and debate with him on religion, politics, and history. But when he arrived at the Jackson home, rather than finding T. J., he was greeted by Laura Ann who gave him some big news.

"T. J. has left for West Point," Laura Ann said excitedly. "I wish you had come a day sooner, he left only yesterday. He didn't think he would be going because another person was appointed but, all of a sudden, he backed out and T. J. got in." Then she added, "You know what this means, don't you Jeremiah."

"I sure do," Jeremiah answered. "It means that there is going to be a General T. J. Jackson, just like he always said there would be. I need his address so I can write and congratulate him."

Although T. J. was not available for lengthy discussions of the weighty matters on Jeremiah's mind, he found that his former teacher, George Talley, was a more than adequate alternative. One or two evenings each week George would come and sit on the porch with the Blake family and they would talk late into the night.

Jeremiah was surprised at the vehemence of George in disagreeing with some of Alexander Campbell's teachings, especially on the subject of slavery.

"How can the man say that slavery is not a sin?" George said heatedly. "How can one man created in God's image treating another man created in God's image like an animal not be a sin?"

At this, the intently listening Abe Blake felt compelled to chime in.

"It sounds to me like Campbell's got Scripture on his side on this one, George," Abe said. "You look at what God told the Children of Israel to do when they went into the Promised Land. He told them which ones to destroy and which ones to make slaves out of. And remember that there was slavery in the New Testament, too, and the Apostle Paul told slaves that they was to obey their masters."

"Yes, Brother Blake," George responded, "but Paul also told Philemon that he was to accept his runaway slave, Onesimus, back as a brother instead of a slave. 'Not as a servant, but as a beloved brother,' were Paul's words, I believe."

"But, Mr. Talley," Jeremiah injected, "since the black race is inferior to the white race, they can never be equals. That's really the crux of President Campbell's argument. Onesimus and Philemon were most likely of the same race."

"That is another thing that I would disagree with Campbell about," George said, warming up to the debate. "How does he know for certain that the black race is inferior, how did you say it, intellectually and physically? How can he be so sure about that? How does he know that their intellectual shortcomings are not due to the way they've been forced to live? I have read about some Negroes who were able to get a good education that proved to have superior minds. Jeremiah, if you had never been to school or church, you had never learned to read or write, and you had been forced to work from sun-up to sundown every day of your life, how intellectual do you think you would be? And physically inferior? If they are physically inferior, why were they brought to this country in the first place? They were brought here to do the hard labor and strenuous tasks that white people cannot or will not do? What white man has the physical strength to do the work that the black man does?"

Jeremiah had a hard time sleeping after some of their deep discussions. He was seeing both his father and his teacher in a new light. Having been raised by Abe Blake, taught by George Talley, and now under the instruction of Alexander Campbell, Jeremiah's mind held at least three perspectives on most issues and he spent many sleepless hours trying to decide what he could accept as the truth.

The three weeks went by quickly and Jeremiah headed back north, wondering how Ben and family had gotten along without him.

A pleasant surprise awaited him when he arrived back at the Givens farm. Kyle, the oldest Givens son, was there with his wife and baby boy, Kyle, Junior.

"I been hearing nothing but good things about you since I got here," Kyle said as he was introduced to Jeremiah. "You must be a good man if you can put up with this bunch."

"Yeah, they're pretty bad, that's for sure," Jeremiah joked, "but they have to put up with me, too, so I guess it's about even."

Jeremiah could see that Kyle's relationship with his father was awkward but that he was overjoyed to be with his mother and share his new family with her and his sisters. Lizzie and Lucy were in constant conflict over who got to care for little Junior and James was obviously very proud of his strong, handsome brother.

"How do you get along with the old man, really?" Kyle asked as he accompanied Jeremiah when he went out to the barn to unsaddle Molly. "Me and him was always fighting about something or other when I lived here."

"The biggest thing I had to get used to was him cussing me out," Jeremiah said. "I was used to being yelled at and criticized all the time because that was the way my papa was, but the cussing was hard to take. Thank goodness he doesn't cuss much now since he joined the church and he seems not to get as mad as he did before."

"Mama wrote and told me that Papa had joined the church and that had made a big difference," Kyle said, "and if it hadn't of been for that I may never have come back here even for a visit. That old man didn't treat me and Alec like we was his sons, he treated us like we was his slaves. I reckon somebody told you that I just up and took off when I was seventeen and as soon as I got a job over on the river I come back here one night and took Alec with me. I think that if the old man had caught me that night he would have shot me."

"Your papa is tough, that's for sure," Jeremiah responded, "but I've seen a lot of changes in him since I came here. When I got here it was like he didn't need anything from anybody else except to do work, but he hurt his foot and we had to do everything for him and then he joined the church and now he seems to me to be a lot easier to live with."

"I don't see much difference, myself," Kyle said. "We've been here three days and he ain't hardly said three words to me. He makes over the baby but that's about it."

"Maybe he doesn't know what to say, especially if he feels bad about the way he treated you," Jeremiah offered. "He's not a man that's likely to apologize but you might get to him in other ways."

"How could I do that?" Kyle asked.

"One of the biggest changes I've seen since coming here is his attitude toward James," Jeremiah answered. "After almost ignoring him for years, I think now the warmest spot in his heart is for James. Why don't you try asking him something about James and see what happens."

By the time Kyle and his family left at the end of the week, he and Ben had made significant progress toward healing the breach that was between them. Kyle found that Jeremiah was right and that the one starting point between the two men was their mutual love for James and, once the ice had been broken, they were able to talk about other things.

As Jeremiah observed the departure events when Kyle and his family were leaving; the embraces, the passing of the baby from one to the other, and the inevitable, "hurry back, now," from Jennie, he was startled by Kyle's final words.

"Lizzie," he said, "we're aiming to come back for your wedding and I'll try to get Alec to come, too."

Lizzie Givens became Mrs. Eldon Tompkins on September 12, 1842, at the Bethany Baptist Church. Despite the fact that Pastor Will Sharpe conducted a beautiful ceremony and the Givens family was happy that Kyle and his family had returned and had, indeed brought Alec with them, it was not a happy occasion for Jeremiah. Not only did Jeremiah have to witness this painful event, he had to participate in it.

Not having any brothers, Eldon asked Jeremiah to stand up with him as his best man so he found himself standing along with Lucy who was her sister's bridesmaid, watching the girl that he adored marry someone that he knew she was settling for.

"Well, college boy," Lizzie teased as Jeremiah approached the couple after the ceremony, "are you gonna kiss the bride?"

As Jeremiah leaned forward, reluctantly, to place a slight, polite kiss on her cheek, Lizzie abruptly turned her face toward his and kissed him squarely on the lips. She was proud of this last bit of tempting and teasing and laughed heartily until she saw Jeremiah's reaction. Lizzie quickly realized that her brashness had stunned Jeremiah and although she had made him blush many, many times, she had never seen him as red-faced as he was now.

"Aw, Jeremiah," she said, trying to lighten the moment, "Eldon don't care if you kissed me. He knows we're old friends, don't you Eldon?"

"Oh sure," Eldon agreed, as he slapped Jeremiah on the back, completely oblivious of the tension of the moment. "If my best man can't kiss her, who can?"

10 *JESUS AND JEREMIAH BLAKE*

Jeremiah graduated from Bethany College in late May, 1845. After the ceremony, President Campbell visited individually with each of the departing graduates.

"Jeremiah, you are one fine lad," the Sage said as he gripped Jeremiah's hand. "You have been an exemplary student. Because God has given you a superior intellect and exceptional abilities, I want you to be ever mindful that He will make great demands of you. He needs you to be His hands and feet so that His will may be accomplished in the dreadful days that lie ahead. I firmly believe that it is His will that this country be preserved but it will only be preserved at a great price. My prayer for you is that you will be prepared to make whatever sacrifices are necessary to do your part in the coming days."

"Thank you President Campbell," Jeremiah responded. "You have been a wonderful mentor and example. If I am able to play a small part in the events of our country, you are the one deserving of the credit. Without the education I received here at Bethany, I would be ill equipped to face the future, that's for sure."

Jeremiah had a lot of good-byes to say before leaving Bethany. His home had been here for four years and the people had become his family. Ben Givens, permanently crippled from his logging accident but able to do most of his needed tasks on the farm reminisced as he, Jennie, and James sat on the front porch with Jeremiah the last evening he was there.

"Jeremiah," he started, "I wouldn't a' give a plug nickel for you that first day when I drove in and saw you setting here on the porch. I thought that this scrawny feller won't be of much help around here, but you proved me wrong. You turned out to be one of the hardest working people I ever saw.

"But it ain't your work that I'm gonna remember most about

ya'. What I'm gonna remember most is what you've done for all of us. I'm gonna remember you hauling me out of the woods and getting me to Doc Pritchard and then taking over the work while I was laid up. I'm gonna remember how good you treated our girls, like they was your sisters, until they got married and left. I'm gonna remember you helping James to learn and helping us to see that he could do things that we wouldn't let him do.

"I'm gonna remember you getting us to go to church, too. That wouldn't have happened if it hadn't of been for you. So when I get to the pearly gates I'm gonna have to tell ol' Saint Peter that I wouldn't be here if it wasn't for Jesus and Jeremiah Blake."

"I'm sure that you'd have a better chance of getting in if you just left me out of it," Jeremiah responded.

Although they all laughed at Ben's last declaration and Jeremiah's response, Jeremiah was deeply moved by what Ben said. He knew that Ben was not one to hold anything back so he meant everything he said, and Jeremiah was humbled by the realization that he meant so much to Ben and his family.

He made a tearful departure the next morning, embracing first Jennie and then James. When he reached out his hand to Ben, Ben grabbed it and pulled Jeremiah to him and held him in a tight bear hug, something that Jeremiah had never experienced from another man.

He went out of his way enough to go by Eldon and Lizzie's farm over near Short Creek and spent more than an hour with them and their two little boys, Jeremiah and Jonathan. Apparently, Eldon had never resented or questioned why Lizzie had chosen the name, Jeremiah, for their first born. After all, he must have thought, wasn't Jeremiah the best man at my wedding and like a brother to Lizzie?"

He spent one night, as had become his custom, with the Hendry family in Old Hundred. Jonas was now a tall, muscular sixteen-year-old well on his way to becoming a skilled blacksmith under the watchful eye of Amos, his father. Lily was fourteen and, Jeremiah observed, becoming quite coquettish. Violet and Rose were as charming as always and the little boys, Jacob and Jesse, were, obviously, the center of Bessie's life.

As Jeremiah approached Nutter Fort, he sadly reminisced about his grandfather, Jeremiah Stevens, who had passed away during the winter of 1843 from pneumonia. He had never known a man who was more gentle or unselfish and, as he neared the familiar house, he wondered if anyone ever saw any of his grandfather's traits in him.

"Jeremiah, honey, I've been expecting you," Grandma Blanche said as she hugged and kissed her grandson. "Let me look at you, now. My, how grown up you've become. You look a lot like your papa looked the first time I ever saw him, and I thought he was the handsomest man I had ever seen, besides your grandfather. You probably know that I picked out your papa for your mama before she did. But I can also see some of your Grandpa Stevens in you."

"I sure hope so, Grandma," Jeremiah responded, "for Grandpa was a remarkable man and even if I didn't look like him, I've always hoped that I could be like him."

As they were eating supper, Jeremiah made a proposal to his grandmother.

"Grandma, would you consider having me live with you for a while, until I get settled in a job in Clarksburg?" Jeremiah asked. "I would pay you, of course."

"Why, that would be the most wonderful thing that I could imagine happening," she said, excitedly. "I get so lonesome rattling around in this old house all by myself and I hate cooking for just one person. I'd be the happiest person in the world if you would come and live with me."

"I'll be back in a week," Jeremiah told Grandma Blanche as he mounted ol' Molly and left the next morning.

Jeremiah found himself treated like royalty when he arrived at home on Melford Creek. His sisters, now aged ten and eight, and little Joshua who was now five, all ran to meet him. As he finished hugging his mother and turned to his father coming toward him with a broad smile, Jeremiah impulsively threw his arms around him and held him in an emotional embrace. Totally disarmed, the normally staid Reverend Abraham Blake found himself returning the embrace and suddenly sobbing on his son's shoulder.

"It's good to see you, Papa," Jeremiah said as the men ended their embrace. "I just want to thank you for everything you've done for me."

"You're more than welcome, Son," Abe responded as he wiped his red eyes with his bandana, "I just wish I could have done more."

11 *THE BEST OF TIMES*

Once he was comfortably settled in Grandma Blanche's home in Nutter Fort, Jeremiah saddled up Molly every day and rode into Clarksburg looking for a position. Since he intended to read the law and pass the bar, he went to all of the law firms and presented them with his credentials and told them of his aspirations. Nathan Fletcher, the older member of the two-man firm of Fletcher and Smith, was impressed by the obvious ambition and intelligence of Jeremiah and he and partner Robert Smith offered him a position as law clerk and runner, which Jeremiah quickly accepted.

As soon as Jeremiah received his first pay he sought out a suitable boarding house in Clarksburg, one with a livery stable where Molly would be well cared for during the week. He spent most of his weekends being pampered by Grandma Blanche at Nutter Fort and worshiping with her at the church where his parents had met. With the exception of the time he spent with his grandmother, he threw himself so completely into his work and reading of the law that he was virtually oblivious to anything else going on in the community around him.

One evening after supper Jeremiah's study of the law was disturbed by a knock on the door of his room at the boarding house. When he opened the door he was faced by a heavy, well dressed, middle-aged man who immediately extended his hand and said, "Mr. Blake, I am Daniel Hayes, pastor of the Baptist Church here in Clarksburg. I met your friend Will Sharpe at our Baptist Convention in Philadelphia last week and he told me I should look you up."

"Well, come in, come in," Jeremiah responded, and then added good naturedly, "I hope that he told you that, in spite of the fact that I attended his church in Bethany, I'm still a Methodist."

"Oh, yes, he told me that for sure," Daniel said, "but I am not here to turn you into a Baptist, I am here because Will thought you could be of help in another endeavor. I was telling him about the Union Debating Society we have started here and he said that your background and convictions could be very valuable in our discussions about secession and slavery, especially."

"Before I can answer you, I need to ask you a couple of questions," Jeremiah said. "Firstly, is your society an abolitionist group? If it is I would not join because I'm not an abolitionist. Secondly, do you really think that secession is likely to happen? I'm convinced that it would be unconstitutional and that there are enough loyal people in every state to keep it from happening."

"No, we are not an abolitionist society; our interest is entirely centered in preserving the Union," Daniel answered. "I was of the same opinion as you about secession until I lived through the events of last week in Philadelphia, but now, I am rethinking my position. You probably haven't heard, but our Baptist Convention had a big fight over slavery and then it split wide open over the question of whether or not we should continue to send out slaveholders as missionaries. When we passed a resolution that we would not send any more slaveholders, the southern states walked out and we hear now that they're going to form their own Convention and Mission Board in the South. It looks like the Methodists and Presbyterians are both splitting over slavery, too. If something like this has happened within the body of Christ, it most certainly could happen in the political arena."

"It sounds like the rhetoric at the convention got pretty heated, then," Jeremiah surmised.

"It surely did," Daniel responded. "I thought a number of times that a fight was going to break out. The moderator even invoked the name of old Adoniram Judson one time to try to quiet the crowd, but then when he called him 'the first Baptist missionary from America,' some pastor from the North jumped up and yelled out that the first Baptist missionary wasn't Judson at all, 'It was George Lisle,' he said, 'but you Southern preachers are ashamed to admit it.' That really got some of them going."

"Was he right?" Jeremiah asked. "I've never heard of George Lisle. Who was he?"

"He was the first Negro preacher ever ordained by Baptists in this country," Daniel responded. "He was a freed slave and he went from Georgia to Jamaica a good forty years before Judson left for India. So, I guess, strictly speaking, he was the first missionary but Judson is the one that's always been recognized for starting the Baptist missionary effort."

After a lengthy discussion of the issues facing the country, Jeremiah said, "I don't know how much time I can devote to the debating society, but I don't see how I could turn you down," remembering the charge that President Campbell had given him after his graduation.

Daniel Hayes proved to be a good and inspirational friend. He was the first seminary trained minister that Jeremiah had known, and the best educated with the exception of Alexander Campbell. Jeremiah had, more or less, always assumed that his father was correct in his belief that if God called a person into the ministry, He would equip that person with the knowledge and wisdom that would be needed and his experience with his father and his close friendship with Will Sharpe had reinforced that assumption. But Daniel Hayes was different.

In Daniel Hayes, Jeremiah found a man in the pulpit who was his intellectual equal, a man as well read in literature, history, and science as Jeremiah and beyond anyone he had ever met in his knowledge of theology and the Bible.

Jeremiah was fascinated to discover that Hayes did not have subjects separated in his mind as did Jeremiah, but he had them all melded together into his life philosophy. Hayes' conversations, sermons, and debates smoothly integrated the scriptures with Homer or Chaucer, and current political events were easily related to similar events in either secular or Biblical history.

Jeremiah loved living in Clarksburg, spending weekends with his beloved grandmother, working for Fletcher and Smith, and participating in the Union Debating Society, all the while preparing to pass the bar.

He pondered on the fact that he had experienced very few of his dark periods since the torturous days following Lizzie's wedding and he surmised that maybe he had outgrown his times of deep sadness. After all, he was on his own now. He had survived the heartbreak of lost love, he had made peace with his feelings about his father, and his mother was happier than he had ever seen her, so it looked like his dark days were all behind him. I can't believe it, he thought, I'm on the verge of becoming an optimist.

One Sunday morning in early September, while Jeremiah was in the midst of feeling that life could not get any better, it did. Soon after he had occupied his usual seat at church beside his grandmother on the fifth row from the front, a tall, slender young woman with long, light brown hair quietly took her place in the fourth row across the aisle from him.

"Who is that, Grandma?" he whispered, glancing in the direction of the newcomer.

"I don't know," Grandma Blanche whispered back, "unless it is the new schoolteacher. That must be who she is."

Jeremiah's heart skipped a beat when, as soon as the service was over, the young woman stood up, surveyed the congregation, and then made a beeline in his direction. As he was about to speak to her, she looked past him and spoke to his grandmother.

"You are Mrs. Stevens, aren't you?" she asked in a voice so soft and melodious that it sent chills up Jeremiah's spine.

"Why yes I am, Honey," Grandma Blanche answered, "I'm Mrs. Stevens."

"Mrs. Stevens, my name is Elizabeth Craft and I've come up from Jane Lew to teach at the school here this year," the melodious voice explained. "Mr. Bailey on the school board suggested that you might have a room available that I could rent."

"Well, I hadn't considered such a thing," Grandma Blanche said, "but it was awful nice of Mr. Bailey to think of me. I guess he knows that I don't need all that room since Mr. Stevens died." Then, turning to Jeremiah she asked, "What do you think of the idea?"

"Well, I'd say it is entirely up to you, Grandma," Jeremiah said, glad to be included in the conversation.

"By the way, my name is Jeremiah Blake," Jeremiah interjected, "and as you may can tell, I'm her grandson."

"I'm pleased to meet you, Mr. Blake," Elizabeth said offering her gloved hand. "I believe Mr. Bailey said that you live in Clarksburg."

"Yes," Jeremiah said, desperately wishing that other

appropriate words would come to him but they would not so all he could add was, "yes, I do."

"Miss Craft, why don't you come home with me and Jeremiah for dinner and you can look at the house and we can talk about you staying with me," Grandma Blanche suggested.

"That is so kind of you," Elizabeth said, "I would love to if it wouldn't be too much trouble."

"It wouldn't be any trouble at all," Grandma Blanche said, "and I'm sure that Jeremiah would enjoy having somebody other than an old woman like me to talk to, wouldn't you, Son?"

Regaining his composure, Jeremiah responded, semi-seriously, "Now, Grandma, you know I never get tired of talking with you but I am sure that having Miss Craft join us will make our time together even more enjoyable."

I wonder, he thought as he rode back to Clarksburg that evening, is this how Papa felt on the Sunday he met Mama? He had only heard bits and pieces of the events of that day, mostly from the perspective of Grandma Blanche, but it appeared that his father had fallen head over heels in love with his mother the first day he saw her.

Since his infatuation with Lizzie Givens, who was really the first love of his life, he had always compared any other girl who had attracted his interest to Lizzie. So, it was natural now that he would draw comparisons between Elizabeth Craft, his brand new interest, and Lizzie.

Funny, he thought, both named Elizabeth, and about the same height. Lizzie was striking looking with beautiful auburn hair and he had always considered her to be the most beautiful girl he had ever seen. But, he thought, Elizabeth is maybe even more beautiful than Lizzie and he surprised himself by realizing that he actually preferred Elizabeth's soft, light hair which perfectly complemented her fair skin.

Lizzie was much more muscular, and he chuckled as he tried to picture Elizabeth stacking hay or pulling a crosscut saw. Also, he could not imagine any of Lizzie's cuss words coming out of the refined mouth of Elizabeth.

He was elated, then, when Grandma Blanche agreed to have Elizabeth live with her. Not only would Elizabeth be company for his grandmother, Jeremiah would have the pleasure of her company every weekend that he could spend at Nutter Fort. Now that Elizabeth was there, he resolved to never miss one.

Jeremiah passed the bar in November and on the first day of the new year, 1846, he proudly saw his name added to the door of the law firm now named Fletcher, Smith, and Blake.

The weekends that he spent with Elizabeth were the most magical moments of Jeremiah's life. He loved sitting in church with her, listening to her clear, cultured soprano voice as they sang the old hymns together. He loved her sense of style and the way she walked. He loved her easy laugh and he fed off her optimistic attitude that he so often lacked.

But most of all, he loved their conversations. He had never before known a woman who could converse on such a wide range of subjects and they would often talk late into the night about religion, music, or even, politics. As the winter wore on and spring approached, their conversations became more and more personal until they talked about little more than their feelings for each other and their desire to be together.

Despite warnings from Elizabeth's family and some misgivings from some of Jeremiah's family about whether or not they were "rushing things," Jeremiah and Elizabeth journeyed to Jane Lew at the end of the school term in May, 1846, and were married in her home church there.

With the money that Elizabeth had saved during her year of teaching and with the salary that Jeremiah was now earning as a lawyer, the young couple was able to rent a house in Clarksburg which had a small carriage building and room for a horse. They quickly became one of the most recognizable and admired couples in the city. Ol' Molly adapted quite nicely to the harness and the sight of her pulling the buggy holding the stylishly dressed couple was a sight, indeed. Elizabeth, wearing one of her bright colored long dresses and matching bonnet, and Jeremiah in his top hat and black suit with a high white collar were so striking that sometimes people would simply stop and stare at them.

They moved into their home in early June, still early enough for the eager couple to plant a garden behind the house. There was already an apple tree and a sweet cherry tree in the yard. Elizabeth took charge of planting the flowers in the front of the house and by the end of the summer, passersby would tell her and Jeremiah that their yard was the prettiest in the neighborhood.

Jeremiah needed to do a little bit of repair work on the clothes line and the grape trellis in the back yard, but in a short time he and Elizabeth were comfortably and happily settled in the exact setting that they had talked and dreamed about the previous winter. Jeremiah was now certain that his dark days were gone forever. He was married to the most wonderful woman he could have imagined, he loved his work, and the future looked bright, so his prayers were now more expressions of gratitude than petitions for overcoming the deficiencies in his life.

"Jeremiah," Elizabeth said one morning after they had been married for nearly a year and a half, "I don't think I can get out of bed this morning. Bring a cold wash cloth and wipe my face. I feel like I'm going to throw up."

Jeremiah quickly got a wash cloth, dipped it into the water bowl and wrung out the water, and placed it on Elizabeth's forehead. He then positioned the empty chamber pot to where Elizabeth could lean over the bed and vomit, which she immediately did.

"What do you think is wrong?" Jeremiah asked, anxiously. "Do you think it was the pork we had for supper last night?"

"No, I don't think so," Elizabeth responded, with a weak but knowing smile, "unless I am badly mistaken, I'm in a family way."

Jeremiah's mind went into a spin as he started to assimilate this new possibility while the love of his life was heaving into a chamber pot. Before Elizabeth had recovered enough to get out of bed, Jeremiah was already, mentally, on cloud nine, preparing a nursery, putting a new fence around the back yard, and hanging a swing from a limb on the apple tree.

"Are you sure?" he asked. "How do you know?"

"I'm pretty sure," she said. "I've been watching the signs and I thought this might be the situation. How would you feel about being a father?"

"Right now, I am mostly concerned about you," he lied, holding back his enthusiasm, "but I think that I like the idea of me being a father and you being a mother just fine."

The baby boy arrived on June 1, 1848. Elizabeth was in full

agreement with Jeremiah's wish to name the baby after one of their mutual heroes, and they named him Andrew Jackson Blake.

The next five years were, for the young Blake family, as near to heaven on earth as life could be. Jeremiah coming home each day to the enthusiastic greeting of his beautiful wife and excited son, Elizabeth caring for little Andy and keeping their home bright and cheery, the couple gardening together, harvesting and preserving fruits and vegetables, going to church every Sunday, and taking long rides in the buggy to visit their families to show off Andy. Life could not be any better than this, Jeremiah thought.

Then the unthinkable happened, Elizabeth came down with what Jeremiah thought at first was a chest cold but, instead of recovering quickly from it, she became sicker and sicker until he had to face the horrible truth; his beloved Elizabeth was terminally ill.

12 *ANDY, YOU HAVE TO GO LIVE AT GRANDPA'S*

Twelve-year-old Andy and his father were close, almost inseparable, which meant that very little went on in Jeremiah's world of government and politics that Andy did not share in or observe. Jeremiah had been his only parent since the death of Elizabeth when Andy was nine years old.

When it was determined that Elizabeth's persistent cough and recurring fever was the dreaded disease of consumption, Andy, at the age of five, was quickly relocated from his Clarksburg home to his grandparent's farm on Melford Creek, about twenty miles away.

Andy still cried when he thought about that dreadful day when his mother and father sat him down in their parlor and said, "We are so sorry, but Andy, you have to go live at Grandpa's for awhile."

He and Jeremiah had left before daylight the next morning in the buggy and arrived as it was getting dark at his grandparent's home. He remembered the discomfort of the chilling winter rain and the seemingly interminable ride as the buggy bumped and sloshed over the rutted and slippery roads as Jeremiah pushed ol' Molly to their destination. But what he remembered most clearly was the uncontrollable grief of his mother at their departure as she clutched him so tightly before telling him good-bye.

Although he had a number of short visits with his mother during the next four years, he never again was able to live with her. The visits that he had with her were confusing and painful to him. When his grandparents took him to see her, Jeremiah was careful to keep Andy at a distance from her. As much as he longed to be held and caressed by her and as much as she desperately wanted to hold him, he could only look at her and talk to her from a distance, and this took place on the front porch to protect him from the disease filled house.

As he looked back, he bitterly thought about all of the changes that resulted from that fateful day when he was just five years old, not suspecting that he would never again experience his mother lovingly putting him to bed, or singing him a lullaby, or kissing his wounds, or preparing his favorite breakfast of rolled oats and buttered biscuit, or telling him a Bible story, or hearing her pray for him. Andy never let himself indulge in these thoughts unless he was all alone because such thoughts always resulted in him sobbing.

It was nearly thirty years after the wedding of Abe and Sally that Andy came to live with his grandparents, his two aunts, and his Uncle Joshua. By this time his aunts, Rebecca and Rachel, were teenagers and seventeen-year-old Rebecca was already making marriage plans.

Even though Andy was only five years old, he was not left out of the stern Blake family work ethic. Every morning, Andy was rousted out of bed at the first hint of daylight to help Abe and Joshua with the chores while his grandmother and aunts were preparing breakfast.

Andy missed his favorite breakfast that his mother had fixed him each morning, rolled oats and buttered biscuit, but he quickly adapted to the breakfasts that his Grandma Sally prepared while he and the other "men-folks" were milking, feeding, and attending to other chores during the first morning hour. Grandpa Blake did not choose to spend the money to buy the rolled oats that Andy loved nor the sugar to sweeten them, but Andy soon discovered that Grandma Sally's breakfasts of buckwheat cakes or fried meat and biscuits topped with gravy, and then more biscuits with molasses or honey were sufficient to get him through the morning.

During the winter months he went to the same one room school that his father had attended. During the summer, he spent each day in the fields with his grandfather and uncle doing the best he could to help them while under the critical eye of Grandpa Abe.

During Andy's four years on the farm, Joshua, who was eight years older, quickly became the little boy's idol. Joshua looked enough like Jeremiah to make Andy homesick for his father but he developed a deep affection for his uncle, too. Joshua loved everything in the out-of-doors and all the time that Andy lived in his grandparent's home Joshua included his nephew in all of his activities.

Joshua loved to fish, hunt, and trap. The results of his successful expeditions provided meat for the table, and the animal pelts which he stretched and dried on triangular boards brought badly needed income into the family.

From Joshua, Andy learned to identify animal signs that told him where they were living, what they were feeding on, and their travel patterns. He learned which animals were out during the day and which were out only at night. He learned to distinguish the barking of ol' Blue, Joshua's appropriately named blue tick hound, so he could tell if he was trailing an animal or if he had the animal treed.

He would hold the lantern at night after ol' Blue had treed a coon or possum while Joshua climbed the tree and, with a stick, poked and prodded until he knocked the animal to the ground where ol' Blue would tackle it and fight with it until Joshua got to the animal and killed it. If it was a possum, Joshua would take out his knife and skin it on the spot, putting the pelt in a sack and leaving the carcass for the scavengers in the woods, but if it was a raccoon it was taken to the house where it was carefully skinned and gutted and then placed in a pan of salt water to soak until Grandma Sally could cut it up and cook it the next day.

Andy learned the technique of loading, packing, and tamping the long rifle that Joshua used to kill squirrels and rabbits, and an occasional deer, but Joshua would not let him fire the rifle until he was big enough to reach the trigger while resting the stock against his shoulder.

"There was a boy that lived up on the mountain that was about your size and he shot a rifle with the stock under his arm," Joshua said, "and when it kicked, the hammer caught him in his nose and ripped one side of it open. The doctor sewed it back up but you ought to see the scar it made. As ugly as you are you're gonna have enough trouble getting a girlfriend without having your nose half tore off."

Andy's favorite activity with Joshua was fishing. The Blake

farm was located less than a mile from where Melford Creek flowed into the West Fork River so Joshua and Andy would spend many relaxing evenings after chores were done on the banks of the West Fork fishing for bass, red eyes, and catfish.

At noon one day in the early summer, Joshua took Andy to the bridge over Melford Creek on the road to their nearest neighbor's house. Joshua laid on his stomach looking over the edge of the bridge and told Andy to join him and tell him what he saw in the small pool in the nearly dry creek.

"I don't see nothing," Andy told him. "What am I supposed to see?"

"What do you usually see when you look into a place like this?" Joshua asked. "Don't you usually see a bunch of minnows swimming around?"

"Yeah, that's right," Andy said. "What do you reckon happened to them?"

"Something ate 'em," Joshua said, "and I think I know what it was. I'm figuring that this spring, when the creek was high, a big old mama bass came up the creek to lay her eggs and then when the creek dried up, she got trapped up here. I'm willing to bet there's a big old bass under that rock over there and if we come out here about dark tonight with a worm on a hook, we can catch it."

Andy could hardly wait for the afternoon to pass. Normally he was fascinated watching Grandpa Abe and Joshua stack hay. They had mowed the hay with scythes two days before and had raked it up with pitchforks and built hay shocks this morning. Now they were using the horses to drag the shocks to a tall pole in the middle of the field. Grandpa Abe and Joshua were each using a horse with a long grapevine attached at both ends to the trace chains hanging from the back of the harness.

Both of the horses were old hands at this operation and they would walk to a hay shock, turn and, while the driver held the grapevine, back into the shock as the driver lifted the grapevine over the shock and anchored it on the ground behind the shock and then the horse pulled it to the stack site. Andy loved this job because Joshua would stick his pitchfork into the hay shock and let the little boy could hold to it and ride to the stack site standing on the grapevine at the back of the shock.

Andy found the building of the haystack to be great fun, too. At first, both his grandfather and uncle used their pitchforks to place the hay on a wooden rail foundation, going around the pole. Andy was given the task, as he held to the pole, of walking around and around and jumping up and down on the hay to tamp it. After the first few shocks were placed around the pole, Joshua climbed on top of the hay and handed Andy to the arms of Grandpa Abe. Joshua moved some of the hay around and tamped it down even tighter. Then, as Grandpa Abe kept pitching the hay onto the stack, Joshua placed it expertly and Andy watched as the round stack began to get bigger and bigger around as it got higher.

"You put a third of your hay in the bottom of the stack," Grandpa commented to Andy as he continued to pitch hay onto the stack, "and then you put another third in the swell, and the last third in the top. Think you can remember that, Boy? You might want to build a haystack yourself, some day."

"I think I could do it, Grandpa," Andy said.

"Your papa was a pretty good hand at it when he wasn't much bigger than you are," Grandpa said. "Did he ever tell you about it?"

"Yes," Andy responded, "but he said he wasn't very good at it. He said you paddled him for not doing it right."

"Aw, I don't remember that," Grandpa said as he frowned deeply. "I may have paddled him a time or two but I don't remember it being for how he was stacking hay."

"I think you've got enough in the swell, Boy," Abe yelled to Joshua after he counted the number of hay shocks that were left. "You can start topping it out now."

"Okay, Papa," Joshua responded, and Andy watched as the stack slowly began to taper toward the top of the pole.

By six o'clock Joshua had created a masterpiece, a perfectly pear shaped haystack, atop which Joshua stood triumphantly. He then caught one of the leather check lines used to drive the horses that Grandpa Abe unhooked from ol' Dan's harness and threw up to him. Wrapping the check line around the stack pole, he held to both ends of it as he deftly slid down the haystack and onto the ground.

"Let's hurry, Joshua," Andy implored as they slowly drove the horses toward the barn, "I want to go see if we can catch that big bass."

90

"Don't be in no hurry, Andy, that old bass ain't going nowhere," Joshua assured him, "and we need to wait until it's almost dark so she won't see us."

So after the horses were unharnessed, the cows brought in and milked, the pigs fed, the stove wood split and carried into the kitchen and lastly, supper eaten, Joshua and Andy were ready to test Joshua's theory.

A few shovels full of dirt dug up in the swamp above the house yielded three nice fat fishing worms and Joshua said, "That should be enough; let's go."

They quietly approached the bridge and after Joshua put the fattest worm on the hook and dropped it into the pool, he handed the pole to Andy. For a while nothing happened and Andy began to believe that Joshua was wrong, maybe that pool just didn't have any minnows in it in the first place.

Then, as he was about to give up and ask Joshua if they could go to the house, his pole was suddenly jerked out of his hands and landed on the rocky creek bed below the pool.

"Go get 'er, Andy," Joshua yelled triumphantly. "Go bring 'er in."

Andy had already begun scurrying down the bank to retrieve the pole and when he did he could not believe the power that was on the other end. It took every ounce of strength that he had to pull the pole up the bank but as he did he was rewarded by a beautiful sight, a fourteen-inch bass flopping on the grass as he pulled it out of the water.

"Andy," Grandma Sally said the next morning at the breakfast table, "I believe that you deserve the first serving since you are the one who provided this wonderful meal for us."

Andy almost burst with pride as he tasted the sweet, salty fish that Grandma had rolled in corn meal and fried golden brown.

13 *SURVIVING DEATH*

The illness and death of his beloved Elizabeth could have been fatal for Jeremiah, too. His dark days, which he thought he had outgrown, returned with a vengeance. The black cloud was back over his life and he was certain that he would never escape it. As long as Elizabeth lived, the activity required of him as her caregiver and encourager enabled him to keep going.

He had prayed, unceasingly, for a miracle, which never happened.

As Elizabeth realized that her death was near she talked, almost exclusively, about what the future should be for Jeremiah and Andy.

"Jeremiah, you must promise me that you will see to it that Andy gets a good education and is brought up in the church," she told him.

"I'll certainly do that," Jeremiah answered.

"I want you and him to be together," she added. "As soon as you can, I want you to get him and you two live together."

"Yes, yes," Jeremiah promised, "I'll do that."

Then Elizabeth tore Jeremiah's heart out when she said, "This is the hardest part but I must say it. When you get ready to marry again, promise me that you will be certain that your new wife will be able to love Andy, too."

Jeremiah clasped Elizabeth tightly and their bodies shook with sobs as they held each other.

"Don't worry about that," Jeremiah pledged, "Andy will always come first and I don't have any intentions of ever getting married again."

"But, just in case you do," Elizabeth persisted, "promise me."

"All right, I promise," Jeremiah reluctantly agreed.

The dark cloud completely closed in around Jeremiah the evening after Elizabeth had been buried. His family and friends brought food and offered to stay with him but he abruptly dismissed them all, preferring to be alone.

He held Andy tightly and told him his mama would want him to be strong and be a good boy while he stayed a little longer at Grandpa and Grandma Blake's house. Then, after embracing his parents and all of the other members of his family and Elizabeth's family, he withdrew. He withdrew deep into himself and retreated into the darkness of the house that he had shared with Elizabeth for the past eleven years, the house that had been the most wonderful place on earth for their first seven years together but which became a place of suffering and death during their next four years.

Jeremiah would have welcomed his own death at this time. He went for days without eating and scarcely slept. He pondered on the words of Solomon, "Vanity, vanity, all is vanity." He mentally relived his entire life and questioned the value of his life and what were once very proud achievements; his education, his profession, his standing in the community, his role in the church, and his association with the elite of Clarksburg, and recognized that in comparison to losing the one he loved, truly, all was vanity.

He reminded himself of Job as he talked boldly, sometimes angrily, to God, asking why this had to happen and why He had not answered his prayers for Elizabeth to be healed. In his despair he told God that he was not the man that Job was for he would never recover from this loss.

However, slowly, things occurred which began to occupy Jeremiah's mind and started a process of change.

One thing that happened was that when he was in the depths of his sorrow, it was as if Elizabeth would speak to him. When he would reach his lowest point he would remember her saying, "I want you and Andy to be together," and his thoughts would turn to their child who looked so much like his beautiful mother and was still living with his grandparents.

The second thing which had a major impact on him was the arousal of his anger when he went back for the first time after Elizabeth's death to the Union Debating Society and concluded that it was becoming an abolitionist organization. At that meeting, Rev.

Daniel Hayes spoke about a book that was causing a major stir throughout the country, *Uncle Tom's Cabin,* which had been written by Harriet Beecher Stowe, who was a sister of the well-known abolitionist preacher, Henry Ward Beecher, a man that Jeremiah considered a troublemaker.

Jeremiah was skeptical from the outset about this book that Rev. Hayes was so worked up about. He knew about the Beecher family and he felt that he did not need to read the book to know that it was just another effort to further the abolitionist movement. Following Hayes' presentation there was a heated debate and, although Jeremiah chose not to speak, he was in agreement with those who were skeptical about the accuracy or importance of the book.

At the conclusion of the meeting, Hayes asked Jeremiah if he would take the book with him and read it. Although not anxious to do so, out of the respect he felt for Daniel Hayes, he agreed.

The book lay unopened until he came home from the law office early Saturday afternoon. He realized that if on the following day he went to the Baptist Church, which he did occasionally, Rev. Hayes would ask him about the book, so he knew that he must take the time to, at the very least, scan through it.

By the end of the first few pages, Jeremiah was livid. Although he had personally only seen a few slaves owned by the wealthier farmers in his home area, he could not believe that slaves, anywhere, were treated like those portrayed in the book. He had never critically questioned the teachings of his father who believed that slavery was biblical and he agreed fully with Alexander Campbell's learned contention that slavery, if practiced as the Apostle Paul instructed, was not a sin.

He failed to see how anyone could disagree with what seemed to him to be perfectly obvious, that the black race was different and inferior. He would not be foolish enough, he thought, to take the word of a sister of an abolitionist rabble-rouser over the teachings and writings of unbiased luminaries like Alexander Campbell and Thomas Jefferson. He was certain that, in most situations, loyal slaves loved their owners and were happy doing the simple tasks for which they were well suited. Even the ones who have harsh owners, he reasoned, were much better off than if they were living in the

94

dark jungles of Africa.

Although Jeremiah tried to reject Harriet Beecher Stowe's book completely, portions of it burned itself into his consciousness and forced him to consider some things. Jeremiah had to admit to himself that he had never been acquainted with a slave. He had never tried to see things from the view of the slave. The power of the printed word was forcing him to consider, for the first time, the humanity of the Negro.

He was perplexed and angered when, in rebuttal to his arguments at the next meeting of the Debating Society, Daniel Hayes paraphrased one of Jeremiah's favorite Shakespearean quotations: "Hath not a Negro eyes?" Hayes asked. " Hath not a Negro hands, organs, dimensions, senses, affections, passions? If you prick a Negro, does he not bleed?"

Although he argued vehemently that this quote did not apply to the Negro slave, the passage did remind Jeremiah of the suffering and sorrow in the world, about which he had once been so concerned. For the past weeks he had been so preoccupied with confronting the Almighty regarding his own plight that he had been blind to the fact that, as great a loss as he had experienced, he still had much to be thankful for.

His prayer that night was his first prayer of gratitude since Elizabeth had died. That night, his anger softened as he thanked God for his parents, his opportunities, his son, and lastly for the privilege that had been afforded him, the privilege of experiencing the love of one of His masterpieces, his beloved Elizabeth.

Jeremiah now saw that the way in which he must deal with his grief was to make some changes in his life. Rather than following his parent's strong urging to move back to Melford Creek, join them on the farm, and follow his father into the ministry, he knew that he must take Andy and make a break from his past and he prayed constantly for guidance as he sought the appropriate new direction with his life.

He left his house in Clarksburg with all of its wonderful and terrible memories and found rooms in a boarding house that would be large enough for him and Andy for the time being. After bringing Andy back to Clarksburg to live with him, he spent every moment with his son that he was not in school. With Andy by his side at the office and in the courtroom, he continued to practice law but he was now certain that this was temporary; something else was awaiting him.

The third life changing event occurred when U. S. Congressman John Carlile came to Clarksburg and spoke to a large open-air audience in front of the County Court House. Jeremiah had been impressed by the then State Senator Carlile when he had campaigned in Clarksburg in 1855 for the seat in Congress.

It had been three months since Elizabeth's death when Jeremiah heard that the Congressman was coming to Clarksburg so he decided to take Andy and go hear him speak.

The Congressman spoke so eloquently and passionately about the dangers facing the country and the importance of keeping the nation undivided that Jeremiah was moved to approach him and offer his assistance to him. After introducing himself and Andy to the Congressman, Jeremiah told him that he was in full agreement with his points of view and would like to offer his services if the Congressman had need of them.

"Well, Mr. Blake," Carlile said in response to Jeremiah's offer, "what I really need is someone who is thoroughly committed to the Union and has enough education to sometimes speak for me and help me with my writing. That person would need to be able to help draft legislation and assist in innumerable other activities."

"I believe that I may have the background that you are looking for," Jeremiah said. "I received my education at Bethany College and I am now a member of the bar. And regarding the Union, let me assure you that I am fully committed."

"Would you be free to travel throughout the district and even to Washington when I need you?" the Congressman asked.

Jeremiah had felt the hair raise on the back of his neck as he listened to the Congressman describe the person that he needed to assist him. He was completely amazed as he realized that there was a good possibility that he would be entering public service, working with the eminent John Carlile.

During the time of loneliness and despair he had experienced after the death of Elizabeth, Jeremiah had harbored doubts and resentment about the way in which the One in whom he had always trusted was managing the universe. He had difficulty praying and when he did pray, it seemed that his pleas were falling on deaf ears. As a result he was humbled as, through what he accepted as Divine favor, he now found himself face to face with an opportunity that exceeded anything that he could have imagined.

"Mr. Carlile," Jeremiah said, fighting the lump in his throat resulting from the emotions of the moment, "I am available to travel anywhere you would need me, as long as I can take Andy, here, with me. I promised his mother before we lost her that he and I would always stick together."

14 *WHO IS DRED SCOTT?*

Going with Congressman Carlile to Washington, D. C., was a monumental step. Nothing in the experiences of Jeremiah had prepared him for life at the seat of America's government.

Washington in mid-summer was not the most desirable place to be. The heat was much more oppressive than in the mountains of Virginia and Jeremiah sweltered through the days wearing his woolen suit at work.

Andy had never experienced the stench that was always in the air, not even when he lived at Grandpa Abe's Farm. Flies swarmed all around and Andy was constantly scratching his mosquito bites. All of these pestilences originated in the ditches that ran along the streets and through the residential area, half filled with stagnant water and sewage during dry days and overflowing on the days when it rained.

The dirt streets, when dry, kept the hot, muggy air filled with a cloud of dust and pulverized, dried horse manure resulting from the constant horse, buggy, wagon, and coach traffic moving over them at a rapid rate. When wet, the streets became slippery, muddy, smelly thoroughfares filled with ruts.

Jeremiah and Andy settled into a comfortable boarding house about two miles southwest of the Capitol. Their days were spent mostly on Capitol Hill where Jeremiah either worked in Congressman Carlile's office or sat with the Congressman when he was on the floor of the House of Representatives.

Andy whiled away these days, usually sitting beside his father's desk reading, or outside exploring the area surrounding the Capitol.

When there was any event occurring on the floor of the House which Jeremiah anticipated would be particularly significant, or when Congressman Carlile was planning to speak, he would take Andy with him to the session.

Andy, although only ten years old, quickly became quite fascinated by the people in government and the topics in which they were immersed.

Jeremiah, not wishing to miss out on the remarkable opportunities to add to Andy's education sought out ways to satisfy the boy's enormous curiosity. He pointed out the most powerful members of Congress to him and introduced him to some of the more approachable ones.

One Sunday, Jeremiah announced, "We are going to the Presbyterian Church today instead of the Methodist."

"Why is that, Papa?" Andy asked.

"I want you to be able to say that you went to church with the President," was his answer.

"So President Buchanan is a Presbyterian, is he?" Andy asked.

"His parents were Presbyterians but he didn't join the church when he was young and now that he wants to, I hear that their churches don't want him," Jeremiah said.

"Why is that?" a puzzled Andy asked. "I didn't think churches were supposed to turn anybody away."

"Well, a lot of them do nowadays," Jeremiah explained, "and in the case of President Buchanan it's about his stand on slavery. The Presbyterians who support slavery don't want him because they say he's too friendly with the abolitionists and the Presbyterians who are against slavery don't want him because they say he supports the slave owners."

"Then why doesn't he become a Methodist?" Andy asked. "We'd take him, wouldn't we?"

"Right now, he'd face the same problem in most any church in the country, at least in the Methodist and Baptist churches that I'm familiar with." Jeremiah explained. "They have about all gone one way or the other on the slavery thing. It's amazing to me that this has gotten so out of hand that even the President of the United States can't join a church."

They got to the church early so they could see the President if he did, indeed, attend services that day. Shortly before the service was to begin, their patience was rewarded as a hushed stir rippled though the congregation and the tall, distinguished, white haired Chief of State entered the sanctuary with an entourage of two men and took his seat in the front row of the church.

"Take a good look, Son," Jeremiah whispered, "you are looking at the President of the United States of America."

One of the few things that had escaped the young lad's attention during his short stay in Washington was that the President was not married, so Jeremiah was slightly irritated when Andy asked, "Where is Mrs. Buchanan?"

Later that week, as Andy and Jeremiah were walking to their boarding house one evening, Andy asked, "Papa, who is Dred Scott? Everybody around the Capitol was talking about Dred Scott today. Who is he?"

"Dred Scott is a slave who was taken by his owner up to the headwaters of the Mississippi River near Canada, into free territory," Jeremiah answered patiently. "Dred Scott claimed that since he was living in a place where slavery was illegal, that made him a free man and now he was a citizen of the United States. What happened this week is that the Supreme Court ruled that he was wrong and he is still a slave."

"That doesn't make much sense, does it?" Andy asked.

"Not until you take the whole ruling into account," Jeremiah said. "Now, pay close attention, this gets pretty complicated but I'll try to explain it. Chief Justice Taney considered this important enough to write the opinion himself, and he wrote that the Court first ruled that the Missouri Compromise, which prohibited slavery in the territories up North was unconstitutional. So that means that since Dred Scott was not living in free territory after all, he is still a slave. Then the biggest thing was when Justice Taney wrote that not only was Dred Scott not a citizen of the United States, neither he nor any other Negro ever could be."

"That sounds strange," Andy responded. "If Negroes aren't citizens of this country, then where are they citizens of?"

"That's a very good question," Jeremiah said. "Based on this ruling, nowhere, really. This means that, in the eyes of the law, they are just like other work animals on the farm, owned by their masters.

Horses and cows can't be citizens so neither can Negroes."

"Papa, can't you and Mr. Carlile do something?" Andy asked. "Why don't you pass a law and change it?"

"No, son," Jeremiah responded, "a law can't change a ruling of the Supreme Court. The only way to change a constitutional ruling is to change the Constitution and that is a very, very difficult process."

"Then what's going to happen?" Andy asked.

"I'm afraid of what's going to happen," Jeremiah said. "This is going to fire up the abolitionists like nothing since Harriet Beecher Stowe's book. Now there'll be another rush by slave owners and abolitionists to see who can settle the territories first and we'll be right back to where we were before the Missouri Compromise."

Jeremiah was right. Public meetings and demonstrations began happening all across the northern portion of the country as the abolitionists fanned the flames and were able to get large numbers of the previously less committed anti-slavery people to join their ranks. Southern slaveholders celebrated their great legal victory and began, once again, to send bounty hunters into the northern territories to capture and return their runaway slaves.

Northern newspapers screamed through their headlines and editorials about the gross injustice of the Dred Scott decision. Southern newspapers applauded the level-headedness and fairness demonstrated by the Supreme Court.

Preachers thundered from their northern pulpits with new vigor about the terrible sin that was sure to bring God's judgment on the nation. Many southern preachers rejoiced as they assured their congregations that God was still in control and that He had led the Supreme Court to uphold His Holy Order and the divinely ordained institution of slavery.

One night, just a few weeks before the election of 1858, John Carlile came to Jeremiah and Andy's room with a stunning announcement.

"Jeremiah, I have decided to withdraw from the race and leave the Congress," he said. "I believe that I can do more good toward saving the Union if I go back to Virginia and concentrate my efforts there. Virginia is going to be the key to this whole thing and I believe that the only hope we have of saving the country is if we can succeed in keeping Virginia loyal to the Union. I don't think that I can get that job done if I am tied up here in Washington all the time."

"What do you want me to do?" Jeremiah asked.

"That's why I'm here tonight," the Congressman said. "You have quickly established a good reputation here and there are any number of members who would hire you as their assistant if they knew that you were available. You just say the word and I'll let a few of them know."

"Well," Jeremiah said hesitantly, "you've caught me off guard but I don't think that I want to work for anyone else here but you."

"Would you like to go back to your law practice in Clarksburg?" Carlile asked. "I'm sure you could do that if you wanted to."

"I went to work for you because I believe in you and the things you are trying to do," Jeremiah said. "I still feel the same way. What can I do that would be of the most help to you?"

"If you really mean it, and make no mistake about it, it isn't going to be easy," Carlile said, "I would love for you to stay with me all that you could. I don't have enough money to pay you much but if you could earn a little money by handling a few cases and you and Andy think you can sometimes come and live like gypsies with me, I would be forever grateful."

15 *GENERAL JACKSON, I PRESUME*

The next two and a half years were hectic times for Jeremiah and Andy. Whenever Jeremiah was about to settle back into a routine in Clarksburg he would get an urgent request from John Carlile to go here or there, speak at this rally, meet with this group, or visit this key individual, so that no routine was possible.

Always accompanied by Andy, Jeremiah began going to the surrounding towns and cities like Fairmont, Grafton, Morgantown, and even occasionally as far away as his favorite city, Wheeling. It was in Morgantown that Jeremiah first met up with attorney Waitman Willey, the constitutional expert and strong Union advocate.

The area that Jeremiah was asked to cover was ever expanding; he went to Elkins, to Buckhannon, and all the way to Parkersburg. Finding places to stay became a bigger problem all the time so he made a proposal to Andy.

"What do you think of the idea that we trade our horse and buggy for a team of horses and a big wagon?" Jeremiah asked. "Then we could take a tent with us and some food and cooking pots and live outside when the weather is good."

"That sounds great to me," was Andy's enthusiastic response, "that might be fun."

With the travel and lodging adjustments made, the two found themselves being asked to go farther and farther from their home base, into the Greenbrier and Shenandoah Valleys, into the communities of Lewisburg and Harrisonburg, moving always in the direction of the state capital, Richmond.

One of the places that Jeremiah was especially anxious to visit was Lexington, where his old friend, T. J. Jackson, was on the faculty of the Virginia Military Institute. Jeremiah wanted most of all for Andy to meet this man about whom he had shared so many stories. He also wanted to be able to probe his friend's thinking about the issues and events that were raging around them.

It was an early fall afternoon in 1859 when Jeremiah and Andy finally arrived in Lexington. With a minimum of inquiry Jeremiah located the Jackson residence and, after tying up the horses, took Andy and knocked on the door. The old friend, himself, opened the door.

"General Jackson, I presume," Jeremiah said grandly.

"No, that's Colonel Jackson," T. J. started to say but then recognized the familiar smile of his friend from long ago and reached out and eagerly grasped his hand. "Jeremiah Blake! I don't believe it! What has brought you here?"

"I came so this lad could meet you," Jeremiah said. "He's heard so many tall tales about you I'm not sure he believed that you existed except in my imagination. Son, let me introduce you to the genuine Thomas Jonathan Jackson. T. J., this is my son Andrew Jackson Blake; he goes by Andy."

"Well, Andy," T. J. said, "if your papa didn't give you anything else, at least gave you a fine middle name. It is an honor to meet you."

"I'm happy to meet you, too, Sir," Andy respectfully responded.

"Come in, come in," T. J. said, "and let me introduce you to my wife."

"Mary Anna" he called into the back of the house, "come in here and meet an old friend of mine, Jeremiah Blake and his son Andrew Jackson."

Jeremiah and Andy were then greeted by a most pleasant woman in her mid twenties who had been married to T. J. for just two years.

"I am pleased to make your acquaintance Mr. Blake, and you, too, Master Andrew," she said with an ease and elegance which testified of her upbringing as the daughter of the president of Davidson College. "I trust you will be staying with us for supper and spending the night here."

"Oh, no," Jeremiah protested. "We have our provisions out in the wagon and we will be just fine if we can get a place to locate for the night."

"Most certainly not," T. J boomed out. "When my old friend from Melford Creek comes for a visit, he stays in my house. I will have someone see to your horses and Mary Anna, you ask the cook to prepare something for these weary travelers to eat."

By the time supper was served, Andy had become completely mystified by the actions of their host. He had never seen anyone like this hero-friend of his father's. He noticed that when Jackson was standing, he was ramrod straight which was not too strange, Andy thought, for a military man. But when Jackson sat down, he was also ramrod straight, never letting his body touch the back of the chair. Most of the time, whether he was standing or sitting, he kept his left arm fully extended straight up in the air. Andy was also fascinated by the strange facial gyrations that Jackson was constantly going through.

When they were called to supper, Andy's amazement continued. Instead of sitting down and sharing the quickly prepared, but adequate meal, Andy watched out of the corner of his eye as Jackson partook of his unique meal standing erect.

"Thomas always has just a piece of bread and a glass of buttermilk for supper," his wife explained. "He went to the Springs a while back for his health and they put him on bread and buttermilk, and he has found that he digests his food better if he eats standing up."

Andy could barely wait until he was alone with his father to ask him about this curious behavior, but wait he must. The old friends had much to talk about.

"We still have some things in common, T. J.," Jeremiah said after they had relocated into the parlor after supper. "Both of us have lost a wife. Your loss was greater, though, as you also lost your son at the same time. I don't know how you survived that tragedy. Just losing Elizabeth almost killed me and if I had lost Andy, I am sure I would have died of grief."

"Well, 'the Lord giveth, and the Lord taketh away,' the Good Book says," T. J. responded, much to Jeremiah's surprise. He had never known his friend to be the least bit religious and he had already been surprised when T. J. had requested that he ask the blessing for the supper.

"Is your father well?" T. J. asked.

"Yes, and still as mean and stubborn as ever," Jeremiah said, smiling.

"The next time you see him, I want you to tell him something for me," T. J. said. "I want you to tell him that I have made peace with God and joined the church. After the way he used to get after me for saying a bad word, not even a cuss word, mind you, I think he would like to know that."

"Well, I'm glad to know that, too," Jeremiah enthused. "How did your conversion come about?"

"I did a lot of thinking during the Mexican campaign," T. J. said. "Any time a man is a witness to all of that suffering and dying, he can't help thinking about things and hoping for something better. You know that I have always tried to be honest and fair and live an upright life, but I began to see that maybe that wasn't enough so when I got here at the Institute, I undertook some serious study."

Without moving his erect body, but, Andy noticed, with increased facial twitching, Jackson continued, "My first wife's family was a lot of help. You know that her father was an ordained Presbyterian minister and the president of Washington College here in Lexington, and the family, especially her brother, gave me a lot of material to consider. After I compared their material with my own study of the Bible, I decided that I could agree with everything they believed except for predestination, so in 1851, I decided to join the Presbyterian Church and they accepted me."

"Tell me something, how this has changed your life?" Jeremiah probed.

"It has given me a sense of forgiveness and peace, and a hope for eternity that I never had before," Jackson answered. "You be sure and tell your father that the boy he once reprimanded is now a deacon and a Sunday School teacher and trying his best to serve the Lord. I want him to know that."

"I'll be sure to tell Papa," Jeremiah assured him. "I wouldn't be surprised if he has a shouting spell when he hears it."

"Oh, yes, Jeremiah," T. J. added, not acknowledging Jeremiah's effort at humor, "there is another thing that we have in common. You wrote me a few years ago that you had joined the Union Debating Society in Clarksburg. Well, I was such a nervous speaker that I decided to emulate you and I joined the Franklin Debating Society, here, to see if I could get over my embarrassment at public speaking."

"Has it helped you?" Jeremiah asked.

"I think it has helped a lot," T. J. responded. "It has even helped me overcome my inability to offer a public prayer."

"Tell, me, T. J.," Jeremiah said, intending to introduce the subject of the Union, when the clock began to strike nine o'clock. Suddenly, as if he had died, T. J.'s head slumped forward and he was asleep.

Mary Anna immediately came into the room, not showing the least bit of surprise. She gently roused her husband and, after excusing herself, led him to their bedroom. After a few moments she returned to explain that, "Thomas follows a very strict regimen," and that "he retires at precisely nine o'clock each night." She also commented that he falls asleep very suddenly and she has a great problem keeping him awake during church services.

As soon as Andy had his father to himself in their bedroom, he began his inquiry.

"Papa, what is wrong with Colonel Jackson?" he asked. "I've never been around anybody like him. He's scary."

"I don't know that anything is wrong with him," Jeremiah thoughtfully replied. "But I will agree that he is different; always has been. You know from your studies that often the most brilliant person may have some unusual habits, and he is certainly no exception. From the time I first knew him he was concerned about his left side being the equal of his right side. Remember me telling you about the time he showed me he could skip a rock with his left hand? Well, it looks like he is still worried that his right side is getting ahead of his left."

"He acts like he's sick," Andy further inquired. "Is he?"

"He has always acted like he is, but I just don't know," Jeremiah said. "It may be that he is the kind of a person who thinks he's worse off than he really is. He has changed a lot over the years but one thing hasn't changed one bit. He has always believed that his destiny is to be General T. J. Jackson and you can tell by the way he stands and sits that he still believes that."

The next morning, T. J. insisted that Jeremiah and Andy accompany him as he conducted the early morning drill and then on to his office before he taught his first class.

Andy had never seen such splendor as now was marching before him. Col. Jackson, in his full military regalia, first stood in front of the cadet companies, erect as always, barking out orders which were followed to the letter. The cadets, also colorfully dressed, stepped smartly and in precise time. After they had gone through their maneuvers, and passed in review, Jackson called them to attention. He then stiffly strode among them, left arm conspicuously pointing skyward, stopping occasionally to quietly commend or loudly reprimand an individual cadet, and then returned to his command position and dismissed them.

The walk to Jackson's office seemed strange to Andy. Col. Jackson walked in perfect cadence, eyes never straying from straight ahead, seemingly oblivious of the cadets he was meeting along the way except for the perfunctory salutes that he returned to them. Andy could not help noticing what appeared to be looks of derision on the faces of some of the cadets as they glanced at Jackson.

Once in his office, Jackson seemed to relax somewhat, but still stood erect as he invited Jeremiah and Andy to be seated. Then, after seating himself stiffly behind his desk, he began to talk.

"Jeremiah, you can tell that this is not a comfortable position for me to be in," Jackson said. "I am a soldier, not a professor, even if I am teaching the tactics of war. I am a field commander and my strengths are in leading men on the field of battle. I have taught myself to overcome all fear and to similarly inspire those who are under my command when on the battlefield, but that does not translate well into the academic world.

"The cadets here do not like me, and frankly, I do not like many of them. There was recently an attempt on my life by a cadet who dropped a brick from a third floor window that just missed my head. I had him arrested but I was then criticized for being weak and not handling the situation within the Institute. I know many of the things they are saying behind my back, but I go on in the knowledge that if they ever find themselves under fire, they will have to admit that I did my utmost to prepare them."

Jeremiah was shocked by the insight and frankness of his friend who, he was coming to realize, was even more eccentric than he had suspected after their time together yesterday.

Finding no way to assuage the frustrations of his friend, Jeremiah sought to change the subject.

"What do you hear from Laura Ann?" Jeremiah asked. "As she has possibly written to you, I have seen her twice during the past two years and she appears well to me."

"She tells me that she and her family are doing well, as you have observed," Jackson said. "How is it that you have seen her, has she been to Clarksburg?"

"No, I was in Beverly with John Carlile once at a Union rally that she and her husband attended, and then I stopped in on them on my way to Elkins back in the spring," Jeremiah explained.

"It doesn't surprise me that she was at a Union rally," Jackson said. "She has always had strong opinions and she and her husband are both loyal Union supporters. Well, I'm glad that you get to see her on occasion."

"I'm curious, T. J.," Jeremiah ventured to ask, "how do you stand on the subject of a strong Union versus state sovereignty?"

"I guess you could say that Laura Ann and I were cut from the same bolt of cloth," Jackson answered. "I would hate to see anything happen to tear down the country and I hope and pray that it will never come to that. That said, if the worst that some are predicting comes to pass I will, as always, be a soldier. You, Jeremiah are the politician; I am the soldier. A soldier takes orders from his commander. In Mexico, I took orders from General Scott. Now I am under the command of the Governor of Virginia. Do you know where he stands on the issue?"

"Yes," Jeremiah said, "he is firmly on the side of the Union."

"Then there's your answer," Jackson said.

Jeremiah was greatly heartened by his visit with his friend, especially with the news that he had embraced religion and that he was wanting the Union to be preserved. He did not want to wait until he was back in Harrison County to share the good news of T. J.'s conversion with his father so he wrote him a long letter telling him of his visit with Jackson and bringing him up to date on many of their other experiences.

After carrying out other assignments in the mountain and valley sections of Virginia, Jeremiah and Andy joined John Carlile in Richmond early in 1860. The weather was unpleasant, cold and damp, and the heavy wagon and carriage traffic turned the streets into quagmires of mud.

Spring, however, began to arrive much earlier than they were accustomed to in Clarksburg. The emergence of the first green leaves, along with flowering of the redbud and dogwood transformed the wooded countryside around Richmond into nature's showplace.

This was accentuated by the profuse show of color in the lawns and gardens of the city's most beautiful homes as the iris, peonies, and lilacs blossomed, wisteria cascaded down from porch trellises, and the apple, peach, and cherry trees in the back yards came into full bloom. By early May, Andy had decided that Richmond must be the most beautiful city in the world.

16 *WHO ELECTED LINCOLN?*

When Andy awoke on the morning of August 17, 1860, the sun was already high in the sky. The activities of the previous evening and the late hour of his getting to bed had resulted in him sleeping much later than usual. He quickly got dressed and ran down to Mrs. Etta's dining room where he found his father in a deep conversation about the events of the previous evening with John Carlile and Waitman Willey at a table in the far corner of the room.

"Hey there, Sonny Boy," Willey, the first to notice Andy, said, "we thought you were going to sleep all day. You better sit down here and have yourself some breakfast."

After being greeted by Carlile and his father, Andy found that he was quickly forgotten as the men returned to their deep discussion of political strategy.

"What about our governor?" Willey asked. "You men know him better than I do. Do you think we can trust him? I like what I heard him saying last night but I question if John Letcher will have enough backbone to hold things together once the real crisis comes."

"I think we all have to help prop him up," Carlile responded. "As long as we have a majority in the state legislature and the decisions are being made there, he won't be put on the spot. I agree, though, if the Calhoun crowd ever gains the upper hand and puts the pressure on him, he might buckle under."

"It appears to me that he is the most levelheaded governor in the South," Jeremiah offered, "and we are fortunate in that respect. I think that our task, now, is to encourage him and commend him for his strong Union stand. We know the kind of pressure he is under from the hotheads so we need to stand firmly with him."

Later in the year, though, their worst fears were realized. In

December, following the election of Abraham Lincoln as President, Governor John Letcher bowed to pressure and made the fateful decision to call for a special session of the Virginia General Assembly to meet in January, 1861. The purpose of the special session was to elect delegates to a convention to "consider the proper relationship of the Commonwealth of Virginia to the Federal Government of the United States."

The summer of 1860 had been an eventful one for Andy. Jeremiah was so deeply involved in state political matters that he could not spend as much time with Andy as he had always been able to do, and felt that, at age twelve, Andy was getting old enough to look after himself, especially since he was ever under the watchful eyes of Mrs. Etta Hatcher and her trusted slaves; Sadie, Jubal, and Jesse.

Andy spent a lot of time in the livery with Jesse, helping feed and groom the horses. Working with Jesse caused Andy to realize how much he missed life on Grandpa Blake's farm, the familiar chores he had carried out and the love he had developed for the animals, especially the horses.

"Masta' Andy," Jesse told him one day when he was helping, "you sure got a way with horses. I never seen a body your age who was as good with horses as you are. How come you know so much about horses?"

"Papa had a great horse named ol' Molly when I was born," Andy explained. "She was real gentle and I remember Papa putting me on her and leading her around the back yard. Molly had been Papa's horse since he went away to college and she lived to be eighteen. She died the same year as my mother, in fifty-six. I lived with my grandparents on the farm for four years when my mother was sick and Grandpa and my Uncle Joshua showed me how to work with their horses."

"I'd say they done a mighty good job," Jesse said. "I ain't never seen nobody better at it than you are."

Andy also made a few friends of boys around his own age that lived near Mrs. Hatcher's boarding house. The one that he spent the most time with was Billy Watson, the son of an old, respected Richmond family. Billy was a year older than Andy and was much heavier. The time Andy spent with Billy was sometimes not of

Andy's choosing but, rather, because Billy sought him out. Andy soon realized that Billy avoided many of the other boys in the neighborhood, boys who teased him about his weight.

Billy knew every nook and cranny of Richmond and delighted in showing them to Andy. Throughout the summer they explored all of the fascinating places in the sprawling city. By hanging out with Billy, Andy got to fish in every stream, catch tadpoles in every swamp, sample the fruit from every fruit tree and berry patch the boys could get access to, and found out which houses had pretty girls living in them.

Billy had opinions on every imaginable subject, opinions Andy figured, that came from his family.

"Somebody oughta' shoot old 'Dishonest Ape' Lincoln," Billy said one morning. "Did you ever see anybody as ugly as he is? He looks just like a big old skinny monkey, don't he?"

"Yeah," Andy agreed, half heartedly, "I don't like him either."

"A man like that don't have no business being the President," Billy said and Andy assumed that he was now quoting the words of his father. "If the people up North are stupid enough to elect him the decent folks in the South ain't gonna stand for it, and that includes Virginia."

"Papa," Andy said that evening, "don't you think it's a shame that the people up North might elect old 'Dishonest Ape' Lincoln who's causing us all this trouble?"

"Andy, I've never heard you talk about anyone like that," Jeremiah said. "What do you mean by referring to Mr. Lincoln in that disrespectful way?"

"Well," Andy said, "me and Billy was talking and ever since Lincoln started running for President there has been a lot of trouble, and you have to admit, he does look a lot like a monkey."

"I am not for the election of Mr. Lincoln, and that is how you will refer to him in the future," Jeremiah said sternly, "but if the people of the United States, not the people of the North, elect him to be our President he will be the President of all the states, whether some people like that fact or not."

"But a whole bunch of states will secede and Billy says that Virginia is going to be one of them," Andy said.

"Andy," Jeremiah said, now in a patient voice, "if you had

studied the United States Constitution like I have, you would know that our country is one big nation, a union, not a confederation of a bunch of little nations. The people who try to secede will be in violation of the Constitution. The only way they could leave the Union would be if the federal government granted it. So, you see, even if they try, they won't be seceding. Instead, they will be in rebellion against their own federal government. I agree with Mr. Lincoln when he contends that the United States will remain the same size it always was, despite the actions of some rebellious politicians in some of the states. There won't be any change in our flag, there will be still thirty-four stars on it."

"Then what's going to happen?" Andy asked.

"I don't know for sure," Jeremiah said. "We are trying desperately to keep the Governor and the legislature here in Virginia from rebelling and, once we have achieved that, I hope we can serve as a mediator between the Federal Government and the rebel leaders. If we can't stop the rebellion here in Virginia this country is in for a lot of trouble."

17 . . *THE AUCTION*

One thing that Billy and others kept talking about and that Andy was looking forward to was the big slave auction that was scheduled for September 12. As the great day neared, excitement was in the air. Posters announcing the sale were hanging all over the city. Billy and Andy had watched all week as a crew of slaves worked, putting the auction platform into place under the close supervision of their white overseers.

On the morning of the sale, Billy was already on the porch of the boarding house at 7:30 when Andy came out.

"Come on, Andy," Billy urged, "we got to hurry if we are gonna get a spot up front where we can see everything."

As soon as they arrived at the auction site, Billy and Andy claimed spots for themselves right at the edge of the platform and planted themselves cross-legged on the dusty street. There was already considerable activity as the owners were signing up with the auction clerks, listing the slaves that they would be offering for sale that day.

Andy had never seen so many black people at one time. He was amazed at the large number of them who were already there, standing around, mostly in small groups, but a few were alone or in pairs. He noticed that some of them were shackled and others were not. He was particularly fascinated by one young woman and a small boy standing quietly by themselves. The boy was leaning against the woman and she had her arm around his shoulders. Andy noticed that these two, like most of the other slaves, kept their heads slightly bowed and their eyes cast downward.

Billy was busy noticing other things.

"Look at that big 'un over there," he said as he pointed to a tall, muscular slave. "I'll bet he don't do no work. I'll bet he's a buck."

"What does that mean?" Andy inquired.

"Don't tell me you don't know what a buck is," Billy said. "A buck is the one that breeds all of the slave girls so the babies will be big and strong and worth a lot of money. If I was a slave, I'd want to be a buck, wouldn't you?"

Andy was incredulous and ignored the last part of Billy's explanation as he asked, "What about their husbands?"

"Oh, that don't matter," Billy explained. "A lot of the owners don't let them get married and even if they are married, they don't care."

"How do you know that?" Andy asked, becoming more and more confused.

"Because they're so dumb, they don't know any better," Billy answered, "My papa says that when they were living wild in the jungle, they just mated with whoever they wanted to, so they're better off here where their owners can pick out the right one for them to mate with."

At nine o'clock sharp the auction started. The market square was now crowded. As Andy surveyed the crowd, he saw the prospective buyers, and sellers with their slaves as he had expected, but he was surprised to see hundreds of others, men in suits and top hats, women in bonnets and long dress finery, and children running everywhere. If it had not been for the reality of the auction, Andy would have thought himself at a Union rally in Morgantown or an annual homecoming at the Methodist Church at Nutter Fort.

The first slave who was brought up on the platform was a slender man in his twenties with his legs chained together. He stood perfectly still as the auctioneer colorfully described him to the crowd.

"Here we have a slave who has been trained to work horses and is an excellent plowman and field hand. He can be a little headstrong but he responds to the whip and he's never been sick a day in his life. Whoever buys him will be getting a good fifty years of productive labor."

While the auctioneer was describing the attributes of the slave, prospective bidders came forward for a close examination. They pulled down his chin to check the condition of his teeth, lifted and moved both arms, felt his arm and leg muscles, and looked at the bottoms of his bare feet. Then the bidding started.

"I got fifty dollars to start, who'll make it sixty," the auctioneer yelled. "I got sixty, now seventy, who'll make it seventy," and so on until the bids ceased and the slave was "sold, to the gentleman on the right over there," and the buyer paid the clerk and led his purchase away.

There followed a parade of people for sale; a teenage girl, a man who appeared to be around sixty years old, a boy who limped on his club foot; but mostly the people offered for sale were strong young men and women looking to be in their late teens. The majority of them were quiet and seemed resigned to their fate but occasionally one of them would have a stern look of defiance and instead of staring down at his feet would look out into the distance over the heads of the audience.

Most of the slaves were barefoot and dressed in simple work clothes. Almost all of the men were naked from the waist up. Prospective bidders were free to come forward and examine the slave being offered for sale in any way they chose. Men's genitals could be checked and the women's blouses could be lowered and skirts raised at the discretion of the bidders. All of this was done to the great delight of Billy.

Billy was able to find something degradingly amusing about each slave that was being sold and shared his humor with Andy who was getting ever more uncomfortable with what he was seeing and hearing.

An unusually well dressed couple who looked out of place and were described by the auctioneer as a skilled maid and butler were offered for sale individually or as a pair, depending on which situation brought the most money. The bidding was heavy and they were purchased as a pair by a prosperous looking couple for over two hundred dollars.

A little after ten o'clock, the tall, muscular slave that Billy had commented on walked, unfettered, onto the platform as the crowd buzzed with excitement.

"Gentlemen," the auctioneer announced, "we have here a magnificent specimen, the highlight of the sale today. Squire Bradford is selling Big Henry, undoubtedly the best buck in

117

Chesterfield County. He is forty-two years old and still has a lot of good, productive years ahead of him. You all know about Big Henry, don't you? A lot of you have had to walk your girls over twenty miles to get to him and you had to pay a pretty penny for his services. Now, today, you have a chance to take Big Henry home with you and let somebody start paying you. So what am I bid for this champion buck?"

"What did I tell you?" Billy said excitedly as he punched Andy on the shoulder. "I told you he was a buck, didn't I? I bet he'll bring more than five hundred."

Billy was right again. The crowd reacted noisily as the bidding passed five hundred, then six hundred, then seven hundred, and cheered when the purchase was made for the whopping sum of seven hundred and seventy five dollars.

It was getting close to noon when the young woman and small boy that Andy had noticed were brought up onto the platform.

"What we have here," the auctioneer said, "is a girl and her young'un. Like I did with the maid and butler, I'm gonna auction them off as a pair and then as individuals and I'll sell them whichever way pays the most."

"This girl is twenty-two years old and in good health. She has been trained for housework, maid service, and looking after children. Come on up and examine her if you're interested in buying her. The little one is hers, he's seven years old and a tough little young'un, even if he ain't very big yet."

Andy, who had become more and more uneasy as the morning had gone along, upon seeing this pair being felt, poked, and prodded, was feeling a strong urge to get up and run away as fast as he could go when Billy punched him in the ribs.

"Look at that poor little pitiful kid up there," Billy said, derisively. "He looks like he's gonna cry. I bet you a nickel he cries before this is over. Wanna bet?"

"No, I don't wanna bet," Andy said emphatically.

The bidding on the mother and child stopped at one hundred twenty-five dollars and then the mother was offered as an individual.

"Now look at this girl again," the auctioneer said. "She's strong, she's been trained, and she's at the perfect age for breeding. She looks to me like if she was bred, she's equipped to nurse two little ones at a time so she could be a wet nurse. What do you think, Sid?" he asked of the man who was, at the moment, loosening her blouse and giving that part of her body a close examination.

"I'd say she could, and then some," the man responded as the crowd erupted in laughter.

Andy looked more closely at the woman. Then he looked at some of the other men who were coming closer to the platform. As he watched, he began to realize that this woman, although sad and downcast, was really quite beautiful. Evidently Billy was noticing the same thing because he giggled and commented, "One of those men is gonna buy her for breeding purposes but he ain't gonna send her out to Big Henry."

Interest in the young female slave was now running high and the bidding went to one hundred and ten dollars, where it finally stopped. Then the auctioneer pulled the little boy a short distance from his mother and offered him for sale. Andy saw a look of terror in the boy's eyes even though he was sure that the boy had not been taught enough arithmetic to be able to calculate that if someone bid more than fifteen dollars for him, he and his mother would be separated.

"I think this one here is big enough to be weaned, don't you?" the auctioneer said as the crowd laughed. "What am I bid for this little feller? You can buy him and make whatever you want out of him."

There was silence and Andy prayed that no one would bid on the little boy.

"Come on, now," the auctioneer pleaded, "someone out there could use this little feller around the house. He's plenty big to carry in the wood or go get the cows, and he's little enough to crawl up in your fireplace chimney and clean it out. He's at just the right age for cuttin' if you're looking to grow your own house slave. He could be a big help to somebody out there. Now what'll you give for him?"

"Aw, I'll take him off your hands for twenty dollars," a man back in the crowd yelled out and Andy's heart sank as he realized the implication of the bid. After a short pause with no further bids, the auctioneer pounded his gavel and said, "Sold!"

"Watch him now," Billy said, "I told you he was gonna cry."

Andy did watch as the young mother was led away, and

although her body shook, she did not make a sound. The little boy was left standing there all alone, his face first puckering and then wrinkling into a grimace of agony and large tears ran down his cheeks as he realized the finality of what had just occurred to him and his mother.

As he watched the little boy, Andy shared in his grief as his mind instantly transported him back to the day he was taken away from his mother to live on his grandparent's farm. He remembered the terrible, helpless feeling he had that day and also on the day he saw his mother's body placed in a grave and covered with dirt. Great salty tears of recognition and empathy were rolling down Andy's cheeks as he saw the little boy peer back over his shoulder for one last glimpse of his mother as she was led away.

Billy was gleeful as he said, "See, look at the little baby crying. Didn't I tell you? He looks just like a monkey with his face all screwed up like that, don't he?"

"Shut up, Billy Watson, I hate you!" Andy spat out angrily at his startled companion as he jumped to his feet and began running with all his might toward the boarding house. Billy took off in hot pursuit but there was no way he could overtake the faster and lighter Andy.

"Masta' Andy," Sadie said when he ran into the boarding house, "are you wantin' somethin' to eat? Your lunch is 'bout ready."

"I'm not hungry," he blurted out and ran straight up to the room he and his father occupied.

Throwing himself onto the bed, Andy gave full vent to his feelings. He pounded his fists on the bed and sobbed into his pillow as he relived the pain he had experienced when he was separated from his mother and he sobbed for the pain he had observed in a helpless, stoic mother and her helpless, fragile child.

As soon as Jeremiah came in from work that evening, Andy poured out his heart to him.

"Papa," he told Jeremiah, "I saw the worst thing today that I've ever seen in my life."

"What was that, Son," Jeremiah asked.

"Me and Billy went down to the slave auction," Andy said, "and it was the awfullest thing in the world, and the worst thing about it was that nobody but me thought it was bad. Billy and a lot of other people thought it was funny."

"What, exactly, went on?" Jeremiah asked, with a puzzled look on his face. "Surely you knew what was going to happen at a slave auction. They were going to sell slaves."

Andy then recounted the emotional trauma he had experienced as he came to identify with the young woman and her little boy who were so callously ripped apart by the auction.

"Papa," he said, "as I watched them, I remembered how I felt when I had to leave Mama and go to live on the farm and I know that they were feeling just like me and Mama felt that day. And it was even worse for them because I got to hug Mama and I could still go back and see her sometimes but they didn't get to even say good-bye and they probably won't ever see each other again. And it was all over five measly dollars."

"Well, Andy," Jeremiah said in the patient, philosophical tone that had always proven so effective when he was instructing his sometimes impetuous son, "remember what I've told you about what Alexander Campbell taught me in college; slavery is not a sin but sometimes the way it's practiced is sinful. It sounds like that's what you saw there today."

Jeremiah's calm, scholarly analysis only served to increase Andy's agitation and he could not hold back his fury any longer.

"Then Alexander Campbell is a big fat idiot!" Andy fairly screamed out. "Slavery is so a sin and I think it's the worst sin there is. Papa, they were looking up the women's dresses and down their blouses and hitting the men with whips if they didn't stand up straight enough to suit them. They even sold one slave named Big Henry that is a buck that a lot of the owners send their women to so they can have his babies."

"There was one more thing," Andy added. "The auctioneer said that the little boy was just right for cutting. What did he mean by that?"

"Well," Jeremiah explained, hoping that his patient tone would calm his agitated son, "you know how, on the farm, your grandpa castrates the pigs and calves when they are small? Well, sometimes people castrate a few of their young slaves, especially if they want to train them to be gentle, obedient house slaves."

Rather than being calmed, Andy was even more upset upon the hearing of this gruesome detail.

"Why in the world would they do a thing like that?" Andy blurted out, almost hysterically.

"The castration of slaves has always gone on," Jeremiah continued, quietly. "Don't you remember hearing your grandpa preach about the Ethiopian eunuch? Do you know what a eunuch is? A eunuch is a castrated man. The Ethiopian eunuch was a slave who had been castrated when he was young so he could serve in the palace. Why, Andy, over in Europe a boy doesn't even have to be a slave to be castrated. If he has a good soprano voice, his parents and the priest might agree to have him castrated so his voice won't change."

"Why do they have to castrate the slaves?" Andy angrily asked. "What difference does that make? That man didn't buy him for his choir."

"Do you remember that big old bull that your grandpa had when you lived with him?" Jeremiah said. "And do you remember the big steer he fattened up and butchered?"

"Yes, I remember," Andy answered.

"Then you tell me the difference between them and maybe in that way you'll answer your own question," Jeremiah said.

"The thing I remember about the bull was that he was mean and we couldn't go near him," Andy said, "but I could pet the steer when I fed him."

"Anything else?" Jeremiah probed. "What was the purpose of the bull?"

"Aw, you know," Andy said, embarrassedly. "He was there to breed the cows."

"All right, then," Jeremiah said, "let's suppose that you are a king or a slave owner and you want a man slave to work in your house. Which would you want; a man like a mean bull or a man like a gentle steer? Take into account that your slave would be working around your wife and daughters."

"It's not right, and I don't care if it's in the Bible," Andy said emphatically. "and besides, that, people aren't animals and they shouldn't be treated that way."

"Andy, you learned a lot out there today," Jeremiah said. "I agree with you that it may not be right, but that's the way it is. I figure that the slaves didn't take it near as hard as you did. They're a lot different than we are and besides that, they're used to it and know what to expect. It hit you hard today because it was all new to you."

Andy really, really wanted to scream at his father that if he believed that then he was a bigger, fatter idiot than Alexander Campbell but thought better of it. What he did finally say was, "Papa, I know what I saw and I don't think they're all that different from us. You're always quoting what Shakespeare said about Jews feeling like we do and bleeding like we do. Don't you think it's the same with Negroes, too?'

"No," Jeremiah answered after a long pause, "I don't think it is. You see, the Jew is our intellectual equal but both Alexander Campbell and Thomas Jefferson wrote that the black race is inferior in many ways and I don't think that their feelings and emotions are on the same level as ours."

Well, Andy thought, now I can make Thomas Jefferson the third name on my list of big fat idiots.

"I know what I saw," Andy said defiantly.

"That's all right, Son," Jeremiah said. "I'm always glad when you have strong opinions about things. Now, go wash up so we can go down to supper."

18 *REBELLION IN RICHMOND*

The Virginia General Assembly, in special session by order of Governor John Letcher in January, 1861, called for an election of delegates to a convention to consider the relationship of Virginia to the Government of the United States. Although Jeremiah and his boss John Carlile had opposed such a convention, they were pleased with the results of the election because the Unionists held a strong majority.

"I've got the information you wanted on all one hundred and fifty-two of the delegates," Jeremiah told Carlile, "and it looks like this: eighty-five supported John Bell and the Constitution Party in the presidential election, thirty-five supported Stephen Douglas and the Jacksonian Democrats, only thirty-two supported Vice-President Breckenridge and the Calhoun Democrats, and none supported Lincoln and the Republicans."

"With that big a majority, we won't have any trouble getting one of our own people elected president of the convention," Carlile said, confidently.

Jeremiah felt somewhat optimistic when the convention met in April. The Unionist majority proceeded to elect John Janney, a staunch Unionist from Louden County, John Carlile's choice, as the convention president. There is no way that the radicals can take over our beloved state now, Jeremiah thought, with Janney as the convention president and since our Governor John Letcher is a strong Jacksonian and a Union supporter.

John Carlile and the other loyal delegates to the convention immediately presented their arguments opposing the concept of state sovereignty. They asserted that a state has no constitutional grounds for secession, and they stated that the states that were claiming to have seceded had not left the Union at all but were, instead, in rebellion.

Jeremiah was proud of his boss John Carlile who, along with Waitman Willey and others, eloquently defended the United States Constitution and argued forcefully for the constitutional principle of the supremacy of the federal government.

Then something happened that made Jeremiah's blood run cold; the debate began to center on whether or not the federal government had the right to use coercive force on the states that were in rebellion. He was alarmed by this turn of events because he remembered clearly what Assemblyman Arthur Boreman had reported at the August 16 strategy meeting called by Waitman Willey. At that time Boreman had said that the Unionists held a strong majority in the state legislature but that there was one important caveat; more than half of the Unionists did not believe that the federal government had the right to use coercive force to keep a state in the Union.

Jeremiah got a sick feeling in his stomach as he realized that, even with the strong Unionist majority in the convention, the battle could be lost over this one issue.

"You're absolutely right, Jeremiah," Carlile said when Jeremiah shared his fear with him. "Unless we can get them off of this technicality and back on the main subject, we are in deep trouble."

Most of the delegates were in agreement with Governor Letcher's oft-stated position that if Virginia could serve as a buffer zone between two hostile forces and deny any movement of forces from either side, Virginia could prevent a civil war and preserve the Union.

The radical delegates, or Secessionists as they called themselves, saw their opportunity and quickly coalesced into a unified force and put into action a determined plan to gain control of the convention.

"Have you ever seen so many strange people wandering the streets of Richmond?" Waitman Willey remarked to John Carlile and Jeremiah as they were walking to Mrs. Etta's boarding house after a long, grueling session. "Who do you think they are and what are they up to?"

"I hear that most of them are from South Carolina and the rest are from the other states that are in rebellion," Carlile answered. "They are up to no good. They're buttonholing any of the wavering delegates and filling them up with all sorts of nonsense."

"Like what?" Jeremiah asked.

"Like Virginia is so important, if she would only vote to secede, the federal government would fold up its tent and let the rebel states go their own way in peace," Carlile answered. "And if Virginia secedes, they say, a new nation would be formed, not as a Union, but as a confederacy of states, and they promise that Virginia will be the 'crown jewel' of that confederacy and Richmond would be its capital."

The men were noticing that the sky was lit up toward the west of the city when a policeman approached them.

"You men ought not be out here walking at this time of night," the policeman said. "Some of these people who are in here are just trying to cause trouble and they've been attacking some people who don't agree with them. I think most of them are over there at their big bonfire, yonder, but you still need to be careful."

"Andy," Jeremiah said to his son the next morning, "I want you to stay close to the boarding house today and don't talk to any strangers. There are some people that have come to Richmond who might be dangerous, especially if they know who you are and who I work for."

"Okay, Papa," Andy replied. "Aren't they liable to try to harm you?"

"I'll be careful," Jeremiah said. "I won't be taking any chances."

As Jeremiah, Carlile, and Willey walked to the convention hall, Carlile asked, "If they can bring the convention to a vote on federal coercion, where do we stand, Jeremiah?"

"The best that I can figure it is you have about fifty uncompromising Unionists, like you and Waitman, who will oppose secession, no matter what," Jeremiah answered. "There are no more than thirty hard core Secessionists, so that leaves over seventy who started out with us against secession but are opposed to the use of force by the federal government."

"Then our course is clear, John," Willey said. "We must prevent that issue from coming to a vote and pray that there is no show of coercive force before we complete this convention."

Willey's prayer, however was not answered. The Secessionists, fully as analytical as Jeremiah, had also counted the numbers and knew that all they had to do was to precipitate an incident involving the federal government and they could get an ordinance of secession. Their strategy, then, was simple. They immediately sent their emissary, Roger Pryor, to South Carolina with the message, "The moment that blood is shed, Old Virginia will make common cause with her sisters of the South."

As soon as they received the message from Pryor, the rebelling South Carolinians fired on the federal installation at Fort Sumter, and President Abraham Lincoln, as they anticipated, had ordered the federal troops at the fort to defend themselves in response to any hostile fire. Five days later, on April 17, 1861, the convention in Richmond voted eighty-eight to fifty-five in favor of an ordinance of secession.

19 . . . *THE BIG FAVOR*

"Gentlemen, we are in a hole but they haven't shoveled the dirt in on us yet," Carlile said defiantly as he sat down at the table in Mrs. Etta's dining room that evening with Willey, Jeremiah, and Andy. "What we've got to do is clear. We've got to cover the state between now and the ratification vote on May twenty-third, and make sure the people get out and vote this thing down."

The news they received over the next few days, however, completely dashed any hopes of stopping the avalanche of events. Governor Letcher, whom they had considered to be their ally moved immediately, without waiting for the required ratification by the people of Virginia, to implement secession.

Jeremiah discovered that even before the final debate of the convention Governor Letcher had ordered Virginia troops to take control of the United States Arsenal at Harpers Ferry and the United States Navy Yard at Norfolk.

"What are we going to do now, John?" Jeremiah asked Carlile upon receiving this devastating news.

"We're going to continue to fight," Carlile said. "What is taking place here is illegal. It's unconstitutional! What that bunch got Letcher to do is to commit treason. We don't have a government here now, our state has been turned over to a bunch of rebels. We have to do what we can to salvage the honor of Virginia and preserve the Union."

"How do we go about doing that?" Jeremiah asked.

"We go back home and put our best minds to work on it," Carlile responded. "We've got a lot of good people who will stand with us, once they understand what's going on. It looks like we might need to hook up with people like Archibald Campbell and Francis Pierpont and the rest of the Republicans up there, the people who supported Lincoln in the election."

"I think it's best for Waitman and me to get out of Richmond as soon as possible," Carlile continued, "so we're going to take the train to where it ends at White Sulphur Springs and go on from there the best way we can. You and Andy should get out of here in the next few days. If you've got room on your wagon, I'd like for you to bring a small trunk of mine with some of my books and papers."

"Is there anything else I can do?" Jeremiah asked.

"Yes," Carlile said, "on your way back to Clarksburg, talk to people and try to find out how they are feeling about what is taking place. If you can, I'd like for you to stop and see my friend, Sam Richmond, down on New River since I'm not going to have the time to see him myself. He's easy to find because he has a ferry and a mill there at Richmond Falls. The best way to get there is to cross the river on the ferry at Hinton and travel down the west side of the river. Sam is a strong Union man and we need to know how much support we can depend on from that part of the state."

The next few days were hectic as Jeremiah and Andy worked hard to get everything together so they could head back toward Clarksburg. One thing that Jeremiah was sure that he must do was to go through Lexington and see what impact the events of the past few days were having on T. J. Jackson. Jeremiah knew that his old friend wanted to see the Union preserved and he hoped that a face-to-face meeting might help Jackson decide how best to accomplish that end. Jeremiah was haunted, though, by his recollection that Jackson had said that, as a soldier, his loyalty was to his commanding officer and that officer was Governor Letcher.

Jeremiah was stunned by the lead item in the Richmond newspaper on the morning of April 21. "Governor Orders VMI Cadets to Richmond," the headline read, followed by the sub-headline which caused Jeremiah's heart to sink, "Under the Command of Col. Thomas Jackson."

Jeremiah spirits sank even deeper as he realized that the die was cast; T. J. Jackson was going to serve in the Governor's Army of Virginia instead of the United States Army and he now hoped more strongly than ever that the Army of Virginia would somehow be successful in preventing an all out war between the Union and the seceding states.

As Jeremiah put the last items on the wagon late in the evening of April 21, in preparation of leaving early the next morning, he was deep in one of his dark moods, certain that things could not get any worse, but he was wrong.

"Mista' Blake," Sadie, the kitchen slave asked in a whisper as he was finishing supper, "could I please have a word with you, Suh?"

"Of course, Sadie," Jeremiah said. "Andy, you go on up to the room and I'll be there in a minute."

Jeremiah was perplexed as he watched Sadie checking all around and when she was certain that no one was watching, she led him quickly into the kitchen.

"Mista' Blake," she said in a very agitated voice, "I gotta know if it's okay if I tell you a mighty big secret. Before I tell you, I gotta have your word that you won't tell nobody. If you can't promise me that, then I ain't about to tell you."

"Sadie, I give you my word," Jeremiah assured her. "If there is something this important on your mind, you can trust me with the information."

"The information is just part of it," Sadie said. "What I really need from you is a big favor."

"What is it, Sadie?" Jeremiah asked. "You know that we are leaving in the morning but if there is anything I can do for you now, I'll do my best."

"Mista' Blake, I know you a fine Christian man," Sadie said as she began to cry, "and that's why I thought you might be willin' to help me."

After she wiped her eyes with her apron, she continued: "I got me a boy named Samuel that's about eighteen years old and he done run away from his masta' and they a-huntin' for him. If they catch him, I'm awful afraid of what'll happen to him. I'm afraid they might even kill him."

"How can I help?" Jeremiah asked. "Do you know where he is?"

"Yessa'," Sadie said in a whisper, "Jesse's hidin' him out in the loft of the livery stable."

Jeremiah experienced a sudden shiver as he realized the danger that was so near. What could he possibly do to deal with this problem?

"Mista' Blake," Sadie said in desperate tones, "my big favor is, would you hide my boy in your wagon tomorrow mornin' and take him out of Richmond to where he could get away? They gonna be lookin' for him soon and they will surely be comin' here just any time, now."

"Oh, my dear, Sadie," Jeremiah responded, "as much as I would like to help you, I could never do that. Helping a slave escape is a major crime and if I was caught I would end up in prison and who would take care of Andy? Besides that, having a fugitive slave with us would put us in danger, too. I'm terribly sorry, Sadie, but I have never broken the law and I can't run the risk of something happening to Andy."

"That's okay, Mista' Blake, that's okay, I understand," the despondent slave assured him. "I sure appreciate you takin' the time to listen to me, I surely do. Now you and Masta' Andy get you a good night's sleep so you can get an early start in the mornin'."

"What did Sadie want to talk to you about, Papa?" Andy asked as soon as Jeremiah entered their room.

"You're not going to believe it," he responded. "She has an eighteen-year-old son who has run away from his owner and he's hiding out there in the livery stable right now. And listen to this, she wanted us to take him with us tomorrow when we leave."

"Well, we will, won't we?" Andy asked excitedly.

"We most certainly will not," Jeremiah responded sternly. "I don't plan to go to jail or put us in danger. We have way too many important things to attend to. We can't be distracted by helping a fugitive slave escape."

"But, Papa," Andy pleaded, "it's Sadie. She is one of the nicest, kindest people I ever saw. What will happen to her boy if we don't help him?"

"He'll be caught and returned to his owners," Jeremiah said.

"What will they do with him then?" Andy persisted.

"Hard to tell," Jeremiah said. "It all depends on what kind of a person the owner is. Let's hope he's a good man."

"That's not too likely, is it?" Andy reasoned. "If he was a good man, Sadie's boy probably wouldn't have run off in the first place."

The discussion between father and son went on late into the night. The longer they talked, the more personal the issue became to Andy and the more emotional he became. His reasoned arguments gradually gave way to tearful pleas. He pictured Sadie and her little boy on the auction block instead of the young mother and son he had witnessed being sold and separated. He again remembered the agony of separation he had experienced when he was taken away from his mother.

"Papa, you say that we have things to do that are way more important than helping Sadie's boy," Andy argued emotionally, "but I remember hearing Grandpa preaching a lot of times about the priest and the Levite who wouldn't help the man that was left in the ditch because they thought they had more important things to do. You know what happened then; the Good Samaritan came along and helped him. Papa, we can't be like that old priest or Levite, we've got to be like the Good Samaritan."

Andy's impassioned pleas finally reached Jeremiah. Although he fully recognized that to help a slave escape was the height of folly and that it went against every rational fiber in his being, Jeremiah finally relented and agreed with Andy to attempt to take Samuel one day's journey, and no more, out of the city.

It was after midnight when Jeremiah tapped softly on the door of the slave quarters in the basement of the boarding house. He was surprised when the door was opened immediately by Sadie.

"Sadie, I've change my mind," Jeremiah whispered. "I'll try to get your boy out of town."

"I was waitin' for you," Sadie whispered. "I knowed you was comin'."

"How did you know that?" Jeremiah asked. "I didn't know it myself until a few minutes ago."

"Oh, Mista' Blake," she said triumphantly, "I ain't stopped prayin' ever since we talked so I knowed you was comin'. I'll get word out to Jesse and he'll have Samuel all ready to go."

Sadie was waiting for Jeremiah and Andy the next morning when they came down the stairs.

"I packed you something to eat along the way," Sadie said, as she handed Andy a large bag. "Ain't nothin' gonna' happen to ya'll now, cause I prayed all night and the Lord is gonna' watch over you. If He's brought us this far, He ain't gonna' let us down now."

Sadie suddenly threw her arms around Andy and held him tight. "Masta' Andrew Jackson Blake," she said, "we sure enough gonna miss you 'round here. You oughta be awful proud of this boy, Mista' Blake. He sure is a good-un."

"Our children are special to us, aren't they Sadie?" Jeremiah said. "I'm forever finding out just how special they are. It was Andy that God used last night to answer your prayers."

"Well, I don't care how He done it," Sadie said. "The important thing was that He heard me and got the message to you."

20 *THE FLIGHT TO SAFETY*

The eastern sky was beginning to show signs of the approaching dawn when Jeremiah and Andy arrived at the livery stable carrying the last of their possessions to put on the wagon and then to depart. They were surprised as they peered through the darkness and saw that their horses were harnessed and hitched to the wagon. The load on the wagon had been shifted somewhat and then covered with the tent canopy.

"Looks like rain, Mista' Blake," Jesse said, despite the fact that the stars were shining brightly in a cloudless sky, "so I moved things around a bit and covered up ever'thing so nothin' gets wet if it does rain."

"I'm much obliged, Jesse," Jeremiah said. "Are you sure that everything is loaded?"

"Oh, yessa', I'm sure," Jesse replied. "I done loaded everything just like Sadie told me to. God bless you, Mista' Blake. You a good man."

"Thank you for that, Jesse, and thank you for all you have done for me and for Andy," Jeremiah said. "We will always be grateful for your service."

"Bye, Masta Andy," Jesse said. "I'll be missin' you helpin' with the horses and all now that you'll be gone."

"Good bye, Jesse," Andy responded, "It was fun working in the stable with you."

At about 7:30, after they had been traveling two hours and had finally passed through the last of the outskirts of Richmond, Jeremiah stopped to give the horses a brief rest.

"Samuel, are you riding okay?" Jeremiah called back at the covered load on the wagon that had been so quiet that he was not certain that anyone was back there.

"Yessa, I'm a-riding jus' fine," came the response from under the canopy.

"I don't see anybody around so you could come out and stretch your legs, if you need to," Jeremiah said.

The canopy rustled and out came, not the immature teenager that Jeremiah expected to see but instead, a large, muscular, fully developed man.

"Well now, Samuel, you are a pretty big man," the surprised Jeremiah said. "How did you fit under that canopy?"

"I jus' made myself little, I reckon," Samuel replied as he smiled slightly.

When Jeremiah started the horses again, Samuel was able to be much more comfortable by sitting on John Carlile's trunk behind the seat where Jeremiah and Andy were sitting. Whenever anyone was spotted along the road they were traveling, he would quickly "make himself little again" and hide under the canopy.

When noon arrived, Jeremiah selected a secluded spot at the edge of the woods for an extended rest. The horses were unhitched and then were permitted to graze on the lush spring grass growing between the woods and the road. Andy got the bag of food that Sadie had given him and he and his father, along with Samuel, settled in to eat and let the horses rest for an hour.

Jeremiah and Andy sat facing the road so they could watch the horses and also see any passersby. Samuel sat facing them, with his back to a large tree trunk so he was not visible from the road.

"Samuel, your mama sure is a good cook, isn't she?" Andy said as he was wolfing down some of Sadie's cold chicken and potato salad.

"I reckon she is," Samuel replied as he was putting away his second ham biscuit. "I never got to try much of her cookin'. From the day I was born, she was always cookin' for white folks and I was always with the other slaves so I had to eat same as they got. Once in awhile she would slip somethin' special out for me to taste. Then Mista' Hatcher sold me off when I was nine and I never seen her again 'til day before yes'day."

"She must have been excited to see you, after all that time," Andy said. "What did she say to you? Did she recognize you right off?"

"She told me I was crazy and fixin' to get myself killed," Samuel said. "She didn't have to recognize me; Jesse done told her I was hidin' out in the stable. I come to him first, night before last, and he went and got Mama."

Suddenly, the sound of hoof beats alerted the trio that someone was coming. An armed man on a large black horse came into view and then stopped and greeted them.

"Howdy, there," the man said. "Looks like ya'll found a good spot to stop off. Would you mind if I got down and set a spell with you?"

"We'd like that," Jeremiah said, his mind reeling, "but we've been here too long as it is and we got a long way to go before dark. Andy, you best be hitching up the horses so we can get on our way."

Andy jumped up and went in pursuit of the horses while Samuel sat motionless, barely breathing. Jeremiah quickly walked past the tree where Samuel was sitting and on toward the road where he could engage the stranger in conversation.

"You ain't seen no big black boy out here anywhere, have you?" the man asked. "I been chasing a runaway named Sambo all the way from North Carolina but I've lost track of him now. I found his mammy in Richmond this morning but she don't know nothing about where he is. I beat the living hell out of her and she still couldn't tell me nothing. If you happen to spot him, there's a big reward out. Be careful if you try to catch him, though, he is awful strong for a black boy. If I was you and I saw him, I'd try to shoot him in the knee and then you could manage him. If you was to turn him in to any sheriff's office you could claim the reward and they'd notify me so I could take him back."

"Thank you," Jeremiah said as he helped Andy finish hitching the horses to the wagon, "I'll be on the lookout for him," and then hated himself as he inadvertently blurted out, "good luck."

As soon as the man departed westward on Jeremiah's chosen route, Jeremiah pulled out his handkerchief and wiped the cold sweat from his face. Only after he carefully checked the horizon in all directions did he call to Samuel to come and get on the wagon. Samuel spent the rest of the day under the canopy.

That evening Jeremiah was careful in selecting a spot where

they could spend the night totally hidden from the road. He found a place where the brushy growth was heavy enough for him to hide the wagon and pitch the tent away from prying eyes.

This was not the scenario that Jeremiah had envisioned when he planned this trip. He had figured that he and Andy would make their way each day to a town with an adequate inn or boarding house and that they would be sleeping on feather tick beds and eating good, hot restaurant food. Now, because of Samuel, they were reduced to sleeping outside on this frosty spring night and surviving on the bag of cold food that Sadie had prepared.

"That was a close call we had today, Samuel," Jeremiah said, intending to direct the conversation toward determining the soonest time that they could part company with him.

"Yessa, it was," Samuel answered. "I thought, sure as anything, he was gonna come around that tree and see me settin' there."

"How do you know it was you he was looking for?" Andy asked, "He said he was looking for somebody named Sambo."

"It's me, all right," Samuel said. "My mama named me Samuel 'cause she didn't think she was ever going to have a baby, like that woman, Hannah, in the Bible. So she said she prayed and when she had me she named me Samuel like that woman did. Then when Mista' Hatcher sold me off, Masta' Davis, the man that bought me, asked me what my name was and I told him it was Samuel but I was called Sam most times. He said that Samuel wasn't no fittin' name for no little black boy and Sam was a white man's name so he was gonna call me Sambo. You and Mista' Blake's the first white folks to ever to call me Samuel but I'd be proud if you'd just call me Sam."

"Well, Sam, what made you decide to run away from your owner?" Jeremiah asked, fascinated by the story Samuel had just told them. "Was he mean to you?"

"Nossa," Sam answered, "he was better to me than he was to any of his other slaves. He always give me the best food and the easiest jobs to do. I run away because I was 'shamed of what he was wantin' me do."

"What did he want you to do?" Andy asked.

"Well, Masta' Andy," Sam said, searching for the right words, "you know how white folks get married and have their little babies?

137

Well, it ain't that way for a lot of black folks. Sometimes the masta' wants his slave women to have big, strong babies that'll be worth lots of money when they's old enough to sell. Instead of lettin' them have their own men, he sends them off to a big buck slave to give 'em a baby."

"Did your owner want you to be a buck? Is that what he wanted you to do?" Andy asked. "Why didn't you? My friend, Billy Watson said that if he was a slave, that's what he'd want to be."

"You never told me that," Jeremiah said, with eyebrows raised. "When did Billy say that to you?"

"At the slave auction, when they were selling Big Henry," Andy explained.

"You've seen Big Henry, then?" Sam said. "I reckon Big Henry's my papa, least that's what Masta' Davis told me and he said he paid top dollar for me 'cause he intended to make as much money off of me as other people was makin' off of Big Henry."

"I thought that Jubal was your papa," Andy said. "Isn't he Sadie's husband?"

"Jubal's sorta like Mama's husband; they look after one another," Sam explained, "but he couldn't be my papa cause he was cut when he was a young-un. No, I reckon Mista' Hatcher just kept marching Mama off to Big Henry 'til I come along."

"You still didn't tell us why you ran away," Jeremiah said.

"Mama says that you a good Christian man, Mista' Blake, so you gonna know what I'm fixin' to tell you," Sam said. "Even when I was little, Mama would pray with me and talk to me 'bout the Lord Jesus. I was glad to find out when I got to the plantation in North Carolina that Masta' Davis was a big man in his church and he let an old slave named Rafe have us a service every Sunday while him and his missus was at church. Rafe couldn't read but he'd learned a lot about the Bible somehow. After I got there, Rafe'd have me read from his Bible and then he'd preach."

"How did you learn how to read?" Andy asked. "You never went to school, did you?"

"No, I sure didn't go to no school," Sam replied, "but Ms. Etta Hatcher thought that Mama and Jubal would be more help to her if they could read so she taught them some and they taught me."

"My grandfather couldn't read, either," Jeremiah said, "and he

138

was a preacher, and a pretty good one, too."

"Well, Rafe was sure a good'un," Sam continued. "He's the reason that I come to the Lord when I was young, maybe ten or twelve. When I was growin' up I wondered a lot about how the Lord could be pleased with things that was going on; things that didn't seem right to me."

"What kind of things?" Andy asked.

Sam answered with his voice filled with emotion, "Oh, there was lots of things, Masta' Andy. It didn't seem right to me what the white men would do to the slave girls, and it didn't seem right to cut little slave boys, and it didn't seem right to breed slave women like animals instead of letting them have men of their own."

"So that's why you left?" Jeremiah asked.

"Yessa', that's why," Sam answered. "They brought this little girl, no more than fourteen, and put her in my cabin and my cabin didn't have no door on it and they just stood there, lookin' in, a-grinnin'. She no more than got into the cabin 'til she started crying and they started laughin' and yellin' at me to go at it. She knew what she was there for and she started gettin' ready, but I decided right then and there that I was not gonna do this. They 'spect us to work their fields, tote their water, fetch their food, and mind their children, and we do all of that. But it ain't right, what they was trying to make me do. There ain't no way I could do that and still serve the Lord."

"What happened then?" a wide-eyed Andy asked.

"They went and got Masta' Davis and he told 'em to tie me to a post and he beat me with a whip 'til I promised I'd do what he told me to," Sam said. "I'm 'shamed now that I let him make me say I'd do it after I hear that man say today that Mama didn't tell him nothin' 'bout me even after he beat her."

"How did you get away?" Andy asked.

"Masta' Davis said that with a whuppin' like that, I wouldn't be no good 'til mornin' so he told them to leave the girl there with me in my cabin and said he'd be back at sunup and I'd better be ready to do my job then," Sam said. "So I knew that I had to do somethin' before mornin', so in the middle of the night I took off a'runnin'."

"How did you know which way to go?" Jeremiah asked.

"You prob'ly know this already, Mr. Blake; all slaves set

139

around on warm nights lookin' up at the stars," Sam said, "and we always look for the Big Dipper and see it pointin' at the North Star. We all know that if we was to ever run away we had to follow the North Star to get to Canada, so that's what I did. Soon as it started to get daylight I'd hide in the woods and do all my travelin' at night. The road I was travelin' on ended up in Richmond and that's how I got there."

"What did you eat?" Andy asked.

"I didn't eat much," Sam responded. "If I was at a creek, I'd catch crawdads and peel their tails and eat 'em, and I figured out that if poke weeds and dandelion leaves and lamb's quarters was good cooked, they'd be okay if they was raw, so I ate some of them. One night I was so hungry I snuck up to a slave's cabin and a woman gave me some cornpone and fatback."

"Did you eat the crawdads and weeds raw?" Andy asked.

"Had to," Sam answered. "I didn't have nothin' to cook in and no way to start a fire and even if I did, I'd a been scared to, cause they could've found me that way."

By this time Jeremiah had decided that it was a little too soon to cut Sam loose so he would alter his route tomorrow. He would use the less traveled roads hoping that the visitor from yesterday had not been there putting people on the alert looking for Sam.

When they came into Buckingham, Jeremiah left Andy in the wagon with the well-hidden Sam while he went into the general store to get some badly needed supplies. He knew that as long as Sam was with them they would need some basic food items so he bought six eggs and replenished the staples in his food chest with enough cornmeal, lard, salt, and cured pork to last them for a few days, until Sam could be let go on his own.

He also bought some items for their meals today, including some sardines. Jeremiah smiled to himself as he thought of the fun he would have introducing Andy and Sam to sardines, remembering his initial encounter with them on his first trip to Bethany.

As he came out of the store, Jeremiah's attention was caught by a group of five young men talking excitedly.

"Think what we could do with five hundred dollars," one of them said, "and all that for just finding just one black boy. He must be somethin' special if he fetches that kind of reward."

140

"I don't know," one of the group said, "it could be risky. That man said he was awful strong and you know he's bound to be running scared. He might be dangerous."

"Aw, you know there ain't never been a black man that can whip any one of us," the first man said. "No matter how big and strong they look, after you hit 'em once real hard they put their arms up in front of their face and start begging you not to hit 'em no more. There ain't no way he's gonna hurt five of us."

"Well, if we're gonna find him, we better get going," another man, who Jeremiah deemed to still be in his teens, said. "The man that was chasing him said he figured he was hiding in the woods somewhere between here and Sprouses Corner, so if we're gonna do it, let's go. Let's go get that five hundred dollar slave."

As Jeremiah headed the wagon west, he was relieved that the slave-hunting posse was heading east to look for Sam. He could not be sure, though, that there was not another posse or two looking for Sam in other directions so he cautioned Sam to stay out of sight until they were safely camped for the night.

When they arrived in Lexington, curious about what was going on with his friend, Jeremiah decided to make a quick call on Mary Anna Jackson, T. J.'s wife.

"Mrs. Jackson, I was just passing through from Richmond on my way to Clarksburg and I wanted to check and see how you were doing," Jeremiah said when Mary Anna greeted him at the door. "I read in the paper that T. J. was called to Richmond."

"Please come in and sit down, Mister Blake," she said. "So many things are happening that you will be interested in."

"You mean more than taking the cadets to Richmond?" Jeremiah asked.

"Oh, yes," Mary Anna said proudly, "now Governor Letcher has assigned Thomas to go to Harpers Ferry and take charge of the arsenal there."

"Will he do it?" a surprised Jeremiah asked. "The arsenal is a Federal installation. If he takes over a Federal facility, he'll be charged with treason, won't he?"

"No, certainly not," she replied, indignantly. "The arsenal is located in Virginia and since Virginia is no longer a part of the United States, then the arsenal is ours just like Fort Sumter now belongs to South Carolina."

"But Virginia cannot secede until the people of Virginia vote on it on the twenty-third of May," an exasperated Jeremiah blurted out. "And even if the people vote to secede it is not going to hold up, for secession is not permitted under the United States Constitution."

Mary Anna's silence at his outburst resulted in Jeremiah calming down and returning to the more personal aspects of the situation.

"How does T. J. feel about all of this?" Jeremiah asked, gently.

"He was very troubled at first," Mary Anna responded. "He gave a lot of consideration to what you had said to him when you were here before and he received a number of letters from his sister, Laura Ann, begging him to give his loyalty to the Union instead of Virginia. But once the decision to secede was made and he got his orders from Governor Letcher, he was the good soldier and embraced the challenge. We are very proud of him."

After leaving Mary Anna at Lexington, it took two hard days to get over the rugged mountain terrain between Lexington and Clifton Forge. The winding roads were steep, necessitating the frequent resting of the horses. A sudden spring downpour made the going slower than usual as the wagon wheels sunk deep into the slippery clay road surface.

As they crossed the mountains Jeremiah pondered, over and over, the conversation he had with Mary Anna Jackson. He was heartsick that his friend had cast his lot with the rebel element for he had no doubt that he would shortly achieve his goal of becoming General T. J. Jackson and that he would be a powerful military leader for the rebels. But the other possibility, that of his friend being convicted of treason and hanged on the same gallows at Harpers Ferry where Jackson, himself, had watched John Brown be hanged was too terrible to contemplate.

The one good thing about going through the mountains was that there were few people and Jeremiah figured that it was highly unlikely that Sam was being pursued this far away from Richmond. Each day he became less concerned about being caught with a runaway slave and let Sam become more of a participant, rather than a stowaway. On mile after mile of isolated terrain Sam rode out in the open and even started taking his turns driving the wagon.

The rains stopped and the roadways hardened, making travel much easier. The trio made good time, passing through Covington and into White Sulphur Springs.

"Andy, I know you've never tasted sulfur water," Jeremiah said as they neared the springs. "Sam, have you ever drunk any of it?"

"Nossa, I ain't," Sam answered. "I don't even know what that is."

"Sulfur water is something that this part of Virginia has lots of," Jeremiah explained. "People come to the springs to drink it and bathe in it and it cures some kinds of sickness. It's funny, all of the water is about the same in all of the springs around here but the names of some of the springs would make you think that it would look or taste different. Here we are at White Sulphur Springs and I know that there's a Blue Sulphur Springs, a Red Sulphur Springs, and a Green Sulphur Springs. There is a Salt Sulphur Springs, a Sweet Springs, and a Pence Springs. They just now got the railroad open to here, but when the railroad gets to all of the springs, I figure that people will flock to them by the thousands."

"Does the water really help people," Andy asked. "Why didn't you bring Mama here when she got sick?"

"I thought about it," Jeremiah said. "I talked to her doctors and they said that the waters had never proven to be of any help with what your mother had. The water seems to help people with rheumatism and digestive problems but doesn't do any good for consumption."

Jeremiah told Sam to stop the wagon at the pavilion beside the spring and he got off and bought three gallons of the precious, medicinal water.

"Here, Andy, is one jug for you, and one for you, Sam, and one for me," Jeremiah said as he handed the jugs up to them in the wagon. "We'll each one drink a gallon over the next couple of days and that will be our spring tonic for this year."

"Can I go ahead and open mine now?" the curious Andy asked as soon as they started to move. "I'm kinda thirsty."

Jeremiah smiled to himself in anticipation of the shock that was awaiting his anxious son.

"Sure, Andy," Jeremiah said, "the sooner you start drinking it, the sooner it will start doing you some good."

His father's approval was all Andy needed and he quickly pulled out the cork and was immediately overwhelmed by an odor every bit as offensive as the smell of the open sewers in Washington in mid-summer.

"Ooh, Papa," Andy said as he cringed from the open jug. "They sold you some water that was bad. Something in this jug is rotten."

"No, Andy," Jeremiah said, fighting to hold back his laughter, "That's what it's supposed to smell like, that's the sulfur. That's what makes it good for you. Go on, try a big drink of it. Hold your nose if you have to."

"I'm not drinking any of this stuff," Andy said adamantly.

"Hand it up here to me," Jeremiah said. "I'll try it first and see if there is anything wrong with it."

Andy handed the opened jug to Jeremiah who was in the driver's seat beside Sam. Jeremiah turned the jug up to his lips and drank down three or four large gulps.

"Man, that is good sulfur water," Jeremiah said as he wiped his lips with the back of his hand. "What's wrong with you, Boy? People come all the way from Philadelphia and New York City to get some of this wonderful stuff and here you are, born and raised in Virginia, turning your nose up at it. Here, try it again."

Andy was reluctant to give it another try but, he thought, all those people from Philadelphia and New York City couldn't be wrong so maybe it was him.

"It don't taste as bad as it smells," he said after bravely taking one small sip from the jug.

"That's why I told you to hold your nose," Jeremiah said. "If you can't smell the sulfur, it tastes like any other water."

Andy was the last of the three to finish drinking his jug of the medicinal water but he finally accomplished it.

"Now," Jeremiah proclaimed, "we are all assured of good health for the whole year."

21 GOING UP NORTH BUT DOWN THE RIVER

The trip through the city of Lewisburg and then down into the Greenbrier River valley at Alderson went without incident. Jeremiah wanted to set up camp somewhere at the base of Keeney's Mountain in preparation for the daunting task of crossing the mountain to get over into the New River Valley.

He found what he was looking for when he spotted a small school building beside the road in the community of Santifee, just west of Alderson.

"Hello, there," Jeremiah called to a man working in a field beside the school. "Do you think it would be all right if we spent the night here in the schoolyard?"

"That'd be fine with me," the man answered, "and I reckon if it's all right with me it should suit everybody else. My name's Flint and this here's the Flint school, so you just make yourself at home. Where you fellows headed, anyway?"

"We're on our way from Richmond to Clarksburg," Jeremiah responded. "I was working for John Carlile in Richmond and when we lost the vote on secession, we had to leave town."

"Yeah, that was something, wasn't it?" Mr. Flint observed. "Do you think we're gonna get a chance to vote on it?"

"It doesn't look like it'll matter much even if we do," Jeremiah said. "Governor Letcher has taken matters into his own hands and started acting like we're out of the Union already."

"Well," Mr. Flint said, "you boys make yourselves at home. If you need anything, just holler."

"Thank you, we will," Jeremiah said as he started the horses and drove the wagon into the schoolyard.

"After we get the horses unhitched and settled in," Jeremiah said, "I'll get a fire started. Sam, if you would, go back along the road and see if you can find some greens that I can put in the skillet after the cornpone is done. Andy, you go across the road to the creek and get us some water."

The creek was not flowing but Andy found a spring-fed trickle of fresh water flowing over a nearly dry waterfall into a small pool. While Andy was dipping water from the pool, he suddenly remembered something from when he lived at his Grandpa's farm.

"Hey Sam," he yelled, "take those greens to Papa and come over here a minute. I want to show you something."

"Look at that pool of water," Andy said when Sam arrived. "Do you see anything unusual about it?"

"No," Sam said, "looks pretty common to me."

"There aren't any minnows in it," Andy said. "That means there's a big ol' bass that got stuck up here from the river and she's hiding under one of them rocks. If I had a line and hook, I'll bet we could catch her about dark."

"You mean they's a big fish in this little hole?" Sam asked.

"Yeah, I'm sure there is," Andy said. "This is what me and my Uncle Joshua always looked for when Melford Creek got low."

"Well, if they's a big fish in there, Masta' Andy, we a-gonna have it for supper, hook or no hook," Sam said as he took off his hat and began using it to bail the water out of the pool and throw it on the rocks downstream.

"Sam, when are you going to stop calling me Master?" Andy asked as he joined in the bailing with his water bucket. "You know my name's Andy and that's all you need to say."

"Now, Masta' Andy," Sam said, looking up momentarily from his bailing, "us black folks was raised to call all white men Mista', and all young white men Masta'. You can't ask me to change that."

"All right, then," Andy said, after a long, thoughtful pause, "us white folks were raised to call you Sambo, so I guess that is what I'm going to call you as long as you call me Master."

Sam completely stopped his bailing and stared solemnly at Andy for a moment. Then, gradually, his face softened into a smile and he said: "Masta' Andy Blake, you're sure one different white boy. If Mista' Blake don't have no concern about it, I reckon I could jus' call you Andy."

"Papa won't mind, I'm sure." Andy said.

Before long, as they continued bailing the water out of the hole, Andy noticed a stirring under one of the big rocks.

"Keep bailing, Sam," Andy said, excitedly, "I think I can see her. Get a little bit more of the water out of here and I'll grab her."

Before Sam had lowered the water enough for Andy to try to catch the fish in his hands, they noticed something stirring under another rock.

"Sam, looky there," Andy yelled. "There's two of them.

Supper was good that night. While the boys had been catching the fish, Jeremiah had built a fire and set up his iron spider that held his black skillet over the fire. He had made a fried cornpone and was cooking the wild greens with salt pork when Andy and Sam arrived with the main course. By the time the greens were done, Andy had scaled and gutted the fish and Jeremiah rolled them in cornmeal and put them in the hot skillet.

"Do you know what would have made this meal even better," Jeremiah asked after the last morsel had been consumed and they were lying on the grass, watching the moon come up over the eastern horizon.

"What?" Andy asked.

"If we'd only had some more of that delicious sulfur water to wash it down with," Jeremiah said, and they all rolled on the grass with laughter.

"Papa, why were you so worried about this mountain?" Andy asked the next morning after they had been traveling up a steep grade for less than a hour and they suddenly were confronted with a wide expanse of level farm fields. "We've already got to the top."

"Not yet," Jeremiah said. "Old Keeney's Mountain is nearly three thousand feet high and we've just gotten up the first step. I happen to know a little bit about this place, it was in the newspaper when I was in college. This is where a man by the name of Clayton crashed in his balloon and the people here took care of him. Now they've named their community after him."

Andy soon realized that his father was right about the mountain. They all had to get off the wagon and walk after they left Clayton and the mountain road got steeper and steeper. During their frequent stops to rest the horses they were able to look back and, seemingly directly beneath them, see the beauty of the farms on the flats of Clayton; the zigzag rail fences, the grain fields beginning to turn from green to golden, and the parallel row patterns of the emerging corn.

It was late evening when they arrived at the banks of the New River at Hinton, where John Carille had advised that they should cross the river on the ferry.

"You'll have to wait 'til tomorrow to cross the river," the ferry operator announced. "I ain't going over again tonight but I'll take you across for thirty cents first thing in the morning."

"Where could we find some good food and a decent place to spend the night here?" Jeremiah asked.

"Well, for another fifty cents I got an extra room you and your boy could stay in," the man answered, "and your colored boy could stay in the barn with your horses. I'm sure the missus can stir up something for you to eat and you can take what's left out to your colored boy after you've had your supper."

"Papa," Andy asked after they had gone to bed, "do you feel right about us to sleeping in here and Sam having to sleep in the barn?"

"Andy, I think Sam is happy to be sleeping in the barn." Jeremiah answered. "He is very fortunate that we were willing to take a big risk in helping him get away from his owner. The problem I'm having is figuring out how we are ever going to get rid of him."

"What do you mean?" Andy asked. "Why do we have to get rid of him? Why can't he stay with us?"

"Sooner or later he is going to get us in trouble," Jeremiah said. "Whenever we get to some point where he can go it alone, he needs to take off on his own. I certainly didn't intend to keep him with us this long."

The next morning after they drove the wagon onto the ferry and they started across the river, Jeremiah was concerned as he observed the ferry owner looking at Sam in a very calculating way. He was relieved when the owner's question had nothing to do with him suspecting than Sam might be a runaway slave.

"This here's a powerful colored boy you got," the man said, speaking as if Sam was not present. "What would you take for him?

148

If you was thinking of selling him, I might be interested. Looks to me like he'd be a good hand here on the river."

Andy's heart did a flip-flop as he thought that his father might be actually considering this offer as an opportunity to free them from Sam. After an extended silence, Jeremiah answered the man.

"I don't think I want to sell Sam, just yet," Jeremiah said. "He's been with me for awhile, now, and I think I'd better keep him."

"Mista' Blake," Sam asked after they were on their way on the west side of the river, "was you fixin' to sell me to that ferry boat man back there?"

"No, Sam," Jeremiah answered. "I couldn't sell you if I wanted to. I don't have a bill of sale or any other proof of ownership so if I tried to sell you the person would know that I didn't own you. But we do need to find the right situation for you to leave. What are your ideas? What are you planning to do after you leave us?"

"What I always heard back in North Carolina was that the only safe place, for sure, is Canada," Sam said. "Then Mama and Jubal told me the same thing. Mama told me to go as far north with you as you'd take me and then head out on my own 'til I got to Canada."

"Well, I guess since we have made it this far, we can make it on to Clarksburg," Jeremiah said with resignation.

"Hey, I have a riddle for the two of you," Jeremiah said after a few minutes. "Are we traveling up or down?"

"What do you mean?" Andy asked.

"I mean, look at the river," Jeremiah said. "Which way is it flowing?"

"It's flowing the same way we're a-goin'," Sam said. "Looks like we're a-goin' down the river."

"That's right," Jeremiah said, "but we are traveling due north. Have you ever heard of anybody going 'down North?'"

"Down North doesn't even sound right," Andy said. "It's always down South and up North."

"Then it sounds like we are going up and down at the same time, doesn't it?" Jeremiah said. "We are going down the river at the same time we are heading up north."

"Then what's the answer to the riddle?" Andy asked.

"I don't guess there is one," Jeremiah answered. "The bigger riddle is why does this river and the West Fork of the Monongahela near your Grandpa's farm flow north and then turn and flow south to New Orleans?"

"Do you know why that is, Mista' Blake?" Sam asked.

"I know what Alexander Campbell told us when I was in college," Jeremiah said. "He said that this river here, New River that flows north all the way up here from North Carolina, didn't always turn south at Point Pleasant like it does now. A long time ago, he said, it kept on flowing on north where the Ohio River now flows south and it joined the Monongahela River at Pittsburgh and went on north and then out east to the Atlantic Ocean."

"That sounds strange," Andy said. "What made it change? Did the world tip up or something?"

"Nothing that dramatic," Jeremiah said. "What Campbell said happened was that there were big ice glaciers up north that blocked the flow for thousands of years and the water had to find another way to go, so it found its way out to the Gulf of Mexico."

"Do you believe that?" Andy asked.

"I'm not sure," Jeremiah said, "but President Campbell had studied science pretty thoroughly and he usually knew what he was talking about. Your grandpa didn't think so, though. When I told him about it, he said that was just a bunch of Alexander Campbell's hogwash since the Bible says that the world is only six thousand years old, so there wasn't enough time for it to happen like Campbell said it did. He said that the rivers flowed that way because that was how God made them."

When they arrived at Richmond Falls, Sam Richmond was waiting for them.

"Mr. Jeremiah Blake, it's about time you got here," Richmond said in a booming voice. "John Carlile is looking for you already. I got a letter from him three days ago telling me to hurry you up, he needs you as soon as you can get there."

"It's good to finally meet you, Mr. Richmond," Jeremiah said as he extended his hand to the powerfully built, gregarious mill owner. "Mr. Carlile holds you in high esteem."

"John Carlile is one of the finest men that Virginia has ever produced, in my opinion," Richmond said, "and if Letcher and the rest of that bunch of traitors in Richmond had listened to him, we wouldn't be in this mess we're in."

After Jeremiah had introduced Sam and Andy to Mr. Richmond, they put the horses out to pasture for the afternoon and went with Richmond to his house where Mrs. Richmond prepared a meal for them. Jeremiah and Andy were served by Mrs. Richmond at the dining room table with Mr. Richmond and his son Tuck, and Sam was given food on the back porch. As the conversation went on around the table, Jeremiah quickly discovered why John Carlile treasured this man. Jeremiah had never met anyone with more conviction or zeal in his devotion to the Constitution.

"I think what we need to do is to shove this thing back into Letcher's face by voting it down in May," Richmond said. "I've talked to people from miles around that come here to the mill or to cross on the ferry and I believe we can win the vote. Most folks around here want to stay with the Union. The biggest obstacle I'm facing is Jeff Bennett up on the mountain. He's hell-bent for secession and he's got the whole Jumping Branch community in an uproar. He's got his boy, Robert, and a bunch of other boys up there just waiting for the opportunity to join a rebel army against the Union. I've tried my best to talk some sense into him but it's no use. I wouldn't be surprised, before this thing is over, if him or me one don't kill the other."

"Do you know why Carlile is in such a hurry for me to get home?" Jeremiah asked, anxious to change the subject.

"I sure do," Richmond answered. "He believes, and I agree with him, that since the actions taken in Richmond are unconstitutional that bunch there have lost their right to govern. He got a resolution passed in Clarksburg that said, in essence, that since there's no legitimate government in Virginia now, loyal Virginians are gonna have to create one. Him and the others are headed up to Wheeling where they intend to set up a whole new legal government for Virginia."

"No wonder he's in a hurry," Jeremiah said. "We'll leave first thing in the morning. Now, I want you to tell me everything you want me to pass on to him."

"I want him to know that we are going to carry the referendum election in this part of the state," Richmond said, "and if it comes to war, my boy, Tuck, and a lot of other boys around here will answer the call to fight for the Union. Tell him that I fully support his endeavor to set up a new government for Virginia and that I have great confidence that he will be successful."

It took Jeremiah and company another five days to travel from New River to Melford Creek. Abe and Sally were overjoyed to see their oldest son and favorite grandson after so long an absence but were made uncomfortable by the presence of Sam. Andy was especially happy to be reunited with his uncle, Joshua.

"Can you stay with us for awhile?" Sally asked, after a long embrace with Jeremiah. "We've missed you so much, we wondered if you were ever coming back."

"I'm sorry to say, we will only be able to spend two nights and that's only so we can rest the horses," Jeremiah told his parents. "John Carlile wants me as soon as possible to hook up with him either in Clarksburg or in Wheeling if he has already gone there."

"What do you think is going to happen, Son,?" Abe asked. "We've been hearing some awful predictions that we are getting close to war."

"I hope and pray it doesn't come to that," Jeremiah answered. "Evidently, what we are going to do in Wheeling is try to establish a new government for the state of Virginia to replace the one in Richmond that's in revolt. A lot of us don't believe that Virginia or any other state has the right to leave the Union so we are going to do what we can to keep Virginia loyal."

"Tell me about your slave you brought here with you," Abe demanded of Jeremiah. "You're the last person I expected to be bringing a slave up here."

"Papa, Sam is not my slave," Jeremiah responded. "He is more of a friend."

"Well, what are you doing with him?" Abe asked.

"Sam is a Christian man who ran away from his plantation down in North Carolina rather than serve as a 'breeding buck' to slave women that were brought to him," Jeremiah said. "He said that he could not do that and serve the Lord."

"I reckon not," the shocked preacher said. "Good for him. What's are you going to do with him now?"

"He came this far with us and plans to head out on his own for Canada," Jeremiah said. "I can take him as far as Wheeling."

Sally calling them to come to supper interrupted their conversation.

"Jeremiah, you sit here and Andy, you sit there next to your Papa," Sally directed and then asked, "Where is Sam?"

"Sam will eat on the back porch, Mama," Jeremiah said. "If you will fix him a plate, Andy can take it out to him."

"Why's he gonna eat out there?" Abe asked. "There's plenty of room for him here at the table. You go get him, Jeremiah."

"No, Papa," Jeremiah tried to explain in his patient voice. "You see, Sam has never eaten in a white person's home and he wouldn't be comfortable in here with us."

"Well, if you ain't going to go get him, I will," Abe said resolutely as he got up from the table. "You tell me he's your friend and a Christian and then you leave him out there on the porch. That ain't no way to treat a friend."

"Oh, nossa, Reverend Blake," Sam protested when Abe invited him to come inside to eat with the family, "I ain't never ate with white folks, I'll just have me a little somethin' out here if it wouldn't trouble nobody too much."

"I'm here to tell you it would trouble me a way too much," Abe said, forcefully. "You're a visitor in my home and I'm gonna treat you the same way I would treat any other visitor. My wife has fixed a fine meal and put it on the table. Now then, you can come in the dining room and eat with us like we want you to or you can set out here and go hungry. I suggest you get up and come on in with me and forget all this foolishness."

"Yessa, Reverend Blake," Sam said politely as he rose to accompany Abe into the house. "You Blakes sure do surprise a fellow."

"Mista' Blake," Sam said to Jeremiah late the next day, "it 'pears to me that Reverend Blake could use some help here on his farm. Some of his fences need fixin', his corn is gettin' weedy, and his hay is near ready for cuttin' and he don't look able to do much heavy work and it 'pears to be too much for Mista' Joshua to do all by hisself. Why don't I just stay here and help 'em for a spell?"

"Sam, you've figured out that this is about as far as we can go together, haven't you?" Jeremiah said.

"Yessa, I have," Sam responded, "but I ain't ready to head off

153

for Canada on my own just yet. If I was to stay here and help your folks, that'd be my way of payin' you for bringin' me with you."

"Papa," Jeremiah said to his father, privately, "Sam has offered to stay here and help you with the farm. What do you think of that?"

"I don't think much of it. I ain't never had a slave and I ain't aiming to start now," Abe said passionately.

"Papa, I told you that Sam is not my slave and he would not be yours," Jeremiah said.

"I know that was what you said," Abe responded. "Just what do you mean by that? How did you come by him, anyway?"

"I didn't buy him, Papa," Jeremiah said. "I brought him out of Richmond as a favor to his mother."

"Well, he's still a slave, ain't he?" Abe bellowed.

"Papa," Jeremiah said, using the same patient tone he so often used with Andy when he was trying to teach him an important concept, "you remember the night we discussed slavery with George Talley and he reminded us of the account in the Bible where Paul sent Onesimus to Philemon and told him to receive him, not as a slave but as a brother? Well, that's what I mean when I'm talking about Sam. He's not a slave any longer in my eyes. Now he's a Christian brother who is in need and he's offering to be your friend and helper on the farm."

"As I recall," Abe said, "you didn't agree with George about that. What's the difference now?"

"I've learned a lot over the past few weeks," Jeremiah said. "I think that the Lord has used Andy and Sam to show me where I have been wrong about some things in the past."

"If he stays here, how will people know that he ain't my slave?" Abe asked.

"You tell them he's your friend and Christian brother," Jeremiah said. "They'll know it's true by the way you treat him."

"I'd have to fix him a place to stay." Abe protested.

"You just decide on the place and I assure you that Sam will take care of the fixing," Jeremiah replied.

"I reckon Joshua could use some help around here," Abe said. "If that's what you want, we can try it for awhile."

"Thank you, Papa," Jeremiah said. "I know that Sam will be happy."

22 *RESTORATION IN WHEELING*

Jeremiah felt a great weight lifted when Sam had chosen to stay with Abe, Sally, and Joshua and Abe had, albeit reluctantly, agreed to let him live there. As he and Andy rode toward Clarksburg they reminisced about all the things they had learned from Sam. Their time spent living with him had provided the closest personal relationship that either had experienced with a black person.

"The thing that kept sticking with me all the time he was with us," Jeremiah said, "was your reminder to me of the Shakespeare quote. 'Does he not bleed?' ran through my mind every time I saw Sam scared or in pain. I'm ashamed to say it, but before I got to know Sam, I just had never thought about Negroes having much in the way of feelings. That's how ignorant I was. You were surely right about Alexander Campbell, too. I wouldn't go as far as you did in saying that he was a what? A big fat idiot; wasn't that what you called him? But he was certainly wrong when he said that the black race was physically inferior to us. Sam is undoubtedly the strongest man that I've ever seen."

"Sam is pretty smart, too, wouldn't you say, Papa?" Andy asked with a smile of satisfaction.

"Yes, Andy," Jeremiah said, "you are right again. Sam is very smart."

Upon arrival at his law office in Clarksburg Jeremiah saw a message from John Carlile: "Get to Wheeling as soon as you can. I need you."

As Jeremiah and Andy traveled on to Wheeling, signs of impending war were everywhere. People were gathered in groups, some talking quietly, others shouting. Young men in uniforms were often visible. It appeared that every man was carrying a rifle. It seemed to Jeremiah that the whole world was about to descend into one of his dark periods.

When Jeremiah and Andy arrived in Wheeling on May 12, 1861, the city was alive with drama and anticipation. Delegates from twenty-seven Virginia counties had already arrived in preparation for the opening session, on May 13, of the Wheeling Convention that had been called to consider a response to the illegal actions of the government in Richmond.

When Jeremiah finally located John Carlile he found him hard at work drafting the statements and resolution proposals that he would present to the convention.

"Jeremiah, I am certainly glad to see you," Carlile exclaimed as he arose from his desk. "I feel like John the Baptist. I seem to be just a voice crying in the wilderness."

"What do you mean?" Jeremiah asked.

"Nobody has the sense of urgency that I have," Carlile explained. "Even Waitman Willey doesn't want us to do anything of substance until after the May twenty-third vote on secession. We can't wait for that. Letcher and his gang didn't wait for that. We need to act fast if we are going to keep Virginia loyal to the Union."

"What are you going to say tomorrow?" Jeremiah asked.

"Basically, I am going to say that the actions taken in Richmond in April were illegal and that the actions of Letcher and his officials constitutes an unconstitutional usurping of power," Carlile said, looking at his notes. "Therefore, we, on behalf of the people of Virginia, have the right and responsibility to form a legitimate government for the state, a government that is loyal to Virginia and is loyal to the United States of America."

Although Jeremiah shared much of Carlile's passion, he was not surprised when, after heated debate, the convention passed Willey's resolution which called for a second Wheeling Convention if the voters approved the Ordinance of Secession on May 23.

When the votes on the ordinance were tallied, the resolution to secede passed and thirty-two Virginia counties then sent delegates to the second Wheeling Convention which was to open on June 11, 1861.

Jeremiah and Carlile worked feverishly for days in an attempt to draft just the right opening resolution to set the stage for the convention.

"What do you want to call your resolution?" Jeremiah asked.

"I am not sure," Carlile answered. "What I think it is, is simply a declaration of the people of Virginia."

"Then why not call it that?" Jeremiah asked.

"Call it what?" Carlile responded.

"Call it 'A Declaration of the People of Virginia,'" Jeremiah said. "You are declaring that because of the treasonous actions of the Richmond government the governor and all state offices are illegal, and therefore there is no legitimate state government in Virginia."

"That sounds good," Carlile said. "I probably won't use the word 'treason' but if I can get the point across that the Richmond government is no longer valid and get that passed as a resolution, then the necessity of forming a reorganized Virginia state government should be seen as an inevitable follow-up."

Before the second Wheeling Convention was held, fighting broke out in Virginia between federal Union forces and the rebels. On June 3, a rebel Virginia force, led by Brigadier General Robert Garnett, was confronted at Philippi on its way to Clarksburg to take control over the railroad. After fierce fighting, the Union forces led by Gen. George McClellan succeeded in driving the rebel forces back past Beverly. McClellan then set up his Union headquarters in the nearby community of Webster.

Soon after the opening of the second Wheeling meeting, Carlile's choice, Virginia State Assemblyman Arthur Boreman was selected president of the Convention.

"Because the government of our State of Virginia has forfeited its legitimacy by engaging in revolution against the government of the United States in its illegal and unconstitutional attempt to secede from the Union, we must now institute a legitimate government for Virginia." Boreman said in his acceptance speech. "We have been given the solemn task of forming a true government for the state of Virginia, a government that will loyally exist within the United States of America and will live within the confines of the United States Constitution."

Two days later, on June 13, John Carlile presented his

resolution.

"Mr. President," Carlile said when he was recognized by President Boreman, "I rise to present a proposed resolution which I call 'A Declaration of the People of Virginia.'"

"Mr. Carlile is recognized for the purpose of presenting a proposed resolution," Boreman announced.

"Mr. President and fellow delegates," Carlile said as he began to address the convention, "the actions of the state government at Richmond regarding secession from the United States of America were, and continue to be, illegal and unconstitutional acts of revolution. All of the officials who have participated in these acts have violated their oaths of office and have committed treason, yes, I use the word treason, against the United States of America. By their actions they have forfeited their powers and the powers have now reverted to the people. Therefore, I propose that this body, on behalf of the people of Virginia, declare all state government offices vacant and reconstitute a state government for Virginia."

Jeremiah was expecting that Carlile's proposal would get a favorable response but he had not anticipated the enthusiastic cheers and applause that erupted when he sat down. Their hard work had paid off, the resolution stirred the convention.

Delegate Dennis Dorsey was then recognized by Boreman to present a counter resolution. His proposal was that the counties that remained loyal to the federal government should separate themselves from eastern Virginia and form a new state.

Carlile rose in opposition to Dorsey's resolution.

"While I am in agreement with much of what is contained in the proposal from the delegate from Monongalia County, I must oppose it on constitutional grounds," Carlile argued. "In order for a new state to be formed from an existing state, the original state must give its approval. Even if the formation of a new state is a judicious choice, we must first form a legitimate government for the State of Virginia that could then agree to the formation of a new state."

Waitman Willey made his strong constitutional case against the creation of a new state. Such an action, he argued, would be "triple treason."

"The first treason," Willey stated, "would be against the United States because the U. S. Constitution prohibits the formation of a new state out of an existing one without the approval of the parent state. The second treason would be against the State of Virginia that has not given its approval. The third treason would be against the newly formed Confederate States of America."

Carlile's resolution, "A Declaration of the People of Virginia," passed overwhelmingly on June 19, and the Reconstructed Government of the State of Virginia was formed.

On the same day, the convention selected an ex-Whig who had become a Republican and was a strong Lincoln supporter, Francis Pierpont, as the new Governor of Virginia.

In his inaugural address, Governor Pierpont emphasized the principles to which he subscribed.

"I believe that the foundation of our democracy is that all power resides in the people," Pierpont said. "The people who are the leaders of the revolution in the southern states are introducing a new doctrine, namely, that all power resides in them and not in the people. We have been forced into the situation we find ourselves today by the actions of these selfish and treasonous men. I stand on the principle that the power to govern in a state belongs to the loyal citizens of that state. I humbly accept the position that you have granted me, and I accept it in the name of all of the loyal citizens of the State of Virginia."

"My first action," the Governor said the next day when he again addressed the delegates, "will be to send a direct request today to President Lincoln for military aid to assist Virginia against the insurrection already underway in our state."

"Our future hinges on what we hear back from Washington," Pierpont explained to the delegates. "If Lincoln honors our request, that means that the President, himself, recognizes us as the true government of Virginia."

"Next," Pierpont reasoned, "we will have to convince Congress to seat our new Senators and Representatives and then, undoubtedly, we will have to argue our case before the Supreme Court."

There was jubilation when word came from Secretary of War, Simon Cameron, that the State of Virginia would receive the requested help from the Federal government.

John Carlile and Waitman Willey were selected by the new Virginia legislature to serve as the U. S. Senators from Virginia, replacing J. M. Mason and R. M. T. Hunter who had left Washington when the Richmond government voted to secede.

Jeremiah and Andy were in the gallery of the Capitol when the Senate voted by a margin of thirty-five to five to accept Carlile and Willey as the Senators from Virginia.

"You know what this means, don't you Andy?" Jeremiah asked, jubilantly. "This means we need to find us a place to live here in Washington, again."

When the issue reached the Federal Courts, the decision was rendered that the President had the power to decide on the validity of contesting state governments and the government in Wheeling, headed by Governor Francis Pierpont, having been recognized by President Lincoln, was, therefore, the legitimate government of the State of Virginia.

The establishment of the Reorganized Government of Virginia, with Wheeling as the new state capital, caused a great deal of reaction. President Lincoln, in a letter to Governor Pierpont said: "The reorganized government which you lead is, I pray, the first of similar governments which will be established in all of the states where legal governments have been replaced by illegal rebel factions. You have set a powerful precedent and Virginia can now serve as a model for the loyal citizens in other states to follow."

Horace Greeley editorialized in the New York Tribune that, "the loyal people of Virginia are the first of all the citizens of the seceded states to disclaim and resist the authority of the Confederate usurpers. The whole country owes her a debt of gratitude."

Jeremiah was struck by the irony of a statement made by Jefferson Davis, the President of the Confederacy that was carried in the newspaper.

"Listen to what Jeff Davis had to say about us," he said to Senator Carlile. "He said that the state of Virginia was a nation, not a federation, and we are all guilty of insurrection, revolution, and secession. John, that sounds just like one of your speeches when you were talking about the Union. Don't you think his reasoning is a little bit hypocritical?"

"A little bit?" Carlile said as he smiled wryly. "It's more than a little bit. It's astounding that a man as intelligent as Jeff Davis couldn't come up with a better statement than that. If he would just open his eyes, he would realize that he is condemning himself."

Jeremiah anxiously sought word from the war, especially from his home area. He learned that on July 11, General McClellan had attacked General Garnett's forces at Rich Mountain and pursued them to Carrick's Ford where General Garnett was killed. He was heartened to learn that loyal Virginia forces were able to repel the next wave of rebel forces that were led by General Robert E. Lee and drove them back into the Greenbrier Valley.

"I wonder how John Letcher is feeling about his theory that Virginia would be the state to preserve the peace?" Carlile speculated to Jeremiah when they were discussing the latest news. "I wonder if he realizes that his actions have now led to two groups of Virginia boys killing each other. If this turns into an all out war he will see that, instead of Virginia being the state of peace, it is the state where the first battles were fought. What a tragedy! And already one of our country's best Generals, Robert Garnett, a man who graduated from West Point and was a hero of the Mexican War has died a traitor, fighting against his own country. And it's going to get worse."

"He might have figured it out by now," Jeremiah said, "but it's too late now for him to do anything about it. Like my papa would say, once you strike a deal with the devil you're stuck with it. The people he decided to throw in with will never let him change course."

23 *THE NEW STATE MOVEMENT*

By late summer of 1861, battles were raging throughout Virginia as Union and rebel forces sought control of strategic sites. Confederate forces under General John B. Floyd moved into the Kanawha Valley in September in a move against the new Virginia Government. Seeking to control the Kanawha Valley and all points south and east, the rebels hoped to reduce the size of the region supporting the Pierpont government.

The rebels were engaged by Union forces led by General William S. Rosencrans and defeated at Carnifex Ferry. The rebels were forced to retreat to Lewisburg and did not again pose a serious threat to the strategic Kanawha Valley.

General George McClellan and General Rosencrans were then both involved in a battle with rebel forces at Rich Mountain over control of the Stanton-Parkersburg Turnpike, the major east-west artery across the center of Virginia. Although it was mostly the actions of Rosecrans' forces which secured the victory, McClellen managed to glean most of the credit and was subsequently summoned by President Lincoln to Washington to become the new commander of the Army of the Potomac.

The weekly letters that Jeremiah received from his mother indicated her steadily increasing alarm over events happening around her.

"We never know when the war is going to break out here," she wrote. "Most of the boys around here have gone off to the army. Some of them have even gone to join the rebels. I think some of them want to fight with your friend, T. J. Jackson."

"Your father is not able to do much work," she also wrote, and then added, " Samuel sends his regards. I do not know what we would have done without him, he and Joshua take such good care of the place."

Jeremiah kept a close watch on the volunteer rosters from the counties around his home and where he knew some of the people. Familiar names started showing up. On the list from Brooke County he saw the names of Rev. William Sharpe's two sons: William Jr., and Seth.

Upon reading the next listing from Brooke County his heart jumped as he saw the name, Jeremiah Tompkins. Could it be, he thought? Then he realized that Lizzie's first son, the one she had named for him, would be eighteen years old and it must, indeed, be him. From Wetzel County he saw that Jacob and Jonas Hendry, boys that he remembered as the little babies of the blacksmith's family in Old Hundred who had joined the Union forces.

"Is something wrong, Papa?" Andy asked as he observed a troubled look on his father's face while he was reading the latest letter from home. "Is something wrong with Grandma or Grandpa?"

"Not exactly," Jeremiah responded, "but let me read you what Mama wrote. 'My heart is broken. My beloved baby, Joshua has joined the army. I'm sorry now that you brought Sam here. Maybe if Sam was not here to look after the place Joshua would not have gone.'"

"That's not true, Papa," Andy protested. "I'll bet Uncle Joshua would have joined up anyway."

"You're right, of course," Jeremiah said, "and Mama probably knows it, too, but she is so hurt that Joshua is going to war and I know that she's scared to death that he won't make it back."

"I hate this stupid war," Andy exclaimed. "Is it true what folks say, that if Lincoln hadn't been elected there wouldn't have been a war?"

"That may, indeed, be true," Jeremiah responded. "But think about it. If Mr. Lincoln had not been elected, and if there was no war, then we could have ended up with no country."

By the middle of 1862, the two Senators from Virginia, John Carlile and Waitman Willey were developing their strategy for the formation of a new state comprised of the inland, mountain portion of Virginia. They were both now of the opinion that their portion of Virginia would be better served by separating itself from the coastal, tidewater regions which had often dominated state politics to the exclusion of the mountain region.

Many favorable factors were in place for the new state formation. The legitimate government of Virginia in Wheeling could give its approval to the formation of the new state from within its boundaries. A majority of members of Congress were favorable to the action. The biggest stumbling block to the formation, though, was the executive branch.

President Lincoln opposed the formation of the new state because he liked the precedent of the Reorganized Government which he saw as a prototype and he still was harboring hopes that the loyal citizens in other states would follow Virginias example. He also intended to reestablish Richmond as the state capital as soon as the war was over and relocate Governor Pierpont and his cabinet there from Wheeling.

Despite the opposition of President Lincoln, Carlile and Willey plowed on ahead with their effort.

"Jeremiah, I am not satisfied with our initial proposal of forty-eight counties. I want you to work with our other staff members and draft up some proposed configurations for the new state," Carlile requested. "Start with the smallest feasible size by including only the solid Union counties and then expand it up to include the whole mountain region so we can discuss it."

Jeremiah found that there were about thirty counties that were solidly loyal to the Union and at least that many more where the loyalty was pretty evenly divided.

When Jeremiah's group presented the alternative state size proposals to Carlile, Willey, and their advisors, they decided that most of the southwestern counties, regardless of their loyalty at this time, belonged in the new state. There was great debate about whether or not to include the Shenandoah Valley counties. If they were included, the new state would consist of sixty-six counties. They finally decided against including all of the Shenandoah Valley counties but did include the counties of Jefferson, Berkley, and Morgan which were close to Washington. The proposed new state would have fifty-five counties.

"We only have one item to make sure that we are agreed upon," Willey asked, leaning back in his chair, "Do we go with the name

'West Virginia' as the convention preferred or do we choose another to put on the bill?"

"I have thought, all along, that we need a whole new name, one that totally separates us from Virginia," Jeremiah said. "You recall that when the proposal was first introduced at the convention the name was Kanawha. I would prefer that we go back to that and name it the State of Kanawha but I'm afraid it's too late for that now."

After everyone expressed their opinions, John Carlile closed the discussion by saying, "I think that Jeremiah is right, there is enough controversy about creating a new state without causing more by disagreeing with the state convention. The bill that I introduce in the Senate will use the name West Virginia."

As soon as the measure was introduced, an unexpected hornet's nest was stirred up. John Carlile got together with Waitman Willey and Jeremiah to make a startling announcement; President Abraham Lincoln had presented to his cabinet that morning, a draft of an Emancipation Proclamation stating that all slaves in the states in rebellion against the federal government would be freed, and he intended to make it effective on January 1, 1863. The proclamation would exempt all Union states and the counties of Virginia that would make up the proposed new state of West Virginia.

Senator Carlile was livid at the President's actions.

"This war is being fought to preserve the country, not change it," the irate Senator angrily declared to Jeremiah and Waitman Willey. "What does he propose to do with millions of Negroes running loose all through the South after the rebellion is put down? They can't be citizens; the Supreme Court decided that in the Dred Scott case. Where does he plan to put them? Is he going to ship them back to Africa? Liberia wouldn't hold all of them. Sometimes I question the sanity of that man."

"John," Senator Willey responded, "I agree that this is going to cause nothing but trouble. I don't know what the man was thinking. But nothing is going to change until after the war is over and then one of two things will have to take place; either the Supreme Court changes its ruling or we'll be forced to work on legislation to amend the Constitution to make Negroes citizens. What we have to do now is keep our focus on the task at hand and get the state of West

Virginia admitted."

"We've got serious trouble, Jeremiah," Carlile said after the first day of debate on the floor of the Senate. "The Republicans and Radical Unionists are insisting that West Virginia be admitted as a 'free-soil' state and Waitman is willing to appease them. Those fanatics are not just trying to save the Union or punish the rebelling states, they won't be satisfied until the institution of slavery is abolished in the entire country."

"Would that be too high a price to pay for statehood?" Jeremiah asked. "It seems to me that this would be a fitting way to further draw the lines of demarcation between us and the Richmond crowd."

"I am no abolitionist!" Carlile thundered. "Jeremiah, you know my position. You know that I support the preservation of the Union and its restoration to the exact same conditions as existed before the war, nothing more, nothing less. And those conditions include maintaining the institution of slavery."

"John, I have never disagreed with you before," Jeremiah said, hesitantly, "but on this issue, I do. As the result of my experiences lately, I've come to believe that slavery is an evil that needs to be abolished, not just in the South, but everywhere it exists, so I guess I am becoming an abolitionist, myself."

"Well, if that's the way you feel," Carlile said, bitterly, "I don't have any further need for your services. My task now is to prevent the admission of West Virginia to the Union as a free-soil state and it sounds like you would not be of any help in that endeavor."

That night as Jeremiah was preparing for his exit from Washington he was called on by Waitman Willey.

"John told me about the two of you coming to a parting of the ways, today," Willey said as soon as he entered the room. "I am no more an abolitionist than John is but I'm not willing to let that stand in the way of the admission of West Virginia to the Union."

"I'm glad to hear you say that," Jeremiah said.

"You know more about the ins and outs of this issue than anybody else," Willey said. "I talked to John about me hiring you to help see things through to the end."

"What did he say?" Jeremiah asked.

"After he got down off of his high horse, he said that it was the right thing to do," Willey said. "John is extremely fond of you, as you know, but he was floored by your strong position against slavery."

"It is only recently that I arrived at a different position from John on the slavery issue," Jeremiah said. "All my life I felt about slavery just as he does, but I have seen things and experienced things that have caused me to change my mind on the matter. As a Christian, I have felt it necessary to repent for my previous feelings. I hope that's not offensive to you, but I feel that strongly about it."

"No, I'm not offended in the least," Willey said with a smile, "I know all about you Methodists and repentance.. We all need to repent once in awhile for something or other. I'll be aware of one thing, though. I know that you'll be zealous in your new conviction. There is never anyone as red-hot as a new convert."

"I think I can keep myself under control long enough to help you get this legislation passed," Jeremiah said with a smile, "that is, if you still want me."

"Come in early tomorrow," Willey said. "We've got lots of work to do."

The bill to admit West Virginia to the Union passed both houses of Congress with comfortable margins despite the strong efforts of John Carlile and his pro-Union, pro-slavery colleagues, a group in the Democratic Party becoming known as the "Copperheads."

The bill now presented President Lincoln with a major dilemma.

24 *SECESSION IN FAVOR OF THE*
CONSTITUTION

President Abraham Lincoln was in his office early, pacing impatiently as he waited for the cabinet to arrive. It was just a few days before Christmas, 1862, and the war was not going well. General George McClellan who had been deemed brilliant in the early fighting in Virginia and credited with chasing the rebels from western Virginia into the Greenbrier Valley had not distinguished himself in the eyes of his Commander-in-Chief since he had been summoned from his headquarters in Webster to take command of the Army of the Potomac, replacing General Irvin McDowell.

McClellan, Lincoln had soon discovered, was not as interested in fighting as he was in his appearance and advancing his own career. He was very visible in Washington, a quite dashing figure as he drilled and paraded the Union soldiers through the streets of the city, always in preparation for a fight, but seldom into a fight. Lincoln realized that McClellan's top priority was not to fight a war but, rather, to replace him as the occupant of the White House at the next election.

After McClellan's forces won the long and bloody battle of Antietam in 1862, in which his army outnumbered Lee's army by two to one, McClellan failed to follow up the victory and capture Lee and destroy his army. The enraged President relieved McClellan of his position, replacing him with General "Fightin' Joe" Hooker who, despite his ferocious sounding sobriquet, also had limited success against the rebel forces.

For the most part, rebel General Robert E. Lee and his most trusted associate, General T. J. Jackson, who had by now earned the nickname, "Stonewall," controlled the Shenandoah Valley. They had, on occasion, even ventured far enough north to be within sight of Washington, itself.

Nothing seems to be going right, Lincoln thought as he paced. He agonized over generals who would not fight, a Congress reluctant to provide enough money to pay or equip the army, an angry General McClelland who was already campaigning against him for the Presidency, an unstable wife on the verge of insanity since the loss of their dear child, Willie, and the terrible toll of young lives the war was claiming; more than twenty thousand at Antietam, alone.

Lincoln's depressed thoughts were interrupted by the appearance of Secretary of State William Seward, the first of the cabinet arrivals. Seward was, as befitted a man of his great wealth, very nattily attired. Since he was a good foot shorter than the President, Lincoln harbored the thought that maybe Seward's ostentatious attire was an effort at compensating for his short stature.

"Good morning, Mr. President," Seward said in a voice that Lincoln recognized as more cordial than usual. He knew that Seward and Secretary of the Treasury Salmon Chase, and maybe a few others, thought that they were much better qualified than he to be president and their contempt for him often showed.

Secretary Seward considered Lincoln an easy target for his manipulation. He was so confident in his own superior intellect that he considered the President quite slow-witted by comparison. Seward was totally unaware that Lincoln had, from their first meeting, figured out his methods and secretly enjoyed a running battle of wits with him. Lincoln knew immediately this day that Seward was there early and feigning cordiality because he wanted to predispose the President to his position.

"Mr. President," Seward said, "I know that the Attorney General does not think that the formation of a new state out of Virginia is constitutional. I want you to know that I consider his position to be wrong for this reason: the Restored Government in Wheeling is incontestably the government of Virginia and can give its approval. The status of the restored Government was settled, once and for all, when it was recognized by you and the Congress, and then upheld in the courts."

"I certainly appreciate your thoughts on this matter," Lincoln said, solemnly. "I know that I can always rely on you to give me wise counsel, Mr. Seward, but you know that I have to listen to everyone before I announce my decision."

Soon the other cabinet members had arrived; Salmon Chase, Attorney General Edward Bates, Secretary of War Edwin Stanton, Postmaster General Montgomery Blair, and Secretary of the Navy Gideon Welles.

"Gentlemen, as you know, I have called you here to give me your advice on the bill that would create the state of West Virginia," the President announced. "I want you to be completely candid in giving your opinions on this bill."

"You must veto the bill," Attorney General Bates said bluntly. "This bill legitimizes an act of revolution against the state of Virginia and it is a breach of the Constitutions of Virginia and of the United States."

"Thank you Mr. Bates," Lincoln said, "but your colleague, the Secretary of State, has a different interpretation of the legality of the matter. He tells me that he believes the Restored Government in Wheeling to be the legal government of Virginia and that the formation of a new state is, indeed, constitutional."

The President did not have to look in the direction of Secretary Seward to know that he was squirming nervously in his seat and that his transparent skin was now bright red as his position, which he had intended to keep secret from his political ally Edward Bates, had been revealed to him. Lincoln felt a little guilty at the measure of evil pleasure he enjoyed knowing that Seward was assuming that this information had been accidentally imparted by a bumbling President who knew next to nothing about politics.

"Mr. President," Montgomery Blair, who was next to speak, said, "the so-called Wheeling Government represented less than half the people of Virginia and the recognition of that government was wrong in the first place."

By the time the dust had settled at the end of the meeting, Chase, Stanton, and Seward had weighed in on the side of approval of the bill and Blair, Welles, and Bates favored a veto.

"Well, Mr. President," Seward said, "it is now in your hands. What is your position?"

"I am grateful to each of you for your counsel," Lincoln said, "but I am going to defer my decision until I can meet with Governor

Pierpont and the Senators from Virginia. I hope to do that shortly after Christmas."

Governor Pierpont had to travel on a cold, snowy Christmas day in order to meet with the President on December 27, along with Senator John Carlile and Senator Waitman Willey.

"Hurry and get dressed," Jeremiah said to Andy that morning. "We can't be late for a meeting with the President.

"Papa, do I have to go?" Andy whined. "You know that I don't like that man."

"Yes, you have to go," Jeremiah said, sternly. "How many boys your age get the opportunity to see the President and be there when history is being made? This is something you will tell your children and grandchildren about. Now, get dressed."

The group of Pierpont, Willey, Carlile, and Jeremiah assembled outside the President's office and entered together, with Andy lagging half-heartedly behind them.

"Governor Pierpont, Senator Carlile, Senator Willey, it is good to see you," Lincoln said solemnly as he shook hands with each of them.

"Mr. President," Senator Willey said, "let me introduce to you my assistant, Jeremiah Blake, who has done a lion's share of the work on this effort."

"Mr. Blake, I am pleased to meet you, your reputation has preceded you," Lincoln said as he gripped Jeremiah's hand, then looking at Carlile, he said, "I've heard a lot of good things about Mr. Blake but, John, I thought that he was your assistant."

"He was until recently, Mr. President," Carlile said with a wry smile. "We had a strong disagreement over whether West Virginia should be admitted as a slave-free state, and you know my position on that issue."

"Yes, John, I know how hard it must have been for you, after all the work you did to get the statehood bill before Congress, to have to vote against it after it was amended," Lincoln said. "I know that you want everything after the war to be as it was before the war, but that is just not going to be possible. The Emancipation Proclamation goes into effect next week and, as of then, the residents of the states in rebellion will no longer own their slaves. Things will never be the same there, again. It seems that the times have dictated to us that we must do things that we otherwise would not have chosen to do."

"Governor," the President said, abruptly changing the subject and turning to Francis Pierpont, "I would like your recommendation on this bill."

"Mr. President," Pierpont responded, "As the Governor of Virginia, I took no part in the movement to create a new state. Initially, I, along with many Union men, was not in favor of the formation of a new state. Now, however, the support of the Union and the sentiment for a new state have become one and the same. I am afraid that if the state of West Virginia does not become a reality now we will lose vital support for the Union."

"Francis," the President responded, "I understand your predicament. This war, which I entered into as a defense of the Constitution, has become different things to different people. People like the Beecher's, William Lloyd Garrison, and Frederick Douglass now see it as a war of abolition and if we are to prevail, I must keep their support."

Then the President added, "There is one other thing that has forced my hand regarding freeing the slaves. It appears that England is close to giving official recognition to the Confederacy. I suspect that England and the other European nations will be less likely to recognize the rebel government if they see that they are fighting a war to preserve slavery rather than fighting for independence."

Turning next to John Carlile, the President asked, "Senator, what advice would you give me?"

"As indicated by my vote on the final bill, I would have to recommend that you veto the measure," Carlile said, forcefully. "I look upon secessionists and abolitionists as twin brothers and I have spent my career fighting them both. My opposition to the admission of West Virginia into the Union as a free state is based on my belief that our effort, as well as the war, has been taken over by the abolitionists and the final bill is not in the interest of the people we represent."

"Senator Willey, your comments, please," Lincoln said.

"I hope, after this thing is settled," Willey said in a voice that was uncharacteristically gentle, "that Senator Carlile and I will be able to mend our fences and overcome the differences that have come between us on this matter. I have encountered no one in my professional life that I respect more that I do John Carlile. I split with John and offered the amendment that West Virginia be admitted as a slave-free state for one reason and one reason only; it would not have passed the Senate without it. I would have preferred that it would have been passed in its original state, as John introduced it, but when I saw that it was going to fail, I considered the compromise necessary in order to save the bill and, in keeping with Governor Pierpont's remarks, possibly save the Union."

"I think that you all know that the formation of a new state was not my first choice," Lincoln said. "I considered what you did in setting up a legal government of loyal citizens in the state of Virginia to be a brilliant maneuver, a true act of patriotism. It has been my intent since then, that after the rebellion has been put down that you, Francis, would move into Richmond with your cabinet and continue your governorship there. I had hoped that the loyal citizens of other states would emulate your efforts. As you all know, initially the legislatures in Alabama, Georgia, Louisiana, and Mississippi, like the legislature in Virginia, all voted to stay in the Union, but through the intimidation and chicanery of the rebel element, those sentiments were overruled. I had hoped that the Virginia plan would be followed by the loyal people there."

"Sometimes we don't get everything we want," Senator Carlile said, dryly.

"I guess not, John," the President said, careful not to reveal his irritation at Senator Carlile. "In any event, you are all invited back here in four days when I will make my final decision known."

"Mr. President," Senator Carlile said, "I respectfully wish to decline the invitation if it is your intention to sign the bill. Is it possible for you to give me an indication of your decision?"

"John," Lincoln said in a mock whisper, "why don't you sleep late that day."

"I will, Mr. President," Carlile said, trying mightily not to show his bitterness. "Thank you."

"Now, then," the President said, motioning toward Andy, "no one introduced me to the young gentleman back there."

"I beg your pardon, Mr. President," Jeremiah said as he tried to cover his embarrassment. "This is my son Andrew Jackson Blake.

He goes with me most places and I hope you don't mind me bringing him here, I thought this was an unusual opportunity for him to see you and experience a historic event. Andy, let me present to you the President of the United States."

"Come here, Mister Andrew Jackson Blake, and let me get a good look at you," Lincoln said as he rose from his chair. Andy suddenly felt very small as his right hand was completely enveloped in Lincoln's large hand and he looked up into the face of the tall, gaunt man who was the President.

"How old are you, Son?" Lincoln asked.

"I'm fourteen, but I'll be fifteen in the spring," Andy answered.

"Where did you get that light brown hair and fair complexion?" Lincoln asked as he tousled Andy's hair with his long fingers and looked at the dark haired Jeremiah.

"I reckon I take after my mother," Andy ventured. "At least, that's what people tell me."

"Mr. Blake," the President said to Jeremiah, "If you wouldn't mind joining the other men in the hallway, I'd like to visit for a few moments with your boy."

Reluctantly, Jeremiah exited the room. What on earth, he wondered, is going on in the mind of this enigmatic giant named Abraham Lincoln. Perhaps he was reminded of his own son, Willie, that he had lost less than a year ago, or could it be that the bright innocence of Andy would provide a brief respite from the arduous ordeal that was the President's life.

In any event, Jeremiah thought, a few moments spent by Andy with the man he had never respected and had often ridiculed might have a favorable impact on him.

"Is your mother here in Washington with you and your father?" Lincoln asked as he sat down and leaned back in his chair.

"No sir," Andy answered, "she died when I was little."

"I'm sorry to hear that," Lincoln said. "Just how old were you when you lost her?"

"I was nine when she died," Andy answered, "but I was just five when she first got consumption and I had to go live with my grandparents."

"That is quite a coincidence, Andy, for my mother also died when I was nine," Lincoln said, leaning forward. "She wasn't sick but a week. She died of milk sickness."

"What's milk sickness?" Andy asked. "I never heard of that."

"It's something that a person gets from drinking milk from a cow that has eaten poison plants," Lincoln explained. "A lot of people in our community got it at the same time."

"That must have been awful," Andy said, and then asked tentatively, "Tell me something; did you pray for her not to die?"

"Yes, I prayed for her," the President said, "and my papa prayed for her, my sister prayed for her, and our whole community prayed for her."

"I prayed for my mama every day for four years but she still died," Andy said. "Why is it, you think, that God didn't heal either one of our mothers?"

"A lot of people think they understand God, but I'm not one of them," Lincoln said. "I've prayed for a lot of things that I didn't receive. I've recently come to the conclusion that sometimes I wasn't praying correctly."

"What do you mean?" Andy asked. "How can you pray wrong?"

"Let me tell you a little story," Lincoln said. "Shortly after the rebellion broke out, a man asked me how I expected to win a war with the South since Jefferson Davis was a praying man. You may already know this, both Jefferson Davis and Robert E. Lee are big time Episcopalians and I'm just a backwoods Baptist so most folks think that those two have a direct line to God and I don't. What I then asked the man was, how did he know that I was not a praying man, too. Then he asked me how I thought God would decide who would win the war if Jefferson Davis and I were both petitioning Him to be on our side. I told him that I would never pray for God to be on my side. 'Then what on earth do you pray for?' he asked. What I always pray for, I told him, is that I'm on God's side, for He is always on the side of right."

"Does that mean you think that God was right when He let our mothers die?" Andy asked, skeptically.

"I don't know that I would say it that way," Lincoln said, "but I don't question God any more. It is His job to see that justice and right ultimately prevail and our job is to do our best as we see it."

"Were you there with your mother when she died?" Andy

asked. "I didn't get to see Mama right before she died because I was at my grandpa's."

"Yes I was, Andy, I was right there," Lincoln said as tears began welling up in his sad, sunken eyes. "She wanted me there to hold her hand. I was there with my papa and sister when she died."

"I wish I could have been with my mama," Andy said as he wiped his own tears on his sleeve. "Did your mama tell you anything before she died?"

"Yes, she did," Lincoln said. "She told me to be a good boy and listen to Papa. Then she told me that she would be waiting for me in Heaven."

"Do you think maybe our mama's might know each other there in Heaven?" Andy asked.

"I surely hope so," Lincoln said. "It would be a sight, wouldn't it, if they were watching us now and hearing us talking about them?"

"Boy-oh-boy, it sure would," Andy responded as a smile began to shine through his tears.

"Andy," Jeremiah said when Andy joined him and they were departing the White House, "do you realize what a remarkable opportunity that was, for a boy of your age to have a private conversation with the President? And I thought you would be telling your children about just seeing him while your papa talked to him."

"Yes, I'm sure glad you made me come with you today," Andy said. "I didn't have any idea that it would turn out this way."

"What did he talk to you about?" Jeremiah asked. "Did he talk about his son, Willie, who died last February?"

"No," Andy answered. "Mostly, we talked about our mothers. Did you know that we were both nine when they died?."

"What do you think of Mr. Lincoln, now that you've met him?" Jeremiah asked. "Has your opinion of him changed any?"

"Papa, I was wrong about him," Andy said. "I think that he's probably the greatest man in the world. I just wish that everybody who hates him could have a talk with him like I did."

"I thought that might be the case," Jeremiah said in a superior, smug tone. "How many times have I tried to tell you what a good man he was but you were too hardheaded to listen? You just had to see it for yourself, didn't you?"

"I guess so, Papa," Andy said and, after a long silence,

cautiously added, "wasn't it sort of like that for you and what you thought about Negroes, until you got to know Sam?"

After another long silence, Jeremiah said, "It wasn't sort of like that, it was exactly like that. Andy, you are undoubtedly the beatin'est boy I ever saw. It seems like every time I think I'm teaching you something it turns out that I end up learning from you."

"It sounds like we're stuck with each other," Andy said as they both laughed.

On December 31, 1862, Andy was present with his father and a host of dignitaries, minus John Carlile, when President Abraham Lincoln signed the bill that called for the admission of West Virginia into the Union.

"I am signing this bill," President Lincoln said, "fully aware of the inconsistencies it presents but I have concluded that the spirit of the Constitution is being followed. The loyal people of what we will henceforth call West Virginia have been indispensable in our struggle against the rebellion. Some have called the formation of West Virginia as an act of secession. Well, if you choose to call it secession, be assured that there is a world of difference between secession against the Constitution and secession in favor of the Constitution."

Then, as he dipped the tip of his pen in the inkwell, the President continued, "Effective on June 20, 1863, West Virginia will become the thirty-fifth of these United States," and he signed the bill into law.

As the group who witnessed the signing began to disperse, President Lincoln sought out Jeremiah and Andy.

"Mr. Blake," the President said, "I don't know how much Andy told you about our conversation the other day, but we talked a great deal about our mothers. Andy, one thing that I failed to mention to you was that my mother was born in Hampshire County. Until the recent unpleasantness, I was always proud to tell folks that my mother came from Virginia. But since the rebellion I haven't felt the same pride so I stopped using that phrase. But now, Andy, that has been changed by the work of your father and other loyal citizens like him. So now, when I am telling someone about my mother I will say proudly, 'she came from WEST Virginia.'"

177

25 . . *LOSING FRIENDS*

Jeremiah and Andy left Washington in the middle of the winter, arriving in Clarksburg in late January.

"Good morning, Nate," Jeremiah said as entered the office and surprised his law partner, Nathan Fletcher, "I see that my name is still on the door. Does that mean you can find something for me to do around here?"

"Hey, Robert," Fletcher yelled to his partner in the other room, "come in here and see who dropped in looking for work. Pick up the broom on your way in here, he looks like he could be trained to use one."

Jeremiah and Andy soon settled into life in Clarksburg again, the first stability that they had experienced since the day Jeremiah had tied his fortunes to John Carlile. Jeremiah rented a cottage and Andy was enrolled in school.

"What grade are you in?" Headmaster Homer Jennings asked Andy.

"I don't rightly know," Andy answered. "I haven't been in school much since I was eleven and I was in the sixth grade. But I've read a lot since then and my papa has taught me when he had time."

"Even though you will be much older than the other students, I have no choice but to start you in the seventh grade class," the headmaster said. "I will ask Mr. Tabor to evaluate you after a few days and we will determine your proper placement."

Within two weeks Andy was deemed by Mr. Tabor and the other teachers to be ready for graduation and he was placed back under the direct tutelage of Headmaster Jennings who directed his studies in preparation for college.

Jeremiah somewhat reluctantly settled back into the practice of law; writing wills, assisting in land transfers, and representing people in court. His heart, though, was still in the political arena.

He was pleased and not surprised when Arthur Boreman, who was no longer a Whig but a Republican, was elected the first governor of West Virginia and the new state government began to function in Wheeling. He thought it was a stroke of genius that President Lincoln had asked the Restored Government of Virginia Governor Francis Pierpont and his cabinet to relocate to Alexandria and continue to function as the legal government of Virginia until the end of the war, at which time they would move to Richmond.

The war news often put Jeremiah into his dark periods. He took no joy from the fact that his boyhood friend, T. J., had become the notorious "Stonewall" Jackson, the most famous rebel general besides Robert E. Lee. He had closely followed Jackson's exploits throughout the war and was not surprised that he was seemingly invincible in battle after battle up and down the Shenandoah Valley between Richmond and Washington.

"Andy," Jeremiah said as he got home from the law office in early May, "I just got terrible news; T. J. Jackson was shot by his own men as he rode into camp."

"He was? Why did they shoot him? Do you think somebody shot him on purpose?" Andy asked, remembering the looks the cadets gave Jackson and the cadet who had tried to drop a brick on him at Virginia Military Institute.

"I don't suppose anyone will ever know, for sure," Jeremiah said. "The news report said that he was mistaken for the enemy."

"I'd think that would be pretty hard to do," Andy said, "considering his uniform and decorations, to say nothing about his odd quirks. He probably had his arm sticking up in the air. I don't see why they couldn't recognize either him or his horse?"

"I don't have answers to any of that," Jeremiah said. "I know that he drove his men hard and I remember him telling us that he expected his men to be as fearless in battle as he was. But what we need to do now is to pray for his recovery. I still have hopes of seeing him after the war and being able to bring about a reconciliation between him and his family, especially his sister, Laura Ann."

Once again, Jeremiah's prayers were not answered. In a few days the news was heralded across the entire country, both North and South; the great rebel general, Thomas J. "Stonewall" Jackson was dead.

Jeremiah was devastated. He had no doubt that his friend had made a wrong decision but he had never considered that their friendship would not be resumed after the war and that T. J. would eventually see that, although he was a valiant warrior, he was fighting for an ignoble cause.

The only thing that Jeremiah could think about doing to commemorate Jackson's death was to go and be with Laura Ann.

He and Andy left Clarksburg immediately and, after leaving Andy with his grandparents at Melford Creek, Jeremiah rode straight to Laura Ann's home in Beverly. When he got in sight of her house he saw that there was a great deal of activity which did not surprise him as he assumed that her neighbors were rallying around her during her time of sorrow. When he got closer, though, he realized that the people here were not neighbors, they were military personnel, mostly wounded Union soldiers.

"Jeremiah Blake," Laura Ann said as she came to the door, "it's good to see you. Whatever brings you here today?"

"I am so sorry that you have lost your brother," Jeremiah said, "and I just wanted to see you and share in your grief."

"Let's go out to the back yard where we can sit down and talk," Laura Ann said. "There are so many soldiers in here and they are making so much noise that I can't hear myself think."

After they sat down on a bench in the back yard, away from the groans and foul odors of the wounded, Laura Ann said stonily, "Jeremiah, you have wasted your time if you came to help me grieve. I don't have time to grieve. I have too much to do taking care of the wounded."

"But you must take time to grieve," Jeremiah said. "You and T. J. were the closest brother and sister I ever knew. He loved you like no one else in the world."

"I know that he did, once," Laura Ann said, "but he changed. I blame it on his two wives and their families. Once he got married, he forgot about his own family and did everything to please them. Do you know they even got him to join the Presbyterian Church?"

"Yes, he told me all about that," Jeremiah said. "I think he had a real conversion, though, and it was based more on his own study of the Bible than on their Presbyterian teaching. He told me that he didn't accept their position on predestination."

"You might be right about that," Laura Ann conceded, "but I will go to my grave believing that they were responsible for him joining in the rebellion against the government. Our family always supported the Union but especially after he got mixed up with Mary Anna and her family he changed. I wrote him at the time of the Richmond vote on secession and begged him to do what his friend William Sherman, did. You knew that they fought together in the Mexican War, didn't you? Did you know that the day the state of Louisiana voted to secede, General Sherman resigned his position as head of the military academy at Baton Rouge and headed north to take his rightful place in the army of his country?"

"I told T. J. that if he took the side of the rebels I would never speak to him again, and I didn't," she said bitterly.

"His belief was that he owed his allegiance to his commanding officer," Jeremiah said. "He told me that he favored keeping the Union in tact but he was under the command of Governor Letcher and would follow his orders."

"I know that was how he explained it," Laura Ann said. "He wrote me that same cock and bull story, but if he had really believed in the Union, then he would have known that Letcher was committing treason and he would not have had any part of it."

"Is that why you are caring for wounded soldiers?" Jeremiah asked.

"Yes, I think it is," Laura Ann responded as she started to cry. "Although, as you said, we loved each other so much, I have been so angry and ashamed that he would fight a war of rebellion against our country that I felt obliged to do something. I couldn't join the army and fight against him so I am doing all I can in this way."

By this time Laura Ann was sobbing. She soon got her emotions under control and said, "I was determined not to cry about T. J.'s death because I just knew that it was going to happen and I thought that his dying might be God's way to shorten the war so there would be fewer men killed and wounded. But then you come here, Jeremiah Blake, and you remind me of the days gone by when T. J. and I were close and, now look at me, I am a blubbering mess."

"Laura Ann, I will not apologize for reminding you of your love for your brother, regardless of the decision he made," Jeremiah said.

"Did you know that they amputated T. J.'s left arm before he died?" Laura Ann asked, still crying. "Do you remember how concerned he always was about having a strong left arm?"

"I sure do remember that," Jeremiah said. "The first day I met him, he showed me how he could skip a rock left handed. When I visited him in Lexington he reviewed the cadets holding his left arm in the air. It must have been a terrible blow to him to lose that arm."

"I just think it is the most ironic thing I ever heard of," Laura Ann said.

"Laura Ann, I know that he disappointed you," Jeremiah ventured, "but I still think it's right and natural for you to grieve his passing. I know that he would have grieved yours if you had gone first."

"You're right, of course," she responded through her tears, "but it is going to take me a long time to forgive him for what he did."

"I understand that," Jeremiah said, "and I'm pleased to hear you use the word 'forgive,' because that's what you know you have to do. I fully expect to meet him again when I get to Heaven and you should, too," and then ventured slyly, "even if he did become a Presbyterian. Surely a few of them will get in."

"Jeremiah, I don't know whether to laugh or cry," Laura Ann said, softening her tone. "If you're right, maybe the three of us can sit down together there and straighten all this out."

"That gives us something to look forward to," Jeremiah said and then bid his friend farewell.

When Jeremiah got back to his parent's place he found that Andy had easily slipped back into life there. He had spent that day once again under the watchful eye of Grandpa Abe, working side-by-side with Sam caring for the animals and putting in the crops. He was also being thoroughly spoiled by Grandma Sally who was catering to his every whim and cooking all of his favorite foods.

"How did you find Laura Ann, Son?" Abe asked, as they all settled down on the front porch.

"She's every bit as tough as her brother was," Jeremiah said. "She has turned her house into a hospital for wounded soldiers and refuses to take any time out to grieve T. J.'s death. She said that she refused to have any contact with him after he joined the rebellion, but I could tell she was hurting on the inside over his death."

"He was a good boy, T. J. was," Abe said. "I remember what a hard worker he was at the mill. It's good that he found the Lord when he did and I'm glad that he wanted me to know about it. Maybe I had a little part in that."

"I think you did, Papa," Jeremiah said. "I'm sure that's why he wanted you to know it."

"Any late news from Joshua?" Jeremiah asked.

"We haven't heard anything since that letter we got from him last week that we already told you about," Sally said. "I worry so much about him, I don't see why this awful war had to happen, anyway."

"Sam," Jeremiah said, "how do you think you will feel as a free man? You do know, don't you, that on June the twentieth, when West Virginia becomes a state, you'll be a free man?"

"Yessa, I know that," Sam said, "but I don't know what all that means. I'll still be black and I know that as long as I'm black I can't be no citizen, so you tell me what it means?"

"It means that the Constitution has to be changed to make you a citizen," Jeremiah said, "and Senator Willey and a lot of other people in Congress are already working on it."

"President Lincoln has said that the slaves in the rebel states are free, too," Abe said. "Now, supposin' the Union does win this war and they are, then, truly free, what happens to the slaves in the other states?"

"Slavery will soon be over in the entire country, I am confident," Jeremiah said. "I think that the constitutional amendment that will make Sam a citizen will also free the slaves in the Union states."

"What do you s'pose is to happen to us black folks, Mista' Blake?" a concerned Sam asked. "Where we s'posed to live and what we gonna do for a livin'?"

"That is a very difficult question, Sam, and I don't have a good answer," Jeremiah said. "President Lincoln has talked of the United

States buying land in Central America and moving the Negroes there but I don't know if that will happen or not. One thing is certain, though, the big plantation owners will need labor to keep their places going so they'll have to hire workers. Maybe a lot of freed slaves can go to work where they want to and get paid for their work."

"I been worried about Mama and Jubal," Sam said, "but maybe Ms. Hatcher will keep 'em on there at her boardin' house. I don't see how she could run it without 'em. One thing I'm lookin' to do soon as the war's over is to go see about Mama."

"You might even find yourself a wife while you are down there," Sally said, smiling.

"No ma'am, Ms. Sally, I ain't about to marry no girl from down there," Sam said.

"Why is that, Sam?" Sally asked.

"I figure Mista' Jeremiah knows why and so does Andy, don't you?" Sam said, embarrassedly.

"I'm not sure what you mean," Jeremiah said.

"Me neither," Andy added.

"Well," Sam explained, "I been told that my papa's a man by name of Big Henry who was used to father children by lots of slave women. I'd be afraid that anyone I was to marry from down there might be my half sister."

"Oh, dear," Sally said, stunned. "I had no idea. Sam, please forgive me for teasing you like that."

"That's fine, Ms. Sally," Sam said, "I know you meant well and I'm 'shamed that you had to know about my situation."

Once back in Clarksburg, Jeremiah kept up his habit of poring through the war news, following every campaign and battle and keeping track of the ever-mounting casualties. He continued to be sickened as he watched the toll of thousands of dead young men grow into the tens of thousands and then, unbelievably, into the hundreds of thousands.

What proved to be even harder for him to deal with were the names that he would find as he searched the lists of the war dead. He felt complete devastation and anguish when he saw the name, William Sharpe, Jr. on the casualty list. Little Will, the kind Baptist pastor's son from Bethany. His heart was broken as he wrote a message of sympathy to Will and Rowena.

184

Not one of the Hendry boys, Jeremiah agonized, when he saw the name of Jacob, the little boy he had seen hiding behind his mother's skirt when he last visited Amos and Bessie's family.

The next familiar name he found was that of Seth Sharpe, Pastor Will and Rowena's second child. As far as Jeremiah knew, the Sharpe's only had two children and now they were both claimed by this terrible war.

Jeremiah was now in his darkest period since the death of his wife, Elizabeth, but the shocks were not over. Scanning the latest list in early July he spotted a name that made his blood run cold; the name was Jeremiah Tompkins.

It was days before Jeremiah could recover from his depression sufficiently to try to write a message of condolence to Lizzie and Eldon over the loss of their first son, the one that Jeremiah knew had been named for him.

26 THE WAR HITS HOME

In early November, Jeremiah received a letter from his mother with the terrible news that his brother, Joshua, had been wounded in a battle at Droop Mountain and that Abe was trying to find out where he was.

"Andy, pack some things, we are going down to Melford Creek," Jeremiah announced to Andy the minute he arrived at home. "Your Uncle Joshua has been wounded and we need to help your grandpa find him and bring him home."

"What's the latest word you have about Joshua?" Jeremiah asked as he entered the front door of his parent's home.

"All we know is that he was shot in the leg," Abe said, "and they are trying to get him and our other Harrison County boys as close to home as they can to treat 'em."

"Do you think they will bring them as far north as Beverly?" Jeremiah asked. "If they do, they may be treated at Laura Ann's place. In any case, that would be a good place to start for it's not too far out of the way toward Droop Mountain and she would know something if anybody did."

"Who do you think ought to go?" Abe asked.

"I think that you and me and Sam should go," Jeremiah said.

"What about me?" Andy asked, anxiously. "I want to go, too."

"You need to stay here to look after your grandma and take care of the livestock," Jeremiah said. "I don't want you to be out there where you might get hurt."

After quieting Andy's protests and trying to assure the tearful Sally that they would be all right, the three men mounted their horses and waved to Sally and Andy as they headed east.

"Brother Blake, it is so good to see you again," Laura Ann said as she embraced the aging preacher. "What's it been, ten or fifteen years since I last saw you? What brings you all the way over here?"

"I'm lookin' for my boy," Abe said in an emotional voice. "Joshua's been shot and we're out lookin' for him. Jeremiah thought that you might be able to help us locate him."

"You don't mean little Joshua, do you?" Laura Ann said. "I remember when you used to bring him with you down to the mill. Surely he isn't old enough to be in the army."

"He was wounded at Droop Mountain, down in Pocahontas County," Jeremiah explained. "We were thinking that they might be brought back this way for treatment."

"That might be," Laura Ann said. "I was told to expect a new batch tomorrow but I didn't ask where they were coming from. You're welcome to wait here and see if he is one of them."

"I don't know what else to do, do you Jeremiah?" Abe asked.

"No I don't, Papa," Jeremiah said. "Let's just stay here and see."

The men unsaddled their horses and released them in the field behind Laura Ann's house where she had directed them and returned to the back yard where she and her husband joined them.

"Laura Ann," Jeremiah said before they sat down, "I want you and Jonathan to meet our friend, Sam. Sam, let me present Mr. and Mrs. Jonathan Arnold."

"I'm pleased to meet you," Laura Ann said, and asked when she extended her hand, "do you have a last name, Sam?"

"No ma'am, I don't," Sam answered. "Not yet I don't, but I been ponderin' that a lot lately."

"I am so proud that West Virginia was admitted as a free-soil state," Laura Ann said. "One thing I don't understand, Jeremiah, was why didn't the President free all the slaves with the Emancipation Proclamation instead of just the ones in the rebel states?"

"I'm not sure, but he may have figured that there were enough Copperheads in Congress like John Carlile who supported the Union but also believed in slavery to possibly negate his proclamation," Jeremiah said. "I am sure, though, that he didn't want to stir up controversy in Missouri, Kentucky and Maryland. The last thing he would want to happen would be for those states to join the rebellion. Another possibility is that he hoped that the Negroes, once they heard that they are free, would rise up in revolt against their masters."

"What is going to happen, then, to the slaves in those Union states?" Jonathan asked.

"That is one of two big issues that has to be dealt with," Jeremiah said. "What has to happen is for the Constitution to be amended to free every slave in the country and to make all Negroes citizens of the United States. I don't know how long that will take, but it will happen."

"Sam," Laura Ann said as she shifted her attention away from Jeremiah and back to him, "you said you were thinking about a last name. Can you tell us what it might be?"

"Well, ma'am," Sam said hesitantly, "I been meanin' to talk it over with Mista' Blake and Reverend Blake before I done anything about it, but I been thinkin' about the name Samuel Blake, if they don't mind too much."

"Why, I think that's a wonderful idea, don't you, Papa?" Jeremiah said.

"Sam," Abe said, "I'd be proud if you was to take our family name. You're one of us, anyway."

The next day dragged on slowly. Morning passed and no word, then the afternoon hours passed and, still, nothing. It was in the early dusk of the fall evening when wagons began pulling in to the Arnold house.

"Where are you coming from?" Jonathan called out to the driver of the first wagon.

"We're comin' up from the south," the driver answered. "We got men from two or three places. Who you lookin' for?"

"Anyone from Droop Mountain?" Jeremiah asked.

"Yeah, I think we got two of 'em in that last wagon back there," the driver said.

Despite his age, Abe was the first to run to the last wagon. The wounded men were wrapped in heavy blankets to ward off the chill of the late fall evening. Neither of them seemed to be awake.

"Joshua, are you in there?" Abe called out in a sob-choked voice.

"Papa, where am I and what are you doing here? Am I home?" the welcome response came in a weak voice.

"You are at Laura Ann's house at Beverly and me and Jeremiah and Sam have come to get you and take you home," Abe said.

"I don't think I'm gonna make it, Papa," Joshua said. "I'm awful weak and I'm burning up. Can you get these blankets off of me?"

Jeremiah and Sam helped the driver get Joshua out of the wagon and carried him into the parlor room that held six beds. As soon as Joshua was placed on a bed, Laura Ann took over. She quickly removed the tattered leg of Joshua's blood-soaked uniform and after calling for a basin of hot water began cleaning his badly swollen, discolored limb.

"What do you think, Laura Ann?" Joshua asked. "I'm gonna die, ain't I?"

"I've seen worse than this make it," she said, in as optimistic a voice as she could muster. "There'll be a doctor here tomorrow and he'll do what he can to fix you up."

"Here, Jeremiah," she said as she handed him a large pair of scissors, "you and Sam cut the rest of his uniform off. The neighbors will have heard the racket of the wagons and they'll be coming here to help any time. We need to get him cooled off, if we can."

By the time Jeremiah and Sam had Joshua's uniform removed, one of the neighbor women was there with a basin and began washing his feverish body. The shock of the cold water cause him to rouse and open his eyes and when he saw his older brother looking down at him, he said in a barely audible voice, "Jeremiah, I want you to know that I did something for you. I helped run the last of the rebs out of your new state. The last we saw of them, they were high-tailin' it for old Virginia."

"You did that for a lot of people, Joshua," Jeremiah said. "One day you'll tell your children about the battle on Droop Mountain."

"You think so?" Joshua said, in a near delirious state. "I ain't so sure. I think you'll have to tell 'em 'cause I might not make it."

"That won't be easy, if you're not here to have them," Jeremiah said, in a gentle teasing voice. "You don't have a bunch of kids somewhere that I don't know about, do you?"

"I guess you're right," Joshua said, his voice fading as he was slipping back into a stupor, "all we got is Andy. You tell Andy."

"I will," Jeremiah promised.

By the time the army doctor arrived the next morning, despite the all night efforts of Laura Ann and her neighbors, two of the soldiers had died. The doctor quickly conducted cursory examinations of the remaining eleven.

"Nothing we can do for that one," the doctor said to Laura Ann at the bedside of one unconscious soldier. "He's too far-gone." As he moved on and examined Joshua, he said, "This one's in bad shape, but maybe we can save him."

"His father and brother are here," Laura Ann told the doctor. "Would you like to speak with them, they're awfully worried."

"Go get them," the doctor said matter-of-factly, "I'll need some help."

"You've got a sick boy here," the doctor told Abe when he, Jeremiah, and Sam came into Joshua's bedside. "His leg is shot up pretty bad and it looks like gangrene is setting in already. The leg's got to come off and it's going to have to be above the knee."

Jeremiah shuddered at this news and his father struggled to keep his convulsive sobs under control. As Jeremiah looked into his brother's face of horror, his knees became weak and he felt like he would pass out.

"Doctor, you were mighty blunt in giving us this information," Jeremiah said. "We need a little time to absorb it."

"I've got no time," the doctor said impatiently, "no time for absorbing bad news, no time for sympathy, no time for sorrow. I'm in the business of trying to save lives and patch them up as best I can. Now either get ready to help me or get out of the way."

"Laura Ann, bring me the whisky and get the table ready," the doctor said. "I'll need you men to help me get him on the table and hold him down during the surgery. Can you do that?"

"Can you boys do it?" Abe asked, almost hysterically. "I don't think I can."

"Yes, we'll do it, Papa," Jeremiah said, "you go out back and wait."

"Here, Joshua," Laura Ann said, "you need to drink this."

"Is that whisky?" Joshua asked, weakly. "Do I have to drink it?

I ain't never tasted whiskey in my life."

"Joshua, there is nothing wrong with you drinking this now," Laura Ann assured him. "I think maybe this is why God gave us whiskey. It will help you get through the surgery. Now, drink as much of it as you can."

Joshua gagged as he tried to gulp the whiskey.

"Just sip it, Joshua," Laura Ann said. "Just keep sipping it."

The doctor, with help from Jeremiah and Sam, got Joshua onto a pallet and they carried him into the next room where the big oak dining table had been covered with a thin pad and a sheet.

After getting Joshua placed on the table, the doctor gave his final instructions.

"Laura Ann, make sure those irons are red hot so we can cauterize the stub as soon as I amputate," he said. "And I want you to see that he keeps the wedge in his mouth so he don't bite his tongue off."

As he placed two heavy leather straps under the table and across Joshua's chest to immobilize his arms, he said, "I'll need you men to hold down both legs. It won't take long. My knife and saw are very sharp because I have to get it done in a hurry so he don't go into shock."

Jeremiah had to steel himself as he felt deathly sick watching the doctor lay out his saw and check the sharpness of his long knife. He glanced at Sam just long enough to see the look of terror on his face.

"Are you all right, Sam?" Jeremiah whispered.

"Yessa," Sam said. "Don't you worry 'bout me. I'd do anything to help keep Joshua alive."

"Joshua, be brave," Jeremiah said to his brother, his voice choked with emotion as the doctor placed a tourniquet on Joshua's muscular thigh. "You know that Papa's out there praying for you. I'd give anything if I could do this for you, little brother."

"I know you would," Joshua said, "but I'm just glad you and Sam are here with me."

When the amputation began, Jeremiah closed his eyes and pressed down with all his strength to hold the injured left leg of his brother as still as possible. It was a Herculean task, for even in his weakened, semi-drunk state, Joshua reacted to the unbearable pain with near superhuman strength. Jeremiah remembered the time that he and Lizzie had held Ben Givens down and listened to him cuss while Doc Pritchard worked on his mangled foot.

Mercifully, the injured leg was severed in less than a minute. Joshua's screams were rivaled by the wailing prayers of his father in the back yard. The doctor, seemingly deaf to the sounds of agony, quickly placed the red-hot irons on the exposed flesh, searing it to create a crust as the odor of burning flesh filled the room.

"Laura Ann, you know how to put tight wrappings over the stub," the doctor said, "and remember to loosen the tourniquet a little bit at a time to keep the blood from spurting through all at once. You boys get him back into his bed so we can get the next one in here.

A sudden chill came over Jeremiah and he shook violently as he realized that he had not loosened his grip and his fingers were imbedded in Joshua's severed leg that he was still holding. "What do I do with this, Laura Ann?" Jeremiah asked weakly as he stared at the leg.

"There's a big box on the back porch, just put it in that," she said. "Jonathan will bury it and any others we have after the doctor leaves."

27. . . *THE HOMECOMING*

Joshua teetered between life and death for the next five days.

"Thank the Lord the weather is cold," Laura Ann said to Jeremiah as they were checking Joshua's stub, "and we don't have to worry about blowflies and maggots. It was really bad here during the heat of the summer"

"I don't know how you and Jonathan are able to hold up to this," Jeremiah said. "I felt like I was going to die just dealing with one person and you take on ten or twelve at a time. How do you keep going?"

"I keep going by just thinking how much better off I am than all those young men out there fighting and dying," she said. "If you stop and think about it, they are doing it for us and the country. So I do anything I can for any of them who are wounded, for I know that I'm in debt to them."

On the sixth day, Joshua's fever finally broke.

"Somebody get me a blanket," were his first coherent words since the amputation. "I'm cold."

"What a welcome sound," Laura Ann said, triumphantly. "Joshua Blake, you are going to make it."

"Not unless you get me a blanket," Joshua said through his chattering teeth. "If you don't, I'm gonna freeze to death."

"He's going to need to stay here for another week," Laura Ann told Abe the next day when Joshua was feeling better and beginning to take some food. "He should be strong enough to travel by the end of next week. You men can go on home and come back then with a wagon to take him home in."

Sally was beside herself with worry as she anxiously awaited their return. When she saw them riding up the road she and Andy ran to meet them.

"Where's Joshua?" Sally demanded. "Where's my baby boy? Did you find him? Is he dead?"

"No, thank the Lord, he ain't dead," Abe told his wife. "We found him where Jeremiah allowed we would, at Laura Ann's place."

"Where is he now?" the frantic mother asked. "Is he going to be all right?"

"You tell her, Son," Abe said as he began to sob.

"He's still at Laura Ann's, Mama," Jeremiah said. "His leg was damaged so bad it had to be taken off and he won't be ready to travel for a few days, yet. She's taking good care of him."

"Oh, my poor baby boy," Sally wailed. "What will become of him now? How will he get along with just one leg?"

"Mama, if we take a good look at all that's going on with this war," Jeremiah said, "we have to recognize that Joshua is one of the fortunate ones. While we were there, we watched seven soldiers die. One of the ones who is going to live had to have both of his legs removed."

"Sally," Abe said, as he struggled to regain his composure, "when it looked like we were going to lose our boy, I didn't think one minute about what shape he would be in, I just prayed all week that God would spare his life. I was willing to take him no matter what condition he was in."

Jeremiah took Sam and Andy with him the next week when he went to bring Joshua home. Jeremiah was anxious to introduce his teenaged son who was nearly as tall as he to his long time friend, Laura Ann.

"This is your boy?" Laura Ann said, feigning incredulity. "He can't be your boy because he is so much better looking than you were when you were his age," she teased.

"He's fortunate that he takes after his mother," Jeremiah responded.

"Andy, I remember the first time I ever saw your father," Laura Ann said in a confidential tone. "I was eleven years old and I was sure, despite what I just said about him, that your father was the handsomest boy I had ever seen. I wouldn't want my husband to hear this, but I told my brother, T. J., that I just might marry that boy some day."

Anxious to change the subject, Jeremiah asked, "How is Joshua? Is he able to travel?"

"I think he can travel as long as you are careful not to jolt or jar him too much," Laura Ann said. "Let's go in and see what he thinks about going home."

"Hey, Andy," Joshua said when they entered the room, "am I glad to see you. I hoped you would come with them to get me."

Andy rushed to his uncle's bedside and gave him an emotional embrace. "I guess you've had an awful rough time of it," Andy said. "I don't know how you stood it."

"I don't know either," Joshua said. "I was sure that my time had come and I was gonna die, but I didn't, so now I'm gonna have to learn how to live again. Maybe you can help me."

"I'd be proud to," Andy replied.

"Joshua, you a lot lighter than you was the last time we lifted you," Sam said as he and Jeremiah carried the pallet out to the wagon.

"Maybe that's because Laura Ann wouldn't feed me," Joshua joked, and then added solemnly, "or maybe it's that big leg I'm leaving behind."

"Oh, Mista' Joshua," Sam pleaded, "forgive me for sayin' what I did. I'd never make light of you losin' your leg. That's the last thing I'd do."

"I know that, Sam," Joshua said. "I didn't misunderstand you, but I can't get that leg off of my mind. You'll think I'm crazy, but I can still feel it. Sometimes it itches and I reach to scratch it and it ain't there. I can even feel like I'm wiggling my toes."

"Other people who have lost limbs have experienced the same thing," Jeremiah said as they were easing Joshua onto the makeshift bed that Sally had prepared in the wagon. "I've heard it called having a 'phantom' limb."

"Well, I've sure got me one," Joshua said. "How long do you think I'll keep it?"

"That I don't know," Jeremiah answered.

The trip home took all afternoon. Sam drove the wagon and Jeremiah and Andy sat and talked with Joshua.

"What was it like, being in the war?" Andy asked.

"Sometimes it wasn't too bad," Joshua answered. "I kinda liked the marching and setting up camp and sleeping under the stars, but the fighting was worse than anything I'd ever imagined. I won't even try to tell you about it, it was so awful."

"Where all did you go?" Jeremiah asked, trying to change the subject.

"The farthest we got was when we set up camp down on New River," Joshua said.

"Were you at Richmond Falls, where Sam Richmond has a mill?" Jeremiah asked.

"Yeah, that was the place," Joshua responded. "How do you know about that?"

"We all spent the night there on our way back from Richmond," Jeremiah explained, "me and Sam and Andy. Sam Richmond is a good friend of John Carlile."

"I didn't know none of that," Joshua said. "All I know is, that after we left there we did the dumbest thing I ever saw. We went up on the mountain and burned down a church and then the whole little town."

"What town was that?" Jeremiah asked.

"It had a funny name, Jumping Creek, or something like that," Joshua said. "I remember the name of the church was the Bluestone Baptist Church. I thought that was a pretty name for a church."

"That was Jumping Branch," Jeremiah nearly yelled out. "That was where Sam Richmond said that a man lived that was leading the rebellion in that area. What was his name, Andy?"

"It was Jeff something or other," Andy said. "It wasn't Jeff Davis, for sure, but something like that."

"Yeah, I remember now," Jeremiah said, "it was Jeff Bennett and Sam said that one of them might end up killing the other one before the rebellion was settled."

"So you think maybe we burned down that little town because Sam Richmond wanted us to?" Joshua asked.

"I don't know," Jeremiah said, "but why else would you have done it? Did you do anything else there? Were any of the people there killed?"

"No, the people just ran into the woods and nobody bothered them," Joshua said. "Some of the soldiers started shooting at any animals they saw. They shot a bunch of horses and cows and just left them laying there to die."

"That's strange," Jeremiah said. "I can't think of any earthly reason for such a raid unless it was a vendetta. If it was, I can only imagine what Jeff Bennett might do if he thinks that his sworn enemy was behind all this?"

It was a heart-wrenching homecoming when Sam drove the wagon into the front gate at the Blake farm. Abe and Sally were joined by Rebecca and Rachel and their children, all anxiously awaiting Joshua's return. Rebecca and Rachel were equally anxious to hear from Joshua about the welfare of their husbands who were serving in the same militia with their brother.

"Joshua, Honey, how are you? Let me look at you," Sally said through her tears as she tried to reach over the side of the wagon and embrace her youngest child.

"I'm doin' pretty good, Mama," Joshua said. "Leastwise I'm doin' a lot better than I was a week or so ago."

"You boys hurry and get him in the house," Sally ordered. "I've got a bed fixed up for him in the front room. Ya'll be extra careful and don't hurt him, now."

Once Joshua was placed safely in the bed and had eaten his fill of his mother's cooking, he was too tired to enjoy the fawning of his mother and sisters and within a few minutes after eating he was asleep.

"Sam, do you think you can take care of things here if we go back to Clarksburg?" Jeremiah asked the next morning at breakfast.

"I reckon I can," Sam answered. "Just as long as Reverend Blake keeps on doin' his part," he added with a smile.

"I'm sure Papa will help you out a lot," Jeremiah said, "even if it's just telling you what you're doing wrong, won't you Papa."

"We'll manage somehow," Abe answered, "but you don't need to be in such a big hurry to leave. Why don't you stay a few more days?"

"I'm sure my work is piling up there," Jeremiah said, "and Andy needs to get back to his studies if he is going to start college next fall. We'll try to come and see about you around Christmas."

28 *THE NATION SURVIVES*

"The proposition that we will be debating tonight is this," Rev. Daniel Hayes said as he opened the December, 1863, meeting of the Union Debating Society, "the tide has turned in the war. Because General Grant had successfully secured the Mississippi and cut the rebels in half and Lee was defeated at Gettysburg, the war will be over within six months. The rebel leaders can read the handwriting on the wall and will sue for peace rather than continue the bloodshed."

Chairman Hayes' opening statement led to a spirited evening as the members agreed and disagreed, sometimes strongly, with his premise.

Before the meeting ended, Rev. Hayes said, "I am glad to see Jeremiah Blake here with us tonight. We have missed you when your duties have prevented you from being here. You have been very quiet tonight. Do you have any words to share with us?"

"Thank you, Dan," Jeremiah said as he stood to address the group, "I have just returned from my parent's where I helped find my baby brother who was wounded at Droop Mountain and brought him home."

Jeremiah recounted, briefly, the ordeal and concluded with, "As Joshua was lying wounded, feverish, and expecting to die, he told me that he was proud of one thing. He said that he was proud that he had helped chase the last of the rebels out of our new state, West Virginia."

Following the outburst of shouts of agreement and applause that were precipitated by Jeremiah's closing statement, Rev. Hayes concluded the meeting by saying, "We are thankful to God that your brother survived his injury. Please relate to him that our gratitude to him for his sacrifice knows no bounds. It is because of him and others like him that we have hope that our country will once again be whole and we will see justice prevail."

Jeremiah was surprised the next day to receive a letter from John Carlile. He had not seen nor had any contact with the Senator since the meeting in President Lincoln's office nearly a year earlier when they had discussed the new state legislation with the President.

"I am saddened to inform you," Carlile's letter said, "that our mutual friend, Sam Richmond, has been killed. He was shot while on his ferry by an unknown gunman who fired from the nearby woods. It is my opinion that Mr. Richmond was probably killed by a cowardly rebel sympathizer who sees that their cause is lost. He was a good personal friend and a great friend of the Union. I consider him a martyr to the cause."

John might be right, Jeremiah thought, or he might be very wrong. Maybe he was killed for his beliefs, as John supposed, or maybe he was killed because someone believed that he had something to do with the raid on the little community of Jumping Branch. Sam Richmond had said that the differences between him and Jeff Bennett would likely end with one of them killing the other, but if Bennett was going to kill him over his support of the Union, he could have done it sooner.

The timing of Sam Richmond's death raised strong suspicions in Jeremiah's mind that Jeff Bennett or someone else from the little mountain town of Jumping Branch might have done the shooting, seeking revenge for the raid on their town.

It was difficult for Jeremiah to concentrate on his work in the midst of the turbulence caused by the war. He and Andy braved the January cold to return to Melford Creek for the funeral of Rachel's husband, James Burns, who died of pneumonia which he contacted in one of the overcrowded sick bay areas where he was being treated for a minor wound.

Daniel Hayes' predictions of an early end to the war were not coming to pass. Although Jeremiah agreed with Hayes that a Union victory appeared now to be inevitable, he did not believe that the rebels would surrender easily, even if faced with that inevitability. He remembered the fervor of the radicals who came into Richmond and intimidated even the governor. He remembered the sermons he had heard in Richmond from preachers who believed whole-heartedly that the way of the South, with its institution of slavery, was ordained of God and that they could never be part of a country governed by that infidel, Abraham Lincoln.

Evidently President Lincoln was of the same mind as Jeremiah, for in the spring of 1864, he made yet another change in the military, replacing General George Meade, the hero of Gettysburg, with Ulysses S. Grant, the blunt, tough warrior who had been so successful in the western campaigns. Grant, who had cut the rebels in half by controlling the Mississippi River, separating the east from the west, had made plans to cut the eastern rebel states in half again by fighting a diagonal line from the Mississippi at Chattanooga through Atlanta and on to the Atlantic Ocean at Charleston. When he was summoned to Washington by the President, Grant left the western army under the command of his assistant, General William Sherman, to carry out his planned "march to the sea."

As soon as Grant took command of the Union forces, unlike his predecessors, he took full advantage of his superior manpower and equipment in engaging General Lee. While General Sherman was carrying out a "scorched earth" policy in the "march to the sea" campaign, Grant used similar tactics for the next year as he pursued Lee down the Shenandoah Valley to Richmond, then to Petersburg, and finally surrounded him at Appomattox.

Grant met with Lee at Appomattox Court House where he, with the full approval of President Lincoln, presented Lee with the most compassionate of peace offerings which Lee readily accepted. In exchange for simply signing a pledge not to again take up arms against the federal government, the rebel soldiers were free to go home.

Confederate President Jefferson Davis, accompanied by his closest advisors including former United States Vice President John Breckinridge, fled Virginia and ordered the remaining rebel generals to continue fighting.

When General Sherman captured General Joseph Johnson and his troops he, like Grant had provided Lee, granted the captured general and his forces a magnanimous peace.

Jefferson Davis and his entourage continued to flee from place to place throughout the South, ordering remaining rebel forces to continue fighting, until he was finally captured while trying to escape disguised in one of his wife's dresses and a sunbonnet.

The celebrations that marked the end of the war were bittersweet to Jeremiah. He could celebrate that the country had been preserved and he was thankful that the slaves in the states which had rebelled were now free. He was heartened to hear that Governor Francis Pierpont had already moved from Alexandria to Richmond and had assumed full executive leadership in Virginia. But despite all of these positive things, Jeremiah has difficulty balancing them with the terrible price that had been paid.

More than six hundred thousand men had lost their lives in the war, including scores of his dear loved ones. More than a million, like his brother, Joshua, had survived but returned home permanently crippled. The scorched earth policy had left thousands of farms and plantations in ruins with homes and buildings destroyed and livestock killed or scattered.

If one third of the soldiers killed in the war were married, he thought, then there are must be as many as two hundred thousand widows like his sister, Rachel, left alone to raise children and manage a farm without the help of a husband.

He was glad that Sam, the slave he helped escape from Virginia, could now begin a new life with the help of friends. But he worried about the plight of the nearly four million other former slaves who had been set free without any plan for their future knowing that the vast majority of them, unlike Sam, were not surrounded by friends who wanted to help them.

The news a few days later put Jeremiah into even deeper depression.

"Andy, I have just received the most terrible news," Jeremiah said, "President Abraham Lincoln has been shot."

"Is he dead? Will he live?" Andy asked, frantically. "Do they know who did it?"

"I don't know if he will live or not, we can only pray that he does," Jeremiah said. "It was evidently done as part of a plot by a bunch of diehard rebels. An actor shot the President at the theater. At the same time, another man broke into Secretary Seward's house and tried to shoot him but his gun wouldn't fire so he stabbed Mr.

Seward and his son and they both may die. When Mrs. Seward, at their home in Auburn, New York, was told of it, she died of shock. Apparently, the third man who was to kill Vice President Johnson lost his nerve. He had his gun pointed at Johnson at close range but didn't pull the trigger."

A few days later the good news was that Secretary Seward and his son would live but then, the final, ultimate bad news arrived; President Abraham Lincoln was dead.

29 *THE AFTERMATH OF WAR*

"Andy, do you think that you can get ready to head off to college by yourself?" Jeremiah asked his son. "The war, the death of so many friends, Joshua's injury, and now the assassination of the President has taken me down so low that I can't even concentrate on work anymore. I'm thinking about loading up the wagon and going all the way back to Richmond just to see how things are. I'd like to go by way of New River to see if I could find out anything about the Sam Richmond thing and I want to pay my respects to T. J. Jackson's widow. I want to go through Lexington so I can visit her and go to his grave."

"That sounds fine to me, but only if I can go with you," Andy responded. "I've been laying off to ask you something, anyway. Would it hurt your feelings if I didn't go to Bethany College like you did?"

"No, I suppose not," Jeremiah said hesitantly. "What do you have in mind if you don't go to Bethany?"

"If I wait a year, I could go to the new Land Grant College up at Morgantown if they get it ready to open next year," Andy said. "That would be closer to Clarksburg and they're going to be offering a lot more courses there."

"Well, that sounds okay, I guess," Jeremiah said, "but I was looking forward to visiting you up at Bethany and seeing some old friends there. But I suppose nothing is keeping me from going up there anyway."

"I'd like to go there with you before I leave for college," Andy said. "Why don't we do that next spring?"

"We'll plan on it." Jeremiah said.

On the first Saturday of May, 1865, Jeremiah and Andy arrived at the family farm at Melford Creek shortly before noon, planning to spend Sunday there before departing for Richmond.

Since Joshua had returned home, they had been frequent visitors, coming to see about him as often as they could. As they arrived, Abe took notice that this time was different, instead of being on horseback they were traveling in their loaded wagon.

"What you got all that stuff on the wagon for?" Abe asked when they pulled in to the front yard. "Looks to me like you're fixing to set up housekeeping somewhere."

"Andy and I are going to backtrack our way down to Richmond and see for ourselves what the war has done," Jeremiah explained. "The summer's a slack time at the office and Andy agreed to put off going to college for another year so we can travel some."

Sunday morning, before they left for church, Sam approached Jeremiah.

"Mista' Blake," Sam said, "since you're fixin' to head for Richmond, how about me goin' with you? Now that the war's over I been figurin' that Mama and Jubal might need my help so it's 'bout time for me to be goin' home and seein' after 'em."

"Well, Sam, I understand how you feel," Jeremiah said. "I'd be worried about you going back there, though, there's going to be a lot of unhappy white folks down there."

"I know that, Mista' Blake, but I gotta chance it," Sam said determinedly. "I don't know what kind of a fix Mama might be in. You know the last we heard was that she got beat up by that man that was lookin' for me."

"Sam, I don't know how we are going to get along here without you but I've always known that, sooner or later, you'd be doing this," Abe said after church when Jeremiah told his parents of Sam's desire to go home to his mother. "You have been a true Godsend to us and we'll never forget what all you done for us. We can't repay you for your help but what I will do before you leave is to write a letter for you to carry with you in case anybody questions you. Sam, I'm gonna write down that you're a Christian man who is honest and trustworthy. I'll ask whoever reads the letter to receive you like I did, like Onesimus was received in the Bible. I figure if the person who questions you is a Christian and knows anything about the Scriptures, that might help."

"Are you planning to come back?" Jeremiah asked.

"I ain't aimin' to, 'specially if I can help Mama and Jubal," Sam said. "I know you folks here need me but I figure Mama needs me more."

Sam's departure with Jeremiah and Andy was an emotional one. Before they left, early on Monday morning, Abe gathered everyone around Sam and, placing his hands on Sam's head, prayed that God would "keep his arms of protection around Sam on his perilous journey" and that he would be a "mighty blessing" to his mother.

"Before we go, I got somethin' I want to say: Reverend Blake and Ms. Sally, livin' here with you folks on this farm in West Virginia has been my Promised Land," Sam said, expressing himself in Biblical metaphors that had been, until now, hidden deep in his personal thoughts. "Mista' Blake," he said to Jeremiah, "you was my Moses, you was the one that led me to the Promised Land. Mista' Joshua, you got the right name. You the one that now has to take over the Promised Land. It ain't gonna be easy, but you'll do it 'cause God's gonna help you."

Turning to Andy he said, "Andy, I ain't never been able to fit you in the Book of Exodus like all of the others. But what you was to me was, you was my very first white friend, and if it hadn't been for you I don't think none of the rest of it would've happened."

Then, after formal handshakes with Abe and Joshua and an embrace from Sally, Sam threw his bag onto the wagon and climbed in to begin his long journey back home.

Evidence of the war was everywhere. Fields were laying idle where there was no one to put in the crops. Stone fences had been toppled to permit the movement of troops. The chestnut rails of the zigzag fences had been used as convenient fuel for fires to keep troops warm on winter nights or to cook the livestock that they had butchered.

Without fences to contain them, horses, cows, pigs, and sheep were roaming free throughout the countryside and chickens were roosting in the trees at night.

There were piles of ashes where barns had been burned and too frequently stone chimneys stood as stark evidence of where a house had once stood. Foul odors and the swarms of buzzards circling ominously overhead gave evidence to the dead animal carcasses that were strewn about the countryside.

The most moving sight, which was also the most hopeful, was the steady stream of men in uniform returning home, weary men, some barefoot, some limping, some hobbling on makeshift crutches, some bandaged, some missing an arm, and some with a patch over a lost eye. During the first two days of their trip most, but not all, of the uniforms were Union blue. It was a common sight to see former foes, one wearing blue and the other wearing gray, trudging home side by side. By the third day as they got farther south, the balance of color had shifted and most were wearing Confederate gray.

"Papa, are we going down on New River to Sam Richmond's place?" Andy asked as they were settling in to spend the night at Fayetteville.

"I don't think so," Jeremiah replied. "I want to see the town that Joshua's unit burned. We're going to Jumping Branch."

When they arrived at the little mountain top community, they found that the people there had made a lot of progress since the raid three years earlier. Some of the houses had been rebuilt and a group of men who were too old to have served in the war were working on a good-sized building.

"Good afternoon," Jeremiah said as he stopped the wagon beside the building site. "It looks like you men have taken on quite a job. What are you building?"

"We're building our church back," one of the men said. "It got burned down when we was raided by some Yankee soldiers a couple of years ago."

"I heard about that," Jeremiah said, wondering what they would think of him if they knew that his own brother had been a part of the raid. "Why do you think they burned down everything, especially the church."

"Most folks think it was 'cause a man by the name of Jeff Bennett went to church here," another man offered. "Jeff was a big supporter of the South and we think they was trying to get him, leastways to punish him some. They set fire to the church first thing, before they burned down anything else."

"I guess they burned his house, too." Jeremiah ventured.

"No, not then they didn't, he didn't live here, he lived out that road yonder," a man said pointing. "He lived way out there on Broomstraw Ridge but I reckon they didn't know that, if he was the one they was after."

"We heard that Sam Richmond, down on New River, was killed after the raid here," Jeremiah said. "Do you think there was any connection?"

This got the complete attention of the entire work crew.

"What do you know about Sam Richmond?" Jeremiah was asked.

"I met him once, just before the war," Jeremiah answered. "He told me then about the bad blood between him and Mr. Bennett and said that one of them was liable to kill the other before the conflict was settled."

"Well, he told you right," a man said. "Now they're both dead."

"Both dead?" a surprised Jeremiah asked. "Jeff Bennett is dead, too?"

"Yeah, he's dead," the man said. "If he wasn't he'd be here workin' on the church. He was the one that got us started on it."

"What happened to him?" Jeremiah asked.

"Back in April, soon as Lee give up, they was havin' a big celebration down on the river and Jeff and his wife and kids was all set to go," a man explained. "Whilst his wife, Nancy, was packin' their lunch, Jeff was settin' on a bench in the yard there havin' a chew of tobacco when three or four Union boys come walkin' by and one of 'em just up and shot him. Nancy told me that she grabbed her kids and run to the woods with 'em, and then them Union boys burned down the house and all the outbuildings."

"Why do you think they did that?" Jeremiah asked.

"Some people figure that Jeff had something to do with Sam Richmond's shooting or maybe shot him hisself," was the answer, "and evidently Sam Richmond's boy, Tuck, was of that opinion 'cause he was the Union boy that shot Jeff."

"That's awful," Jeremiah said. "What will happen now? Has Tuck been arrested?"

"Don't look like nothing is gonna happen," a man said. "The

high sheriff says he ain't got no proof that it was Tuck that done the shootin' even though everybody knows he's the one that done it. Soon as Jeff's boy Robert got home from the war he tracked Tuck down and beat him 'til he almost killed him. He would have killed him, too, if they hadn't a pulled him off of him. Maybe it's all over now. I sure hope so."

"Wasn't it awful, what happed to Sam Richmond and Jeff Bennett?" Andy said as they headed down the mountain into the New River valley. "I liked Mr. Richmond, he seemed like a good man."

"He was a good man," Jeremiah said, "and the men there at the church certainly thought that Jeff Bennett was a good man, too. The rebellion and the war caused a lot of good people to do some terrible things. I shudder every time I think that my baby brother actually killed other boys just like himself, all because some people got it into their heads that they were more important than the Constitution."

"Do you really think that's what happened?" Andy asked.

"I've thought about it and thought about it," Jeremiah responded, "and I'm convinced that's about what it boils down to. I can't come up with any other answer."

"Do you mean it wasn't about slavery?" Andy asked.

"By the time the war was over, it was," Jeremiah replied, "but not when it started. Slavery was a festering issue but it could have bean dealt with in other ways than war. The slaves could have been bought by the government for a lot less money than the war cost and six hundred thousand young men would still be alive. No, the war started out as a test of the Constitution and the strength of the Union."

The door to the Jackson home in Lexington was opened by a black woman who asked who she should tell Madam was calling.

"Tell her it is Jeremiah Blake and I have come to pay my respects to her late husband, General Jackson," Jeremiah said.

"Mr. Blake, you are not welcome here," Mary Anna Jackson said abruptly as she entered the room. "I am sure you are here to gloat and I will not tolerate you nor any other Yankee in my home."

"Mrs. Jackson, you have misunderstood my intentions," Jeremiah tried to explain. "Although T. J. and I took different paths,

I have never stopped considering him my friend and I was greatly saddened by his death. I simply wanted to express my sympathy to you and visit his grave."

"Mr. Blake, I have no desire to hear anything you have to say and I would thank you not to desecrate a great man's resting place by your presence there," Mary Anna said, icily. "You northerners will never understand what you have done to us. You have made war against your superiors and now you have destroyed our way of life. You are not welcome here, Mr. Blake, I ask you to please leave."

30 *RICHMOND REVISITED*

"You didn't stay long," Andy said when Jeremiah returned to the wagon. "How was Mrs. Jackson?"

"She was very angry and informed me first thing that I was not welcome," Jeremiah said. "She even told me not to desecrate T. J.'s grave by visiting it."

"Do you think she's like that just because she's bitter that General Jackson was killed?" Andy wondered aloud.

"It could be, I suppose," Jeremiah said, "but I got the impression it's more than that. Mrs. Jackson was born and raised a Southern aristocrat so I'm sure that she believes that the North is nowhere near the cultural equal of the South and that the war ended up as a victory of the crude over the refined. What she said was that we had destroyed the South's way of life."

"What if everybody here feels that way?" Andy said. "If they do, we'd better be careful."

"You're exactly right and, Sam, that applies double to you," Jeremiah said. "You may be in even more danger than Andy and I. You are going to meet up with a lot of angry, disappointed men who are looking for someone to blame or take out their anger on. You could get into trouble if you just look at someone wrong."

"I know all that," Sam said. "I ain't about to cross nobody. All I'm wantin' to do is see about my mama."

The first stop in Richmond was at Mrs. Etta Hatcher's boarding house.

"Mista' Blake, would you mind goin' in first," Sam asked, "Ms. Hatcher ain't seen me since they sold me off and she sure wouldn't know me now."

"Of course," Jeremiah said as he jumped from the wagon and went to the front entrance.

"Ms. Etta, do you remember me," Jeremiah said upon his entrance into the foyer.

"Jeremiah Blake, of course I remember you?" Mrs. Hatcher said, excitedly. "Law have mercy, you're the last person I expected to see. What on earth brought you here?"

"I was brought so low by the war that I couldn't work so Andy and I just loaded the wagon and took off to survey the damage and see what was left of the country," Jeremiah explained, "and we ended up here."

"Andy's with you, is he?" Mrs. Hatcher asked. "Where is that boy? Why didn't he come in with you?"

"He's out in the wagon and we've got someone else out there," Jeremiah said. "We brought Sadie's boy, Samuel, to see him mother."

"Sadie's Samuel? You brought Sadie's Samuel?" the incredulous Mrs. Hatcher asked. "Where did you find him? Last I knew of him he had run away from the plantation down in North Carolina, where we sold him to. A man came through here looking for him four or five years ago. How did you end up with him?"

"It's a long story, Ms. Etta," Jeremiah said. "How is Sadie? Is she still here?"

"Yes, she's still here," Mrs. Hatcher said, "and she's all I've got left, such as she is. She hasn't been the same since that man looking for Samuel beat her. I think he broke some of her ribs when he was kicking her and she complains a lot, especially when the weather changes."

"What about the others? Jubal and Jesse and the girls you had?" Jeremiah asked.

"Oh, Jubal died in sixty-three," Mrs. Hatcher said, "and soon as the war was over, Jesse got himself a big job with the new governor to work in the livery over at the Capitol. I don't know where the girls went, they just took off without saying a word, after all I'd done for them. Can you believe that?"

"I'm sorry about Jubal," Jeremiah said, "and I know that Samuel and Andy will be, too. Would you like to go get Sadie while I go get the boys?"

"Samuel, Samuel, is that really you?" Sadie cried when she saw her son. "What are you doin' here? Did you come to see 'bout your old mama?"

"Yes, I did, Mama," Sam said, dwarfing his mother as he enveloped her in his strong arms, "I come to see 'bout you and Jubal."

"Oh, Honey, Jubal ain't with us no more," Sadie said. "He come down with the grippe real bad winter 'fore last and the Lord took him on home."

While Sadie and Sam were engrossed with each other, Mrs. Hatcher's attention turned to Andy.

"Andy, you're a grown man and a fine looking one, at that," she said. "How old are you now, anyway?"

"I'm seventeen," Andy answered. "I was thinking about starting college this fall but when Papa said that he wanted to come back down here I decided to come with him and start college next year."

"Do you have a room available for a few days?" Jeremiah asked. "Andy and I might like to stay here for a week or so."

"I haven't been taking any new boarders since it's only me and Sadie for it," Mrs. Hatcher said. "Besides that, the only people looking for rooms are Yankees and its not wise to provide food and shelter to any of them. The only boarders I have now are five gentlemen who have lived here for years. But, in your case I'll make an exception. Just don't tell anybody that you're a Yankee and you can even have your old room back."

After they had unloaded the wagon, Andy drove the horses into the livery stable, unhooked and unharnessed them, rubbed them down, and put out feed for them, just as he had helped Jesse do dozens of times. He thought of Jesse and resolved to find him when Jeremiah went to see the governor.

"Papa, when do you plan to go see Governor Pierpont?" Andy asked the next morning.

"I was thinking about going first thing this afternoon," Jeremiah answered.

"Good," Andy said, "I want to look around some this morning and see if I can find Billy Watson."

"You'd best be careful, Andy," his father warned. "Remember the differences you had with him when you were younger. He may be very hostile toward you now."

"I know that, but I'm still going to try to see him," Andy said.

As he strode through familiar neighborhoods of Richmond, Andy was startled by the changes that had occurred since he had left nearly five years ago. Hollow shells of buildings and piles of bricks and stone were all that was left of entire blocks of the city that had been burned during the war. The once immaculately cared-for lawns and flower gardens were, for the most part, neglected and weed infested. Many of the once white picket fences were now dingy and falling down. Houses were in need of repairs and paint. It was like the once proud city had lost its soul.

Even though Andy could imagine the strain that the war had placed on Richmond as the capital of the Confederacy, the destruction and deterioration evident in what he had once considered the most beautiful city he had ever seen was very depressing.

As he neared the familiar street where the Watson's lived, Andy became very apprehensive. What if his father was right? What if Billy's childhood prejudices had become even more hardened? Would he, like so many others, seek to exact what he deemed to be justice after the fact?

Billy's mother answered his knock on the door.

"Good morning, Mrs. Watson," Andy said. "I'm Billy's friend, or I used to be, I'm Andy Blake."

"Why Andy, I never would have known you, grown up and all," Mrs. Watson said. "Please, come in and sit down."

"I was hoping to see Billy," Andy said as he was seated on the davenport. "Does he still live here or is he anywhere around close?"

"Oh, Andy, Billy's dead," Mrs. Watson said in an emotional voice. "He died on the early this month in the army hospital. He was wounded at Petersburg on April the second, protecting General Lee as he was helping to move our capital from Richmond to Danville. He would have made it, but he got the smallpox while he was in the hospital and that's what killed him. He was wounded just a week before General Lee surrendered and then he died after the war was over and I never even got to see him."

"I am so sorry," Andy expressed, "that is such a tragedy. Billy and I were good friends."

"I know you were, Andy, but we have to take comfort from knowing that Billy is with the Lord," Mrs. Watson said, giving Andy hope that she would now relate an account of Billy's spiritual regeneration. Instead, she said, "We know that all of our boys who died in the war are in Heaven because they were fighting for a holy cause and opposing evil, don't we?"

Andy was able to grunt out something that resembled, "I suppose so," before rising to tell Mrs. Watson again how sorry he was about Billy's death and bidding her goodbye.

"Papa, I want to see if I can find Jesse instead of going with you to meet with Governor Pierpont," Andy said as they walked past more burned out blocks of Richmond on their way to the Capitol. "I doubt if the Governor would remember me anyway."

"Oh, he'd remember you, all right," Jeremiah said, "but if you want to try to find Jesse, you go ahead."

A number of blue-uniformed soldiers were patrolling the grounds around the Capitol. Jeremiah and Andy were stopped by the officer in charge and asked about their business.

"I am Jeremiah Blake and this is my son, Andrew, and we are friends of Governor Pierpont," Jeremiah explained. "I would like to call on the Governor as a matter of courtesy and my son would like to locate a friend, a Negro named Jesse, who works in the Capitol livery."

"Wait right here, Mr. Blake," the officer said, "I'm sure you understand the reason for our caution." Then he instructed one of his soldiers to inform the governor's appointment secretary of Jeremiah's request to see the Governor.

"You may go in to see the Governor now, Mr. Blake," the officer said after the soldier returned, "and your son is free to go to the livery stables."

"Mr. Blake, I'll bet you don't remember me," the young man who was the Governor's appointments secretary said as he stood and extended his hand. "I'm Noah Weatherspoon from Wheeling. I was a legislative page when the Reconstructed Government first convened there. I remember you because you were always with Senator Carlile."

"I'm sorry that I don't remember you, Noah, but that was an eternity ago," Jeremiah said. "How do you like Richmond, so far?"

"It is not the most pleasant place right now," Noah responded. "I don't know how long it will be before things here to return to normal."

"If you listen to the people here, things will never again be normal," Jeremiah said, "not to them they won't. That's what makes the Governor's job so difficult."

"Speaking of the Governor, he is anxious to see you," Noah said. "Come this way."

"Governor, thank you for seeing me," Jeremiah said as he strode across the large office to his friend behind the mahogany desk.

"Jeremiah, it is good of you to come," Governor Pierpont said as he stood to greet him. "What brings you to Richmond? I hope you're looking for a job, I could sure use you right now."

"No, I'm not looking for a job," Jeremiah answered. "It's not that I've soured on government and politics but I'm not ready to get back into it yet; maybe in a few years. I came to Richmond just to retrace my steps and see if I could make any sense out of the tragedy we have experienced. I've been so saddened by the death and suffering that took place during the war and, now, the continued hardship that the war has caused, that I couldn't yet settle back into the routine of every day life. I had to do something and my mind kept bringing me back here."

"I guess you could say, in one way, that I am fortunate in that I cannot settle back into any routine," the Governor said, "because every day brings new challenges, challenges which neither I, nor anyone else, have ever faced before."

"I have thought a lot about how difficult your task must be," Jeremiah said.

"My task would have been so much easier if we hadn't lost President Lincoln," Pierpont said. "I know what he had envisioned for the country after the war for we had discussed it many times. He really announced his intentions in his second inaugural address; 'with malice toward none' he said, and he meant it. He intended to provide full forgiveness and restored citizenship to all who were willing to lay down their arms. Now, the people who are demanding revenge have President Johnson's ear and he is already making things difficult."

"How is he doing that?" Jeremiah asked.

"Well, the first thing he did was to have Robert E. Lee indicted here in Federal Court," the Governor explained. "General Grant took care of that, though. He went straight to the President and said that he would resign from the army if the charges against Lee were not dropped."

"Does Grant still have that much power?" Jeremiah asked.

"He surely does," the Governor said. "I fully expect for him to be our next President."

"You are probably right," Jeremiah agreed.

"I think you will appreciate the problem I am working on today," the Governor said. "President Johnson has requested recommendations from a number of us on just how the country should deal with the rebels. Should they all be treated as traitors? Should they be denied citizenship and have their property confiscated? Should Jefferson Davis and the rebel governors be singled out and hanged? There are some people high up in government who are very bitter about what these people put the country through and are wanting revenge."

"I don't envy you your task, Governor," Jeremiah said. "Would you venture to tell me how you are leaning on this matter?"

"I was working on my response to the President when I was told that you were here," the Governor said. "So far, I had said that I can speak only about things here in Virginia and my priority is to help heal the wounds of the war here. What I intend to add to that is that, although the majority of Virginians were loyal to the Union until the radical element were able to force a vote to secede, by the war's end the citizens had become nearly unanimous in their support of the Confederacy. If we were to carry out an Old Testament 'eye for an eye, tooth for a tooth' strategy, punishing those now believed by the people here to be heroes, the schism between North and South would be widened even more. So I intend to ask President Johnson to use the New Testament principle of 'turning the other cheek' and granting forgiveness and full citizenship rights for the rebel soldiers and showing mercy even to the leaders of the rebellion. If we believe that secession was illegal and, thus, never occurred, then the states never ceased to be a part of the Union and the people of those states never ceased to be United States citizens. 'Mr. President,' I will say, 'I recommend that the states which sought to form an illegal Confederacy and the citizens living in those states be fully

216

restored into the United States.'"

"Have you had any personal contact with General Lee?" Jeremiah asked.

"Yes, indeed," the Governor responded, "he has come to see me frequently and has assured me of his full support. Although vanquished, he seems to now have accepted the new order of things in a remarkable way. I did not think highly of him while he was waging his fierce war against us but now I have found many things about him that I can admire."

"Will he help in healing the great chasm that now exists between North and South?" Jeremiah asked.

"Yes, I think he will," Pierpont responded. "Already when he speaks of the United States he refers to it as 'his country.' I consider that very significant. But more than that, let me tell you what happened at the Episcopal Church here only last Sunday. When the service reached the time for communion, the first person who went forward to the altar was a Negro. No one else moved and the priest just stood there, not knowing what to do. The congregation began getting noisy and sounding hostile and then it was Robert E. Lee, himself, who first stepped out and went forward to kneel beside the Negro."

"What happened then?" Jeremiah asked.

"The discontent died down and most of the congregation went forward and took communion," Pierpont said.

While Jeremiah was with the Governor, Andy was wending his way through the maze of buildings on the Capitol grounds. When he found the livery he inquired of the first person he saw, "Does a man named Jesse work here?"

"You lookin' for Jesse Hatcher?" the man asked. "Jesse Hatcher works here; you'll find him in the back stable over there."

"Jesse, I thought maybe you could use some help," Andy called out when he spotted his old friend.

"I could use some good help," Jesse responded, surprised but smiling broadly as he turned from the horse he was currying to greet Andy. "Ain't got nothin' here for no citified white boy, though. What you doin' here anyway, Masta' Andy?"

"Papa's in visiting with the Governor," Andy said, "but I said I'd rather see you than him. How long has your name been Jesse

Hatcher?"

"Ever since I come here lookin' for a job and they told me I had to have me two names," Jesse answered.

"Why did you choose Hatcher?" Andy asked.

"They wasn't much time to think and Hatcher was the only one I could come up with," Jesse said.

"You could have chosen Blake," Andy said, "Sadie's boy, Sam, did."

"Did he now?" Jesse said. "If I'd a knowed that, I surely woulda done it, then me and Samuel woulda been sorta like brothers. Jesse Blake, now that sounds good, but I think Jesse Hatcher sounds pretty good, too."

"How have things changed for you now that the war is over?" Andy asked.

"Biggest change is I get paid and I had to get my own place to live and I'm fixin' my own food," Jesse said, "leastways 'til I get married. You 'member Flora, don'tcha? She worked for Ms. Hatcher. Well, me and Flora gonna get married next month and then she'll be doin' my cookin' for me."

"Sure, I remember Flora," Andy said. "Ms. Etta said that she didn't know what happened to Flora or the other girls. She said they just took off."

"They was like me, able to get jobs that paid more than Ms. Hatcher would. They all workin' in that big hotel over there," Jesse said, pointing to a building still standing in the center of the city.

Jeremiah and Andy stayed in Richmond less than a week. Jeremiah realized that he would not, could not, find the peace he sought here, nor anywhere else, for that matter. He was, however, heartened by his visit with Governor Pierpont, realizing that this good man was going to do all that was in his power to ease the hatred and suffering that was on every hand.

Leaving Sam was difficult but necessary. For the first time since he had been sold as a youngster, Sam and Sadie, his mother, could be together. As Andy watched them get reacquainted and revel in their love for each other, he wondered about the mother and little boy he had seen separated at the slave auction he had witnessed. He silently asked God to reunite that mother and child as He had now reunited Sadie and Sam.

218

31 *BACK TO BETHANY*

As the spring of 1866 arrived and Jeremiah and Andy were planning their trip to Bethany, Jeremiah's mind kept drifting back to an earlier time, when he was a naive sixteen year old, excited about learning and experiencing life on his own. He knew that he could not fully transmit his nostalgic feelings to his son but he was pleased that Andy wanted to accompany him on his pilgrimage.

On the first day of May, they set out. The visit with Amos and Bessie Hendry in Old Hundred was bittersweet. The Hendry's were happy to see Jeremiah again and get acquainted with Andy, but a pall was on the occasion because of the loss of their son, Jacob, in the war. Time had not been kind to Amos, either. No longer able to do the heavy lifting and hammering required of a blacksmith, he had turned the shop over to his oldest son, Jonas. The years of hard work had left him stooped and looking even older than his fifty-nine years. The most pleasant part of the visit was listening to Bessie tell about the lives of their children and grandchildren.

Jeremiah was disappointed when they arrived in Bethany to learn that Rev. Will Sharpe and his wife, Rowena, no longer lived there. After their two sons were killed, the current pastor of the Baptist Church told him, Will accepted a call to a church in Pennsylvania. "He was a broken man," was the way the pastor described Will.

As they drove past Bethany College, Jeremiah pointed out the building where he had attended classes and listened to the great lectures of Alexander Campbell. Near the old building a new, much larger edifice was under construction.

"We'll stop at the college before we leave Bethany," Jeremiah said, "but first I want to go to see the Givenses."

Jeremiah's heart began to race as they rode the three miles from Bethany to the Givens farm. Andy noticed that his father was quieter now than he had been on any other portion of the trip. What Andy could not know were the thoughts that were whirling around in his father's mind.

Jeremiah was recalling the first time he had come this way, riding ol' Molly and accompanied by the helpful young preacher, Will Sharpe. He remembered his day after day travels over this road during his years at Bethany College. The one reminiscence that dominated his thoughts, though, was the day that he and Lizzie were returning on the milk wagon from their deliveries and Lizzie had grabbed his face and kissed him. For many years that day and event had resided only in the deep recesses of his mind, but today, being here at the scene where it had happened, the memory was suddenly overwhelming.

As they drove the wagon into the yard, Jeremiah saw an old man sitting on the porch that he knew must be Ben Givens. When he saw him stand up, supporting himself with a cane, he knew for sure it was Ben.

"I'm looking for a place to live while I go to Alexander Campbell's college," Jeremiah yelled from the wagon. "Some Baptist preacher said you were the person I ought to see."

"Jennie, get yourself out here and look who musta broke outta jail," Ben said, recognizing Jeremiah immediately.

"Jeremiah, I just can't believe it's you," Jennie exulted as she started hugging Jeremiah while he was still shaking hands with Ben. Jeremiah was surprised at the strength of this woman who had to be in her seventies. "This here must be your boy, Andrew, that you wrote us about," Jenny said as she sized up Andy, "My, ain't he a fine looking young man?"

"Andy," Jeremiah said, "these two people were parents to me while I was in college. One of the main reasons I'm glad you came with me is so you could meet Mr. and Mrs. Givens."

Andy was then subjected to a greeting from Jennie that was every bit as effusive as the one his father had just received, after which he shook hands with Ben.

"Papa has told me a lot about you and your whole family,"

Andy said. "I have been especially looking forward to meeting James."

"James should be coming back to the house pretty soon," Ben said. "He's out at the barn lookin' about a heifer that's gonna freshen for the first time. If he don't come in pretty soon, I'll yell for him."

"How has he been getting along," Jeremiah asked.

"He's a wonder, that boy is," Jennie said. "You know, he's a deacon in our church and he teaches the men's Bible study class every Sunday. Our preacher, Brother Taylor, says that he's the best Bible teacher he's ever seen. James has hisself a little stool that he pushes in front of the church and then hops up on it and just teaches away."

"He does his half of the milking and does most of the work around the barn," Ben said. "I've got one older fellow working as a hired hand that does most of the fieldwork and I do the rest of the milking. Now that the war's over, I might be able to hire some young fellow to help around here. Since the war started Jennie, here, has had to go with James on the milk run to do the delivering."

"If you don't mind," Jeremiah said, "I'd like to go out to the barn to see James. If you will excuse us, we'll see if we can surprise him out there."

The scene at the barn was not what Jeremiah had expected. Instead of James merely observing a normal delivery of a calf, he was in the midst of a desperate struggle to save the life of the calf and maybe even the life of the young cow that was lying on her side.

"Get me that rope over there," James ordered the second they entered the barn. "The calf is coming out backwards and I've got to get it out before it dies."

Andy grabbed the rope and gave it to James who made a quick slip knot and put it around the barely exposed rear hooves of the calf.

"Give me a hand here," James said. "Help me pull."

Realizing that time was of the essence, both Jeremiah and Andy grabbed the rope and began pulling.

"Don't jerk; keep the pressure steady," James instructed.

The steady pull on the rope soon did its work and the next time that the cow convulsed with a labor pain, the slime covered calf slipped out onto the dry straw on the floor of the barn.

James immediately took the head of the seemingly lifeless calf in his hands and stripped the mucous from its mouth and nose. As he opened the calf's mouth, it suddenly shuddered and began breathing.

"I think he's gonna make it, thanks to you two," a grateful James said, smiling broadly. "It took me a minute to realize that it was you, Jeremiah, but I shouldn't have been surprised, you always seem to show up at the most opportune times."

"James, it is wonderful to see you again and be able to introduce you to my son, Andy," Jeremiah said. "Your folks told us how well you are getting along."

"Yes, I am doing well, thanks to Jesus and Jeremiah Blake," James said as he laughed. "We say that a lot around here, Andy. Did your papa ever tell you why?"

"No, but he's told me so much stuff, that must be the only thing that he missed," Andy responded.

"It's a long story but I'll give you the short version," James said as he watched the young cow begin to stir. "While your papa lived here with us he did a lot for us. He brought me books from the college and helped me understand them. He got me out of the house and put me to work. He got me to church and helped lead me to the Lord. He probably saved my papa's life and then, most certainly, helped save his soul. When your papa was leaving after he finished college, my papa told him, 'When I get to the pearly gates I'm going to tell Saint Peter that I'm there because of Jesus and Jeremiah Blake.'"

By the time James had related this to Andy, the young cow had gotten to her feet and was administering motherly care on her offspring, licking every inch of its body with her wide, rough tongue. Within a matter of minutes the calf, also, was on its feet, wobbling and searching for his mother's life-giving milk.

The crisis over, Jeremiah and Andy walked and James hopped back to the front porch of the farmhouse.

"Tell me about the rest of your family," Jeremiah requested. "How are Lizzie and Lucy and your other two sons?"

"The boys are both doing good, still working over on the river," Jennie said. "Their boys all got back from the war. Lucy's second boy lost his right arm but she and her bunch are getting along okay, I reckon."

Why, Jeremiah wondered, was she leaving Lizzie until last? Had something happened to her. Of course, Jennie could not know that Lizzie was first on his mind.

"Poor Lizzie is having it rough," Jennie said as Jeremiah's heart sank. "After losing her oldest in the war and then Eldon dying, she's left with that farm and she and her other three young-uns are trying to run it. I don't know how she does it."

"I knew about her son being killed," Jeremiah said, "but I didn't know about Eldon. What happened to him, he wasn't in the war, was he?"

"No, he just took sick and up and died," Ben said. "He got a bad stomachache and then he swelled up and died in a week. The doc said it must have been his appendix. When it goes, he said, there ain't nothing can be done. It was a bad way to go, though."

"I am so sorry to hear that Lizzie has lost Eldon, too," Jeremiah said. "Andy, we are going to have to change our plans a bit. Before we go to visit the college we have to go over to Short Creek and see about Lizzie."

"You're not going to be in a hurry to leave, are you?" Jennie asked. "Couldn't you spend a week or two with us? We'd sure love to have you."

"Maybe we can stay for a couple of days," Jeremiah said. "We are going back through Morgantown to look at the new college they are building. Andy wants to be one of the first students there."

Three days later, after departing early, Jeremiah and Andy arrived at Lizzie's farm at about eleven o'clock in the morning. Finding no one at the house, they tied their team of horses to a tree and walked past the barn and out into the fields. After they reached the summit of the hill behind the barn they saw four people busy at work in a bottom land field along the creek.

A tall young man that Jeremiah knew must be Lizzie's second son, Jonathan, was walking behind a shovel plow being pulled by a horse, laying off rows in the freshly harrowed field. Lizzie's two daughters were reaching into bags that they were carrying and dropping seed corn into the rows.

The fourth person was a strong looking woman wearing a long

skirt and a broad brimmed sun bonnet who was following the girls and covering the corn with a hoe. Jeremiah knew that had to be Lizzie.

One of the girls was the first to notice the visitors and ran quickly to her mother. Lizzie wiped her brow as she lifted her head and turned toward Jeremiah and Andy.

"Oh, Lordy, I don't believe it," Lizzie said as she dropped her hoe and ran toward Jeremiah. She threw her arms around him and sobbed uncontrollably.

"I knew about your son but I didn't know about Eldon until I visited your parents this week," Jeremiah said when Lizzie regained her composure. "I am so sorry about both of your losses."

"Kids, this is the 'college boy' I've told you about," Lizzie, wiping her eyes, said to her children who were standing in stunned silence because they had just observed their mother behave in a way they had never seen before. "This is Jeremiah Blake, the one we named your brother after. Jeremiah, this is Jonathan and this is Polly and this is Nellie, my baby. This young man with you must be your boy, Andrew."

"Yes, this is Andy," Jeremiah said. "We hate to interrupt your work, but I just had to see you and express my sympathy to you."

"Don't worry about interrupting us," Lizzie said. "We're late getting the corn planted in this field. It's been a wet spring and this field is low anyway. Girls, you take Andrew and run on ahead and get something started for dinner. Jonathan, you can finish laying off the rows and then you can unharness ol' Pete and help me finish covering the corn after we eat."

"Lizzie, I don't know how you have survived all that you've been through," Jeremiah said, as they began walking slowly toward the house. "Just losing your boy was enough to destroy you, but then you lost Eldon, too. How have you kept on going?"

"You know that I'm made of pretty strong stuff; after all, I'm Ben Givens' daughter," Lizzie said as she took off her sunbonnet and shook out her gray streaked auburn hair, "stronger than most, it turns out. Losing Jeremiah was the most terrible thing I've ever experienced but I think it was even harder on Eldon than it was on me. He just gave up on everything; the farm, the other kids, why, he didn't even want to eat. I couldn't get him to go to church with us anymore and he was the one who had gotten me into the church in the first place. It was like he was mad at God. I'll always think that he made himself sick by grieving so much. I kept going because I had to. What other choice did I have? I could either keep going or I could give up, too, and where would that leave the girls and Jonathan? The thing that I'm most thankful for is that Jonathan got home from the war in one piece. With him here to help, we're managing better than most people. How is it with you?"

"Up until this moment I thought it was pretty bad. My parents are getting older and Papa is in poor health, my brother Joshua is trying to learn to walk on a peg leg, Andy is wanting to leave me this fall to go to college, and I haven't been able to concentrate on work for more than a week at a time since the end of the war," Jeremiah said. "But after seeing what you are going through, I'm ashamed of myself. If I had your strength, I'd be Mayor of Clarksburg or running for Congress or something."

"What are you going to do?" Lizzie asked. "You can't quit any more than I can."

"I know that and I guess that I've been just wandering around waiting for a sign or something to happen to give me a new direction," Jeremiah said. "I want to go tomorrow and see old Alexander Campbell at Bethany College. He is a wise man and I have been hoping that he might inspire me again."

The noon meal that Polly and Nellie had prepared under the skeptical eye of Andy consisted mostly of leftovers from the previous day's supper.

"Jeremiah, I remember that you say a nice blessing," Lizzie said. "We've been pretty neglectful about that since we lost Eldon. Would you please ask the blessing before we eat?"

Jeremiah's voice choked as he carefully worded his prayer, thanking God for His blessings while being aware of the pain and suffering that this family had experienced and thanking Him for the food which was meager, to say the least.

"Papa," Andy commented after he and his father were on the road to Bethany that afternoon, "that was about the saddest situation I've ever seen. The father and oldest brother gone, and a woman trying to run a farm with her son who's not much older than me and her two teenaged girls. I don't think they have enough to eat, do you?"

"They're having it rough, all right," Jeremiah answered, "but Lizzie told me that she feels like, compared to most other families, they're the fortunate ones. Did you see their garden there behind the house? They've got fruit trees and berry vines, too. It won't be long 'til they'll have an abundance of food to eat and store up for next winter."

"Of course I remember you, Jeremiah," Alexander Campbell said after Jeremiah reintroduced himself to the now elderly Sage of Bethany and introduced Andy.

"Your accomplishments in life have provided me with a great deal of satisfaction," Campbell continued. "I know of your law practice in Clarksburg and I also know of your work in helping to establish the Reconstructed Government of Virginia and in the formation of the new state of West Virginia. Andrew, your father is a living example of the value of education and enlightenment. I knew, early on, that your father had exceptional potential and it has warmed this old man's heart to live to see him realize that potential."

"He has told me about you and your college all of my life," Andy said. "I think that before he makes any important decision, he considers what he learned here."

"President Campbell, the thing that I remember most," Jeremiah said, "is you telling me at graduation that our country could be preserved but only at a great price. No one ever spoke truer or more prophetic words. I was reminded of your words every time I learned that a friend had been killed. I remembered them again when my brother was wounded and nearly died, and, again, when I went back to Richmond to see the effects of the war. I remembered them when I heard that President Lincoln had been shot and then when he died and I remembered them again yesterday when Andy and I visited an old friend of mine who lost her son to the war and her husband to grief and is trying to hold her family together and scrape out a living on her farm."

"The war was far more devastating that I had ever imagined," Campbell said. "Many men who had been our students here were killed. There are now thousands upon thousands of widows and fatherless children. It will take decades for the schism between the rebelling states and the Union to heal. And what is to become of the

226

Negro race that has now been loosed in our midst?"

Campbell's question stirred Andy's emotion. He remembered what his father had told him about the Sage's teaching on race. He knew that it would be inappropriate for him to challenge this revered man and he wondered what Jeremiah might do if the conversation on this topic progressed.

"I believe that President Lincoln, had he lived, would have implemented my proposal to set up a separate area for the Negro," Campbell said, "probably somewhere in Central America, but now, neither the Congress nor President Johnson are interested in dealing with this problem. There is no way that two such unequal cultures can ever live in harmony."

Andy was proud of his father's response.

"During all of the horrors and turmoil of the war," Jeremiah said, "I was fortunate to become well acquainted with a few Negroes who have become my close friends. My experience with them has caused me to change my mind about the differences between our races. I have come to believe that the difference is not inferiority, rather it is the great gap in opportunity and education. One friend, Samuel, a young black man that we smuggled out of Richmond in our wagon, lived with my father and mother all during the war. The only education he ever received was that his mother taught him to read when he was little. He became a Christian on a plantation in North Carolina where he read the scripture for the illiterate slave preacher who conducted Sunday services. He ran away when his owner tried to force him to serve as what is referred to as a 'buck,' a man who impregnates slave women who are brought to him. He said that he could not obey his master and serve the Lord. After he came to Melford Creek, he not only kept the farm going and looked after my parents, he spent countless hours with my preacher papa reading and discussing the scriptures."

"I appreciate hearing of your experience," Campbell said, "but I would caution you to not over-simplify the matter. It is wonderful that you have befriended this one man but there are millions of Samuels out there and only one of you. What is to become of the rest of the Negroes?"

"I believe that the answer is in the Book of Philemon; I'm sure that you know it well," Jeremiah said. "We who are Christians now have the task of receiving our former slaves as our brothers. The solution is in the hands of God's people."

"That day might come," Campbell said, "but neither you nor I will live to see it. Maybe Andrew, here will see it, but I doubt it. If what you envision is to ever come to pass, it will take generations."

"You appear to be in good health, President Campbell," Jeremiah said, ready to change the subject.

"Yes, the Lord has blessed me with a goodly measure of health and strength," Campbell said. "What about you? What are you doing with your life now that the state of West Virginia has been established and the war is over?"

"To be honest, with the exception of practicing just enough law to pay for our basic needs, I am doing nothing," Jeremiah replied. "I have prayed for months that the Lord would show me what He would have me to do."

"I could certainly use you here at Bethany," Campbell said. "I started work on a new main building to house the college back before the war. I don't know how much longer it will take for it to be completed. I am getting much too old to oversee that work and attend to my academic duties, too. If you are interested, you could come and help me with completing the building and also teach a curriculum on law and government."

"I don't claim to know anything about architecture or construction," Jeremiah said, "and would I be qualified to teach? I haven't pursued any studies beyond what I had here."

"Don't worry about that, my lad," Campbell said. "I have employed the best of architects and I just need someone to help me with the day to day tasks that keep occurring. Now, with regard to your credentials, I know of no one who is more qualified to instruct. Your experiences, alone, would make you a most valuable asset to the college."

"That is very generous of you," Jeremiah said. "Are you sure you would want me here? Do you remember that I am a Methodist?"

"Yes, I remember your strong commitment to the denomination of your father," Campbell said. "I would wish for you that you could travel the same spiritual road as I and come to similar conclusions, but that is certainly not a prerequisite for you serving as

228

a professor here."

"In that case," Jeremiah said, grasping the old man's hand, "I would be honored to work for you and teach at your college."

It was a rare day, indeed, when Jeremiah Blake could be described as jubilant but this had become one of those days.

"Do you realize what just happened, Andy?" Jeremiah said as they departed the college.

"Sounds like you got yourself a job," Andy responded.

"Don't you see, it's so much more than that," Jeremiah said. "It is the answer to prayer; it is the sign that I have been waiting for. If I were to describe it in terms that Sam uses, I would say that it's like I've been in the wilderness since the war and now I've been shown the Promised Land."

"Are we heading home, now?" Andy asked.

"Not just yet," Jeremiah said, "I've got to do something else before we go home."

"Let me guess," Andy said, smiling. "We're going back up to Short Creek, aren't we?"

"Yes we are," Jeremiah said as they headed their horses back north. "I am going to tell Lizzie Tompkins that I will be moving to Bethany and ask her if she would be willing for me to come calling."

"I have an idea that her answer will be in the affirmative," Andy predicted.

32 . . SAM'S CALLING

As soon as he arrived back at home in Clarksburg Jeremiah feverishly set about getting everything in order for his move back to Bethany where he would begin classes in early September. First he informed his law partners, Nathan Fletcher and Robert Smith, of his decision to leave the firm.

"This doesn't come as a big surprise to us, Jeremiah," Fletcher said. "It has been obvious for a long time that your heart has not been in your work here. We have never complained because your good name has brought a lot of business our way even while you were out gallivanting around the country. If you don't mind, we may leave your name on the door for a while longer, no sense quitting on a good thing."

Jeremiah then held an auction where he sold his household furnishings and he and Andy went to spend the rest of the summer at Melford Creek where they could be of help to Jeremiah's parents and Joshua on their farm and his widowed sister, Rachel, on her farm.

To their great surprise, when they arrived at the farm they were greeted not only by Abe, Sally, and Joshua; Samuel also met them.

"Sam, I am shocked to see you here," Jeremiah said. "When did you get here and why did you not stay with your mother in Richmond?"

"As you're fond of saying, Mista' Blake, it's a long story," Sam replied. "First off, Mama don't need me as much as I figured she would. Ms. Hatcher done sold her boardin' house and she and Mama moved to a nice house on Maple Street. They're takin' care of each other right well."

"I'm glad to hear that," Jeremiah said, "but why did you come back here?"

"I'll be gettin' to that in a minute," Sam said. "Your papa already knows why I come back, don't you Reverend Blake?"

"I sure do, Sam," Abe replied smugly, "and I'm gonna help you all I can."

"Well, don't hold me in suspense any longer," Jeremiah said. "Tell me the whole story."

"Mista' Blake, you ain't the only one that's been searchin' for some answers," Sam said. "Ever since I run off from Masta' Davis, I been prayin' and lookin' for the path that God wanted me to travel. After I saw that Mama was okay, I kept thinkin' about comin' back here. It don't 'pear to me that livin' in Richmond now is gonna be much different than before the war. White folks are still orderin' us around down there and beatin' up on them that don't listen. If a black man fights back, a whole bunch of 'em takes him out and hangs him. I don't see no sense in livin' in a place like that when I can live here."

"I don't blame you," Andy said. "You can live here and help Grandpa and Joshua run the farm."

"Them ain't exactly my plans, either," Sam said. "As Reverend Blake knows, I believe that the Lord is callin' me to preach. I know that I ain't got much education but I can read and that's more that a lot of black folks can do. Since I got here, Reverend Blake's been schoolin' me in the Bible, gettin' me ready to start preachin'."

"Where are you going to preach?" Jeremiah asked.

"I don't think it will be in one of your papa's churches," Sam said with a wry smile. "I done seen the looks we get when I go to church with your folks and how the other folks look down on them for bringin' me. What I been doin' is goin' to Clarksburg and gettin' ready to start a church there that black folks can go to. More and more black folks are gonna be comin' this way and they're gonna need somebody to help 'em and I figure that the best help they could get would be comin' from a church they could go to."

"Have you had any success getting started in Clarksburg?" Jeremiah asked.

"Oh, yes," Sam responded, "We been praisin' the Lord for the way He's been workin' things out. I went to all the churches there, and at the Baptist Church the old preacher, Reverend Hayes, told me he's a good friend of yours. Reverend Hayes and his church done rented a place for us to meet and we're gonna have our first service on this comin' Sunday."

"Can white folks go there, too?" Andy asked. "If they can, I'd like to be there."

"Unless somebody bigger than me gets in the way, anybody that wants to come is gonna be welcome," Sam, the young giant, replied.

Jeremiah, Joshua, and Andy accompanied Sam into Clarksburg for his first service. The room was adequate but the congregation of less than twenty had to stand through the entire service because there were no seats. Sam spoke without a pulpit or podium of any kind, using his Bible as his only prop.

"This is the day that the Lord has made, a most grand and glorious day," Sam began in a strong melodious tone that completely surprised Andy. He had no way of knowing that Sam was preaching in the style of Rafe, the old slave preacher who had led him to the Lord.

"This is the day that the Lord's gonna start a mighty work here in Clarksburg," Sam continued, his voice rising and falling with each sentence, "the day that He's gonna send down His Holy Ghost and lift us up, the day He's gonna get somebody on the road to Heaven."

Jeremiah, also, was amazed at the eloquence and passion of Sam as he progressed deeper and deeper into his sermon. He had preached for nearly forty-five minutes before he finally opened the Bible and read from the fortieth Psalm, the same passage that Reverend Abraham Blake had used in his third sermon at the Methodist Church at Nutter Fort.

"I waited patiently for the Lord and He inclined unto me and heard my cry. He brought me up also out of an horrible pit, out of the miry clay, and set my feet upon a rock, and established my goings. And He has put a new song in my mouth, even praise to our God."

"You ever been in a pit?" Sam suddenly asked the congregation in a voice that had the impact of a sledge hammer, to which they answered aloud in the affirmative. "You ever been in a hole that you thought you'd never get out of?" Again, more response.

"What pit you been in? What hole you been tryin' to get out

of?" Sam asked rhetorically. "I'll tell you some holes I been in. I been in the pit of slavery, down in North Carolina. Any of you been in the pit of slavery?"

Andy could distinguish the varied responses of "yes," "uh-huh," and "sure have," that came from the group.

"We all been in the pit of slavery, but God used a good man, Abraham Lincoln, to bring us out of the miry clay of slavery," Sam preached as a chorus of "amen's," encouraged him, "and set our feet on the solid rock of freedom."

"I was in a pit down in Richmond, hidin' in a horse barn," Sam continued, "when God used a good man and his boy, Jeremiah Blake and his boy, Andy, standin' back yonder, to bring me out of the miry clay of old Virginia and set my feet on the solid rock here in West Virginia."

"There ain't a one of us that ain't been in the miry clay of sin, lost and away from God," Sam said, "but God sent a good man, His own Son, to lift us out of the miry clay of sin and onto the solid rock of His Son, Jesus Christ."

By the time Sam extended the invitation for people to respond to God's call to repent, which Jeremiah knew came from his papa's instruction to Sam, more than two hours had passed. Andy, thinking about his tired feet and legs, wondered if anyone would come back the next Sunday. He was pleased to see, though, that the entire group of worshippers went to the front of the room and knelt with Sam for the closing prayer.

"While we are here in Clarksburg, let's go and see Daniel Hayes," Jeremiah said.

"Daniel, I want to thank you for the help you have given to my friend, Sam, here," Jeremiah said when they arrived at the home of the now white-haired Baptist preacher. "We attended his first service this morning and it was truly a blessing."

"I'm happy that we could help Sam get started," Hayes replied and then asked, "How many did you have in attendance?"

"Countin' the white folks here, we had about twenty," Sam responded.

"That's a good start," Hayes said. "Is there anything else you need?"

"They will be needing some benches or pews," Jeremiah said.

233

"Do you think you could help with those?"

"I'll speak to some of the men in our church and see if we can do something," Hayes said. "Anything else?"

"I was thinking that somebody needs to ordain Sam," Jeremiah said. "How should we go about that?"

"I think you know that I put a premium on education for clergymen, Jeremiah," Hayes said, "but I realize that this is a special case. I'll talk to our deacons and see if we can ordain Sam."

Sam's ordination service was set for the first Sunday in August.

"Reverend Blake, I want you to preach my ordination sermon," Sam said, as soon as the date was set.

"Sam, you know that I ain't preached for the past two years," Abe responded, "not since I can't hardly get around no more."

"I know that, but I ain't takin' 'no' for an answer," Sam said. "And more than that, I want you to stay up there with me for a couple of weeks and preach us a revival. Settin' around here with you, talking about the Scriptures, I can tell you still got a preacher's heart and I need that with me."

Getting Abe and Sally to Clarksburg for the first two weeks of August took some doing but was accomplished with Jeremiah making most of the arrangements. He contacted his father's friends, a fellow Methodist preacher and his wife there who were happy to have Abe and Sally to stay with them. Jeremiah and Andy arranged to stay with friends and Sam stayed in the homes of members of his fledgling congregation.

"The first time I laid eyes on Samuel Blake, I said, 'Lord, what have You brought to my door?'" Abe said as he opened the ordination sermon.

A crowd of thirty-five or so sat more or less comfortably on the wooden benches that some of the members of the First Baptist Church had built.

"I asked my son, 'Jeremiah, why did you bring this slave to me?'" Abe continued. "He told me that he had not brought me a slave; he said that he had brought me a brother, a brother in Christ like Onesimus, in the Book of Philemon. I have known Samuel for six years, now, and I can truly say of him, just as the Apostle Paul said of Onesimus, 'He is a beloved brother who has been profitable to me and will be to you.' Therefore, just as Paul said, 'I beseech thee for my son Onesimus,' I say, I beseech thee for my son, Samuel. Let me tell you this, Samuel is both my brother and my son, in the Lord, and it is fitting that he chose our family name to be his own."

Following the sermon, Daniel Hayes led in a ceremony of laying on of hands in which he, Abe, and three deacons from Hayes' church took turns placing their hands on the kneeling Sam's head while saying a prayer of dedication.

The revival began that night. The Reverend Abe Blake got a new lease on life. He had given up preaching partially due to his aches and pains and partially due to the fact that no congregation seemed to need his services anymore, especially since he was usually accompanied by his young black friend. But suddenly, like the old warhorse that stirs when he hears reveille, the old preacher was restored to active duty.

The crowds grew night after night and, urged on by the enthusiastically vocal congregation, Abe, alternately holding to the new pulpit or propping himself up on his cane, preached some of the most powerful sermons of his life. By the end of the two weeks, more than fifty people had come down to the newly constructed wooden altar at the front of the church and prayed a prayer of repentance and professed their faith in Jesus Christ.

The baptismal service on the third Sunday of August was a marvelous event. A large crowd, both black and white, gathered on the banks of the West Fork River to observe the strong, tall, black Reverend Samuel Blake, assisted by the weak, stooped, white Reverend Abraham Blake, baptize the new church members, many of whom had to overcome their fear of water, never having had their entire bodies submerged. Abe, standing in shallow water, would take each person to be baptized by the hand, say a word of encouragement, and place the person's hand in Sam's hand who would then lead the person into the deeper water and, after saying, "I baptize thee, my brother (or sister) in the name of the Father, the Son, and the Holy Ghost," dip the person backwards under the water and quickly up again. He then took the person back to Abe for assistance in getting back on shore to waiting family members and friends.

As he observed the ceremony and listened to the emotional

rejoicing of the crowd, Jeremiah's mind took him back in time and he relived the day at Bethany when he watched Will Sharpe baptize James Givens and then was totally surprised when Ben Givens had hobbled out into the creek, asking to be baptized, too.

After Sam had baptized all of his new members, he asked Daniel Hayes to give the closing prayer.

"Before I pray," Hayes said, "I want to say that I have never seen the power of God so prevalent as I have seen here for the past two weeks. In this short span of time we have seen Samuel Blake ordained into the gospel ministry and we have seen a large number of people come to the Lord. We have seen the size of this young church, only a few months old, more than double in size. Surely the Lord is in this place."

33 *SO DO YOU, MRS. BLAKE*

As Jeremiah neared Bethany in early September, 1866, he felt like he was light enough to float in the air. It was as if his life was just starting over. As he anticipated his new life in an academic setting, surrounded by intellectuals and challenged by eager students, all under the watchful eye of the great Sage of Bethany, himself, Jeremiah could barely contain his exuberance.

He was also excited because he knew that he would be welcomed by Lizzie any time he could arrange to go calling. Last spring, when he and Andy had gone back to Lizzie's farm to tell her that he would be moving to Bethany, she had made it very clear that she would be pleased to see him if he was so inclined.

The building of what Alexander Campbell called "the Main" was a daunting task. President Campbell had hired architects who designed the structure to resemble buildings in Glasgow, in his beloved Scotland. It was designed to contain not only classrooms and faculty offices, but also a library, laboratories, a museum, an assembly hall, and a place of worship. After four years of construction, work had been stopped in 1862 due to the war and was just now getting back into full swing.

Jeremiah settled into a small office in the familiar surroundings of the old building where he had attended classes many years before. The ample college library provided him with the necessary background information to develop the materials for his first class: "The Proper Role of the Federal Government and the States Under the Constitution of the United States."

His separation from Andy had occurred on a hill overlooking the Monongahela River at Morgantown. Leaving Andy there had been emotional but he realized that it was necessary. He felt that he had fulfilled his pledge to Elizabeth to keep Andy with him. Andy was now a good two inches taller that his father and Jeremiah considered him fully capable of making proper life decisions.

Both Andy and Jeremiah were disappointed that the new

college was not ready to open this fall but Andy wanted to stay there, anyway. Morgantown was, like Bethany only more so, undergoing a construction boom. Work was underway on new buildings while older existing buildings were being renovated.

Andy was able to get work as a carpenter's apprentice, working for the builder who was in charge of converting the Woodburn Female Seminary into the focal center of the new institution that would be the state's Land Grant college. Even though he had to delay his plans for another year, Andy was determined to be one of the first students here. He was excited by the opportunity that he would have to study science, humanities, and agriculture, as well as receiving training in the military cadet corps.

Jeremiah knew that it was better for Andy to be on his own in Morgantown and attend college there than to come with him to Bethany even though their first separation in years was painful. When he would look for Andy or start to say something to him and then realize that he was no longer at his side, he associated his feelings with those of his brother Joshua who needed to scratch his leg that was no longer there.

"Jeremiah, my lad," President Campbell said after sitting in on one of Jeremiah's early lectures, "I surely did the right thing by bringing you back here to instruct. I did not think it possible for a man of my age to learn anything new, but I was wrong. Your lecture was so instructional that it even opened these tired eyes a wee bit."

"Thank you, President Campbell," Jeremiah responded, "I never knew that any work could be as rewarding as this. I find that I have so much emotion bottled up inside me regarding the war and the Constitution that it is liberating to be able to release it through my lectures to people who are willing to hear me."

After a few weeks of living in a rented room, Jeremiah found a white, weatherboard, two story house on a quiet street that was for sale. The fact that he was associated with Alexander Campbell and had a steady income was all that the local bank president needed in order to make him a loan and Jeremiah bought the first house that he had ever owned.

Every Sunday morning Jeremiah attended the Bethany Baptist Church where he marveled at the gifted teaching of James Givens. Although James would often mention that the new class member,

Jeremiah Blake, had been his mentor, Jeremiah knew that James had progressed far beyond the rudiments of the faith that he had been able to impart. He did not have to ask James if he had, like Abe Blake, prayed for wisdom, for it was apparent that he had done so and that it had been granted.

The pastor, Randolph Taylor, was an adequate but very doctrinaire Baptist preacher. Sometimes Jeremiah's face burned a bit when Brother Taylor would hammer away on the Baptist beliefs that if a person is truly saved they can never lose their salvation and that immersion is the only acceptable mode of baptism. Jeremiah felt that this was directed at him, knowing that he was probably the only person in the congregation that was not in full agreement with the pastor on these issues. Otherwise, though, he enjoyed the services, especially since it gave him weekly contact with James and his parents, Ben and Jennie.

After church each Sunday, Jeremiah rode the hour and a half trip over to Short Creek where he had Sunday dinner with Lizzie Tompkins and her three children and then spent the rest of the afternoon with them. His prediction to Andy that the food would get better at the Tompkins household after the garden started producing and the fruit on the trees started to ripen proved to be accurate.

Since Lizzie had spent most of her teen years working in the fields with her father, Jeremiah had assumed that her culinary skills would never match those of her mother or her sister, Lucy. After just a couple of Sunday visits to Lizzie's, Jeremiah realized just how wrong his assumption had been. As he was enjoying the crisp fried chicken, boiled new potatoes, various fresh garden vegetables and fruit dessert, he had to admit that even her mama, Jennie, could not do any better than this.

At Christmas time Andy came to Bethany to be with his father.

"What do you think of the house?" Jeremiah asked soon after Andy's arrival.

"I like it," Andy responded, and then mischievously probed, "how long do you plan to live in it by yourself?"

"Funny you should ask," Jeremiah said. "I haven't told anyone this but I've been giving considerable thought to asking Lizzie Tompkins to marry me. What would you think about that?"

"I think that if you haven't done anything to scare her off since the last time I saw her, she'll say 'yes,'" Andy said.

"That's not what I meant," Jeremiah said, "I want to know what you would think if I was to marry again."

"I would think that it's about time," Andy answered. "How do you feel about it?"

"I've weighed it over and over in my mind," Jeremiah said. "You mother tried to talk to me about it right before she died but I didn't want to hear it."

"Do you remember what Mama said?" Andy asked.

"All that I remember her saying was that when, not if, mind you; when I get married again that I make sure that the woman I marry loves you, too," Jeremiah related through the lump that formed in his throat.

"That sounds like her," Andy said. "So now all you have to do is ask Lizzie Tompkins if she loves both of us."

"I believe that your mama was thinking about you being a bit younger," Jeremiah said. "It wouldn't have been any trouble when you were young and cute, but I'll have to do some persuading now."

On Christmas day, Jeremiah and Andy rode over to Short Creek to spend the holiday with the Tompkins family. Jeremiah had bought a dozen oranges and large bag of peppermint candy to take, along with a box of dominoes and a checkerboard and checkers. He was pleased to be able to find a box of dainty lace trimmed handkerchiefs as a gift for Lizzie.

They arrived to find the house as festive as Lizzie and her children could make it. They had a small cedar tree in the corner of the parlor decorated with ribbons and popcorn. Lizzie and the girls were busy in the kitchen fixing the Christmas dinner. Andy soon became comfortable in these surroundings and stood in the kitchen door teasing Polly and Nellie as they worked and giggled.

Jeremiah and Jonathan sat in the parlor while dinner preparations were being completed.

"It looks like you had a pretty good year on the farm," Jeremiah said. "What are your plans for next year?"

"That depends a lot on Mama," Jonathan answered. "She's got a lot of ideas about how everything ought to be done."

"What would you do different if she didn't make all the decisions?" Jeremiah asked.

"I'd like to switch over from milking so many cows and raise some sheep and hogs," Jonathan said. "I'd maybe keep a few head of cattle, but not like her and Papa have. I don't like all of that milking and delivering but that's what she knows."

"Well, she tells me all the time that she's Ben Givens' daughter," Jeremiah said with a smile, "and that doesn't make her easy to get along with, sometimes."

"That's for sure," Jonathan said, returning the smile.

Christmas dinner was a feast; roast chicken and cornbread dressing, potatoes and gravy, leather britches beans, parched corn, cucumber pickles, beet pickles, and hot biscuits with jam and jelly, and then apple pie for dessert made from Lizzie's own dried apples.

After the feast was eaten and the dishes cleared, Andy and Lizzie's children became involved in games of dominoes and checkers at the dining room table and Jeremiah and Lizzie went to sit in the parlor.

"Jonathan tells me he'd like to make a few changes in the farm operation," Jeremiah said.

"Oh, he would, would he?" Lizzie asked, frowning. "What kinds of changes, pray tell?"

"I think he'd like to quit milking so many cows and get a little flock of sheep and a brood sow or two," Jeremiah said. "How does that sound to you?"

"We don't know anything about sheep or hogs," Lizzie said, "except how to butcher and eat them. Why would he want to do some fool thing like that?"

"That's just the way young people are, sometimes," Jeremiah said. "They don't want to listen to us; they want to do things their own way. When I was talking to him he reminded me of myself when I decided that I was going to leave the farm and go to college. That sure wasn't what my papa wanted me to do."

"What are you saying, Jeremiah Blake?" Lizzie said, warming up to the subject. "Are you accusing me of being too bossy? Are you saying that I should just sit back and let that boy tell me what to do? How long do you think we'd keep our heads above water if I did that?"

"What I'm saying is that the boy might need for you to give him some room to operate," Jeremiah said. "He might have some good ideas if you were to give him a chance to try them out."

"Well, just how do you propose that I do that, all-knowing Professor Blake," Lizzie fairly spit out, now in full fury, "sit all day in my rocking chair and daub my nose with those fancy little handkerchiefs you brought me?"

"No," Jeremiah said slowly. "What I propose is that you marry me and you and the girls come and live with me; then Jonathan could run the farm any way he wants to."

"Jeremiah Blake, you've been teasing me, just to make me mad," Lizzie said, "and then you spring this on me. I've half a mind to turn you down."

"Since you're not saying no," Jeremiah said. "let me ask you more formally; Lizzie, will you marry me?"

The commotion that ensued in the parlor attracted the attention of the game players in the dining room and they came into the parlor in time to be totally shocked by seeing their parents locked in a passionate embrace.

The wedding was set for the first Saturday of April at the Bethany Baptist Church. Jeremiah could see from his front room window that the crowd was gathering early. Andy, who had come up from Morgantown to be his father's best man, found that he needed to be a calming influence on his nervous father.

"How does my moustache look?" Jeremiah asked. "Do you think I need to trim it a little bit more?"

"No, Papa," Andy teased, "you've cut too much off already. What you need to do now is shave it off completely."

"Thanks, but no thanks," Jeremiah said. "I thought that maybe you'd be of some help today but I guess that's too much to ask."

"Papa, you look fine," Andy assured him, "and Lizzie is so struck on you that she wouldn't notice if your moustache was gone, or if your hair and teeth were gone too, for that matter."

A great surprise awaited Jeremiah at the church. When he entered and looked to the front, he saw that Reverend Taylor was not alone. Standing beside him was Jeremiah's friend and benefactor, the former pastor, Will Sharpe; a much older Will Sharpe but Will Sharpe, nevertheless.

Jeremiah could not contain his jubilation. He rushed straight to the front of the church and embraced his old friend.

242

"Jeremiah," Reverend Taylor said, "I knew how much Brother Sharpe meant to you and Lizzie so I wrote and told him about your wedding and he wrote back and said he would like to be a part of the ceremony."

"Thank you very, very much, Brother Taylor," Jeremiah expressed gratefully. "Seeing you, Will, is the best thing that could happen on this day."

"Aren't you forgetting something, Jeremiah," Will said. "Are you sure that seeing me is the very best thing that's happening today?"

"I was so excited to see you that I almost forgot that this was my wedding day," Jeremiah said. "Let me rephrase that, please. Will, seeing you is the second best thing that could happen today. What about Rowena? Is she here, too?"

"Right back there in the third row," Will said as Jeremiah turned and saw her sitting just behind where Ben and Jennie Givens were sitting with all of their other children and grandchildren.

As Lizzie came down the aisle on the arm of her son, Jonathan, and attended by her daughters, Polly and Nellie, she was also surprised to see Will Sharpe but could not react beyond flashing a broad smile at him as the ceremony was beginning.

"Did you know that Brother Sharpe was going to be here?" Lizzie whispered to Jeremiah.

"No," Jeremiah whispered back. "Now hush."

Will Sharpe led Jeremiah and Lizzie in their exchange of vows and then Reverend Taylor intoned: "By the powers vested in me by Almighty God and the great State of West Virginia, I now pronounce you man and wife. You may now kiss the bride."

Jeremiah took Lizzie into his arms, pulled her close and kissed her warmly.

"Mr. Blake, you sure do kiss good," Lizzie purred in his ear.

Jeremiah, no longer the tongue-tied youth who did not know how to respond the first time he had heard those words from Lizzie, whispered back, "So do you, Mrs. Blake, so do you."

THE END

About the Author . . . .

Paul Dodd is a native of Griffith Creek, in Summers County, West Virginia. He holds a degree in Agricultural Education from West Virginia University and a Master of Public Administration from Harvard University. During his 37-year career with the U. S. Department of Agriculture he held positions in Hinton, Wayne, and Princeton, West Virginia, and in Ohio, Florida, and New York.

He was the New York State Conservationist for the last 14 years of his government service career.

Dodd is currently an adjunct professor of political science, teaching at Syracuse, NY, and Orlando, FL for Columbia (MO) College.

He is the great-grandson of Robert Bennett and the great-great-grandson of Jefferson Bennett who are included in the book.

He is married to the former Rose Marie Jones of Hilldale, West Virginia and they live in Baldwinsville, New York. They have two sons, Douglas and Michael, four grandchildren, and one great-grandchild.

Dodd is the author of *If My People Who are Called Baptists - A Layman's Challenge,* and *The Gospel According to a Mountain Momma.*